SU

Book 1 of

REBORN
THE BOOK SERIES

Torrie Q. Jones

Sun: Reborn the Book Series by Torrie Q. Jones

Published by Reborn the Book Series, LLC

Published in the United States of America

www.rebornthebookseries.com

For permissions contact: TorrieQ@rebornthebookseries.com

Cover Design & Layout by KLS Designz & Print: www. klsdesignz.com

Editor: I A.M. Editing, Ink LLC

Line Editor: Fluky Fiction

ISBN: 978-1-7370421-0-5

LCCN: 2021913778

First Edition

DEDICATIONS

First and foremost, I want to thank myself for committing to completing this body of work. I made a plan and stuck with it! So, thank you and you go girl!!!! To the special people in my life, you know who you are! Thank you for all the love and encouragement. Shout out to my kids for not being complete teenage horrors and for sticking to the script while I concentrated on my new world. Special shout out to Big Val & Mal. I wouldn't be here without you! Love you always.

To the many people I call friends, family and enemies, thank you very much! My life experiences have given me nothing but an excitement for telling my story in a unique and fascinating way! I love you all!!!

To my rider that's no longer here, I finished it bitch! ♥ RIP Queen!!!

REBORN THE BOOK SERIES

By

Torrie Q. Jones

CHAPTERS

PROLOGUE

The Ultimate High watched as many futures began to manifest. Its next course of action would start with the plans that started so long ago. "Have you decided on my proposition?", it asked, staring at the woman. "I have detailed your orders and responsibilities. Will you accept my terms?"

The petite woman bowed her head, still unsure if she was ready to go back after all this time. Head still low, she continued, "As I do not understand the full extent of my purpose, I am swayed to ask, why me?" She gripped her hands together nervously. "As I am not of your world, I am hesitant in knowing I can complete what you ask of me."

"You are the most competent person for this project. This is a long-term assignment and will require as much discretion as possible. There is trouble coming. We are going to start mobilizing and must be prepared for what is to come. I have given you the information you will need for all your charges. Seek, guide, and protect. Contact will be made when necessary. The rest of your instructions will be given at the gates."

As the continuation of the last set of plans comes into play, the next series of events will determine the outcome of all. The beginning of the end caused the rebirths to commence.

ADAM

Planted at his desk, lost in thought of the days when life was simple, not playing accountant, manager, salesperson, and celebrity stylist at times. Adam began to drift away from the papers he was reading to a night he remembered when his life changed forever. Fire in his hands, a dog-like being eating something, Kisha screaming, blood everywhere, body shaking, eyes burning. The feeling of electricity flowed through his veins. Adam snapped back into reality as some of the papers on his desk caught a spark and started a small fire.

"Got dammit!". Adam yelled as he put the fire out and made a mental note to contact his partner, Peggy, to order a new desk, the third one in six months. Peggy thought he smoked too much. Adam laughed at the thought of her yelling at him about ordering a new desk. Tired of work and thoughts of the past, he decided to see what New York City's beautiful nightlife could bring him.

Not having heard from his godfather, Mikael, Adam stopped by his house. Of course, for the past three months, the cleaning woman had repeatedly stated, "No, Monsieur Adam. Monsieur Mikael has yet to return. Please come back when he is present. Je Vous Remercie, thank you,", before closing the door. Adam didn't understand her behavior since she was always nice to him in the past. Adam knew Mikael was away for a business trip, but it'd been two months since he checked in.

As he searched for something to do that night, Adam got into the white BMW M6 convertible he bought himself as a birthday gift and turned up Lloyd Banks' "On Fire," enjoying the vibe as it blasted from the speakers. With the wind blowing and music playing, Adam zoned out to ride in the crisp spring night air. The music was abruptly interrupted by a phone call.

"What's good?", Adam yelled. "You're interrupting my damn music. What you want?", he asked as he glanced at the speaker irritably.

"Hey, baby!" Jasmine hollered. "I was calling to see if you wanted to meet me at the club. I miss you. What's up?"

Adam rolled his eyes. "Nah, I'm good, Ma. I got shit to do." Her version of hanging out at the club meant him spending thousands of dollars on her and her friends to act like she was his girlfriend, with the night ending with a threesome. Adam's dick jerked at the thoughts of the last time.

"I have to get up and open the store in the morning, so you go have fun for me, and I'll hit your sexy ass later." He smiled, knowing he wouldn't.

"Come on, baby. You know you want this tonight. I got Rebecca, the one you like, with me. We will fuck the shit out of you later, Daddy. Come on. I want to ride your face while Rebecca is riding that big dick!", she yelled out.

Rebecca screamed in the background, "Yes, girl!"

Adam laughed and grabbed his hardening dick. "Come on, don't tease me. I have to get up in the morning. I got you when I get off."

Adam knowing his dick would win the battle if he didn't hang up, he ended the call. Not that Jasmine wasn't sexy. Adam couldn't help but sleep with her since she was a freak. "Whoooooooo!" Adam yelled into the night sky as he thought of the last time, they were together. He just wasn't in the mood for the bullshit that came with dealing with a female like Jasmine. Lots of drama, alcohol, drugs, and sex. She was young, beautiful, and loved sex and money. It was just too much for Adam sometimes, especially lately, with him having problems controlling his "powers." He didn't know what the fuck to call it. The thoughts began flooding his mind. The feeling of his hands warming returned. Startled by a honking horn, Adam peeled off to ride once more.

No destination in mind, Adam called the number left on his voicemail.

"Hello, you have reached Taki Mashiro. I am unable to answer your call. Please leave your name and number, and I will contact you at my earliest convenience." *Beep.*

Adam quickly hung up. "Damn.", he whispered. He didn't know how this conversation would go. Good, bad. However it went, he couldn't help but smile as he remembered his former best friend, Kisha. Takisha Williams, as he knew her. Strong, intelligent, fly, and sassy. Beautiful did not define Kisha in Adam's eyes. He always thought of her as a dark-skinned Wonder Woman. His nickname for her was Amazon Queen. He sat and reminisced on his first time meeting her. Kisha was in a fight after school in sixth grade and beat a girl up. When the girl's friends jumped in and started hitting Kisha, Adam almost jumped in until Kisha held her own, literally fighting all four girls. Adam walked her home afterward.

Since then, he loved him some Kisha. It was almost like love at first sight, and it didn't help that they lived in the same building. However, he settled with being her best friend and the person that brought sunshine in her life, as Kisha's life was very different from his. Outsiders never knew where she came from. Adam felt awful about her situation, but Kisha never allowed him to pity or feel sorry for her. That is what he loved about her most.

As the night sky and wind slowed down, Adam realized he was home. "Fuck it." he said as he parked into the garage of the penthouse suite, he bought himself three years ago.

As he exited the elevator, Adam powered off his two phones and smartwatch. He was never much for religion, but he indeed believed there was more to this world than we knew. Adam thanked that being for allowing him to succeed and prosper in this crazy world as he entered his walk-in closet. He took off his clothes to shower and thought long and hard about the "issues" he had been having. He attempted to remember the scenes that plagued his mind as he slept.

After a long shower, Adam lit a joint he had rolled earlier and stepped onto his balcony to smoke. House rules: no smoking inside. As his high took him to the calmness he continually searched for, Adam decided it was time for bed. He set the alarm for six to open the store for a filming. Adam had scheduled a music premiere party for one of those reality stars starting at ten. One of Adam's famous clients plugged him into using his sneaker store for reality show recordings, which allowed a nice extra chunk of change for the store as well as free exposure.

FIRE, FIRE, FIRE, FIRE, HEAT, HEAT, HEAT, HEAT! So hot, it's so hot. Why am I so hot? Burning, Burning!

Adam jumped up, smelling smoke, panting, sweating, and groaning, seeing a circle of fire around him and the smoke detector going off. He reached for the fire extinguisher next to his bed. The thought of him having a fire extinguisher next to his bed sent chills down his spine.

Adam put out the fire and checked the phone to make sure the doorman downstairs didn't call up to check on the fire alarms. He had his apartment soundproofed and a separate fire sprinkler system installed to assist in the "issues" he always had. This was yet another night of him waking up on fire as he continued to put out the rest of the flames with no sign of burns, marks, or anything on his body. Just a big circle around him with everything burnt within. Being used to this, Adam began to clean up the mess that brought so many questions, pain, and confusion.

"What is wrong with me?" Adam whispered as he collapsed to the floor.

Adam stood, looking around and knew sleep would not be in his cards for the night. After cleaning up the residue and evidence of a fire, Adam decided to get ready for the premiere and head to the store, even though it was 4 a.m. The best thing about his place was that it was right in the heart of NYC, where the city never sleeps, just like him. Lights, yellow cabs, tourists, weirdos, and restaurants were still going as he stepped foot on the sidewalk.

Adam walked to the pizza spot a couple of blocks away to grab a couple of slices and a soda to stop his growling stomach. He believed he spotted Mikael. Running towards the man and grabbing him by the shoulder, Adam quickly realized it was not him. He apologized for startling the man and continued to order his food. After he ate the greasiest pizza in the world, Adam decided he would walk to his store. It was a long walk, but it was better than waking within a circle of flames.

As he enjoyed his brisk early morning walk, Adam's mind started to flood with thoughts-thoughts of fire, thoughts of heat, thoughts of the sun. He swayed from the flood of images that entered his mind. *FIRE, FIRE, FIRE, FIRE, HEAT, HEAT, HEAT, and HEAT* is all he could decipher from the chaos in his mind. He felt the warmth, felt the lines of electricity under his skin that were once called his veins. Grinding his teeth in agony, Adam fell to the ground. He looked around for assistance to no avail.

Adam quickly started to practice the breathing techniques that his godfather, Mikael, taught him during their training. His godfather, whom he considered an uncle, always told him he needed to know how to defend himself. While learning physical strength was necessary for a man, his godfather also felt the need to strengthen one's mind.

As Adam began to focus on his breathing, he slowly felt the sensation subside. Adam heard, "What do we have here?", from a scratchy voice from behind him as he stood up from the ground. Adam was no joke in the fighting department, so he jumped up in a stance to prepare to defend himself, confident he could beat the crap out of some punks trying to rob him. His eyes met a red glare with scaly, human-like skin attached to it.

He shouted as he jumped back, "What the fuck?!" Adam blinked twice to see a demon-like creature with two more like it behind him staring at him like a tasty meal. Immediately retreating, he heard both a snarl and a snapping sound that seemed to ring out in unison. Adam didn't know who or what it was, but something was right on his heels.

The run reminded him of the days when the police would sic the dogs on everyone in front of his buildings. Adam sprinted down the street like his life depended on it. *Good ole days*, he thought. With the silence behind him, he took a quick glance back. Adam noticed no one was chasing him anymore. He smelled a stench of burning flesh but kept hightailing it up the street.

When he ran across the street, Adam saw a police officer. "Right when I need him.", he said out of breath, headed towards the officer.

The officer noticed Adam running full-speed ahead and shouted, "STOP. POLICE! DON'T MOVE! GET ON THE FUCKING GROUND!", and proceeded to draw his weapon.

Adam narrowly escaped becoming another statistic. He fell to the ground, yelling, "SOMETHING IS CHASING ME! HELP! HELP ME!" As the officer began to pat him down to make sure he had no weapons or drugs.

The officer held Adam's hands behind his back. "Calm down, calm down. I'm going to check you for weapons, and then I'll let you stand up." He held a tight grip on Adam's hoodie to assist in helping him stand. The officer asked, "What's up? In a hurry big man? You screamed something was chasing you. On that shit this morning, son?".

Adam, dressed in sweats and a hoodie, standing at six-foot-seven, towering over the officer, stared in disbelief. *What do you expect from NYPD at five o'clock in the morning?* "Some idiots were trying to rob me. I ran for help until I ran into you." He shook his head, unsure of what really happened back there.

The officer replied, "Well, do you know what they look like and what they had on?"

Hesitantly, Adam answered, "Nah, they jumped me from behind."

"You're a little too big to be running from people son. Maybe you should take some self-defense classes. I thought you were a big ass truck about to run through me the way you came from across that street." He grabbed his gun as he walked away. "You be safe kid. Get home out of these streets!"

Stunned at the morning's events, he was unsure if he was more confused by the "things" chasing him or the weird-ass officer who thought he was a big ass punk. Laughing to himself, he said, "This shit really just happened to me. What the fuck?!"

No longer in the mood for a brisk walk, Adam pulled up the ride-sharing app to see if anyone was near his location. Having lost an hour to the bullshit that just happened, he needed to get to his store. While ordering his car service and texting Peggy his ETA, an unknown call came through. Aggravated, he answered, "Who this?"

"Boy, who you think you talking to? I have to talk to you at once! Meet me at the brick house, NOW!", the angry voice yelled.

"Uncle Mike! What the fuck, man? I've been looking for you for months! YO?!"

"Stop it with the dramatics and just get to the house. NOW! I already called Peggy and told her you won't be at the shoot today. It's okay. You don't need to be on TV anyway. NOW!!" *Call ended.*

Adam gaped at his phone in disbelief. *This is a new number. Mikael was gone when I changed numbers. How the hell does he know about the damn filming?* The tingling feeling returned. He continued waiting for Lyft as he changed the destination. Staring at the sky, he asked, "What the fuck is going on?"

TAKI MASHIRO a.k.a. TAKISHA WILLIAMS

"Why did I come back here?" She asked herself as she sat in the office. Lately, she started to hate almost everything in her world. Let's correct that. Dislike almost everything in her world. For a while now, her nights had been filled with screaming, panting, sweating, and a calling for something she couldn't seem to find. Before she returned to the United States, Taki lived a somewhat fulfilled and content life in Japan.

She left the U.S. at seventeen and was part of a foreign exchange program senior year until returning six months ago. She graduated from college and became an anthropologist at a young age. Taki achieved "gaming God" status with an X-Box league and trained in a few of Japan's martial art styles to escape the reality that she didn't want to deal with. Taki enjoyed her life in Tokyo until her symptoms started getting worse.

Unfortunately, due to those issues, she had to look for help on the outside. The social worker who assisted her all of these years was one of the few people Taki trusted with her health concern. She introduced her to Martial Arts and her sensei. They both became great fixtures in Taki's life to assist her with the condition she had. Taki's sensei suggested she move back to the U.S.

Taki was supposed to be practicing the arts to help her in controlling her temper and energy, but it just made her more of a lethal weapon. Her sensei was very tough and rigid on her. She never understood why, but she finally acknowledged Taki as one of her best students.

Due to her inability to continue to assist Taki in her issues, she suggested coming back to the states to find answers. As those thoughts returned, Taki whispered, "Bitch, you know why you back!"

Startled by the knock on her office door, Taki jumped.

Her co-worker, Michelle, asked, "Hey Taki, can you fit another meeting for the twentieth at eleven a.m.?"

"Sure, I'm available at that time." She rolled her eyes as her colleague closed her door. "Whatever." Taki scoffed. Being one of the youngest translators at this United Nations office, she sometimes found office politics and cattiness part of her job description. Not allowing herself to be aggravated, Taki grabbed her purse and keys and flew out the door. "Shit, it's Friday and payday. I'm out! Later bitches!!" She threw up the peace sign in the air.

Headed out to enjoy the beautiful afternoon, Taki felt like a million bucks. She rushed to handle whatever business she needed to address before her day got ruined by her episodes. For almost a decade, fits of pain would just come on to her, mostly at night. She woke up, panting, sweating, and screaming. Last night was one of the worst episodes she'd ever had. She woke up around three a.m. in so much pain, scared, confused, and in a circle of sweat. Unable to explain the outbursts and lack of sleep, you could say Taki hadn't been one of the most pleasant people lately.

Today she felt great, ready to get off to a great start to her weekend. The phone rang, disturbing her. She continued to walk to the train station. "Hey, baby? How are you?", a low, licentious voice chimed in.

"Hey boo, I'm good. Leaving work. About to head home. What's up?" Taki answered sweetly.

"I wanted to see you tonight, maybe get some dinner and a movie?" Mark asked excitedly.

"Unfortunately, handsome, I have some work to do and I'm going to help Michi in Japan with a project. You know the time difference. I have to get some sleep." She said sheepishly. Taki knew damn well that the Call of Duty Event on her Xbox One was the real reason she didn't want to spend time with him. She stopped herself from giggling. "Don't worry, boo. I will make sure I make it up to you when I can. Kisses." She hung up.

She wasn't with the frilly shit getting off the phone. Mark had been trying to get her to say she loved him as he said to her. Unfortunately, she didn't feel that way and explained to him she would not be using words that were not true. He thought Taki was just being a hardass. Not really knowing her, she allowed him to believe his assumptions. She didn't want him to get to know her like that anyway and just really enjoyed his company when they were together.

Sweet guy, ambitious, tall, and attractive. This was the best way to describe Mark. Taki thought she liked him because he reminded her of someone special from her past. That was as far as it went, but he was the token guy. Brilliant, compassionate, successful, and ALL male. She wondered if he loved her, because sometimes it came across as if he used her just as she used him for companionship. For a while, it made them both happy.

She walked down the steps to her train. Taki thought of a voicemail she left earlier. "Hey, It's Takisha. Give me a call when you get this. I'm back in NY and need to speak with you. Please call me back." The message played back in her head. She wasn't sure if her plea would be heard. Shit, it had been ten years. "Would I have returned the call?". She laughed. "Hell yeah, and he would too!"

Continuing home, Taki stopped by the grocery store and then nail shop to get her eyebrows waxed before she reached her apartment. She had a great basement brownstone apartment on the Upper West Side of Manhattan that she absolutely loved. She got a great deal back when she was in Japan since the person was moving to Tokyo. They switched residences, making things a lot easier for Taki when she moved back. Getting rid of her place in Japan was unnecessary, in her opinion. Still, her sensei insisted on her leaving everything and coming back to the states permanently.

"Dammit!" She shouted as she remembered she didn't get her dry cleaning. She needed it since she would be dealing with a very sophisticated client next week. Since it was Friday, Taki chalked it up as a loss and decided to wait until tomorrow to get it.

Just two hours before her gaming tournament, she decided to call that number one more time to make sure he understood she meant business. *I did sound helpless. Let him know Takisha needs to speak with him.* She laughed at herself. Her thoughts were interrupted when her cell phone rang.

"GIRLLLL!!!! Why didn't you tell me you were playing in the tournament tonight? I just realized when I saw your screen name on the roster. Meinu (bitch), you know I can't beat you! No fair!" Screamed Taki's best friend, Michiko Tanaka, Michi for short.

Michi was how Taki got her nickname. In the streets of Brooklyn and in school, people shortened her name to Kisha. Michi told Taki she was more honorable than many people born in her culture and decided to give her a Japanese nickname, meaning plunging waterfall. Michi says that's how Taki fell into her life. After Taki adopted her sensei's last name when she completed high school, the moniker Taki Mashiro was born.

"Seikō o dama~tsu! (Shut the fuck up), you know damn well if there is prize money, I'm playing. Need something to keep up with this shoe and sneaker fetish I got." Taki said jokingly. "Deadass, do you need the money, Michi? I can give it to you. Fuck the tournament. What's up? You good?" She questioned.

"Girl, you know I'm good. Just wanted to kick some ass tonight since my best friend is across the fucking globe, instead of being here with me singing our hearts out at karaoke and stuffing our faces with sushi! I just miss you. That's why I really called," Michi spoke shyly. Neither girl was much with the mushy stuff, but they always let each other know they loved each other. Michi's family somewhat adopted Taki since they found out her story in Japan. Even though they weren't her exchange program guardians, they treated her as one of their own and always welcomed her in their hearts and home.

"I miss you too Mama." Taki said with a warm feeling in her chest. "I gotta get you out of Tokyo, girl. Come to the states and visit. I can find you a nice piece of chocolate when you get here!", she said playfully. "Girl, I have to feed myself and get ready for these matches. If I win, I'm buying you a ticket for you to come to visit me for the holidays. I can't spend another Christmas here without at least another member of my family.", Taki said.

"Oh shit, I'm twerking in my chair!!!". Michi yelled through the phone. "Twerking in my chair! I can't wait. You know your ass is going to win, so just book my ticket, and it's on! Love you! Saraba da! (Bye)." Taki heard Michi disconnect the call.

Taki somewhat hugged her phone as if Michi could still feel her and then decided to make dinner. She committed to a clean way of eating by doing alkaline vegan meals. So far, it had been two weeks, and she felt great. Back in NYC, Taki had dumped the balanced diet she was used to and knew that she gained a few pounds. It's just that she looked the same with a bigger butt and breasts. Taki did not claim that ugly word—fat. However, she was definitely not in the Vogue model category due to her curves.

She stood at five feet nine inches, two hundred and twenty pounds. Taki was what some people would consider a "Brick House." Natural caramel bronze-like colored skin; jet black, thick, coarse hair that reached the middle of her back, luscious triple D breasts, and an ass that most women nowadays pay for. The true definition of a video vixen. Taki recalled a few rappers from the neighborhood that would always try to talk her into being in their little block party videos, but to no avail.

Her martial arts training undeniably helped put some more definition in those curves. With her use of a vegan eating guide, she figured she could afford to lose a couple of pounds. Roasting some vegetables with quinoa, Taki ate her dinner, adding a bowl of blueberries and strawberries as a snack for her tournament. She set up her gaming area and grabbed her headset and controller; she was ready to kick some ass.

A sudden knock on the door stopped her in her tracks.

"WHAT THE FUCK?!" Taki said, frustrated. "Who is it? Better be a good fucking reason you're at my door. If I miss the first round, I'm cussing you the fuck out!" she grumbled on her way to the front door.

LADY M

"This place is disgusting. How could Takisha choose a place with so much negative energy in the air?" M said, wrinkling her nose. She felt as if her shoes shouldn't even be touching what was considered the ground. Not being a fan of NYC, Lady M, as her little annoying charge called her, continued her stroll down the dirty streets. "Where in all fire did those raggedy things come from?" she continued, talking to herself. "How did they get here? This is not what I am here for. That boy better be lucky I sensed them when I did, or he would have been done for."

She stopped to make sure she was at the correct address then began walking to the side door, knocking, making sure whoever was inside could hear. Defensive mode kicked in when she heard cursing and yelling towards the door as if there was a threat. M unsheathed her twin arm blades, standing at defense as the door opened.

"WHO THE FUCK IS IT?!" Taki yelled and immediately jumped back in shock, meeting M's deadly stare.

M quickly assessed the area and found no threat. "Well, such language for a beautiful woman such as yourself. I thought there was a threat in the house. Don't ever do that again. I almost cut your head off." She smiled as she spoke.

Lady M, as Taki nicknamed her when they first met, stood at five feet, two inches tall with flawless, caramel colored skin and hair that was always pulled back into a sleek ponytail that reached the arch of her back. She always dressed as if she was going to a business meeting. Skirt, blouse, jacket, and knee-high heeled boots. Very stylish and incredibly chic with her small frame. She was petite in height and size but moved like a murderous snake.

"Well, isn't it the queen of Hell herself? What did the world of lowly peasants such as me do to deserve to be in your presence?" Taki rolled her eyes, annoyed. She continued, "Come in. You interrupted something important that I was doing, so this better be good. Just FYI, threats are usually on the other side of the door."

M shuffled by Taki through the door to close it and continued through the walkway to go back to her sitting area. M scanned the room for any clues of the information she received while she watched Taki sit on the couch and pick up some device and start talking. "Hey, my bad guys, come on. I'm not with the shits today. Don't fuck with me! I'm winning this shit tonight, and you pussies are going to be mad!" Taki said excitedly.

M, speechless at her language, sat in the chair and just watched as Taki did whatever it was, she was doing. M began to get lost in her thoughts. She remembered why she came to check in on her young charge. She looked at Taki with a sense of familiarity and awe. Every now and again, she would stare at Taki with a look of wonder as if she *knew* her. Of course, she'd been her charge for about fourteen years now, but there was always something more that she felt when she looked at Takisha.

M spoke over all the noise from the picture box. "Takisha, turn that off now. We have to speak about your condition. I might have something that could help."

She reflected back to her conversation with her boss. *"She has to get through this herself. DO NOT INTERFERE; she will overcome it all."* Still, after fourteen years on the sideline with this young woman and watching Taki go through so much pain and torment, M felt she deserved some relief from the pain.

"I have contacts that are working on a serum. It can assist you with the sleep issues that you've been having." M watching Taki continue to mess with the device, "Turn off that gadget and pay attention NOW!" M stated calmly through clenched teeth.

Taki recognized the seriousness in the tone of M's voice and quickly yelled into the headset, "Guys, I have to go! Michi, kick-ass!" She disconnected and turned off the console, waiting for M to speak.

"I still have not found any solution to your predicament. The only thing I can suggest is this serum that I have. It should assist you in sleeping.", M spoke calmly. "Any new episodes since we last spoke?" She already knew the answer since M herself felt the surge of energy.

Taki answered quickly, "The one I had yesterday was fucking, I mean, really crazy. There was a puddle of sweat in my bed. I found it weird because it was in a complete circle. This shit is creeping me out. I have black sheets, but I still could make out a complete circle of sweat."

M pondered what could be the cause of this phenomenon and assessed that the energy surge was getting much more potent than it had been in Japan. She shook out of her thoughts. "Just try this. Take about one teaspoon right before bed." M revealed a small bottle of a cough syrup-like substance. "Do NOT take more than what I said, or it will have dire consequences. This is a new psychological drug that hasn't been tested thoroughly but has been useful for sleep deprivation." She repeated what her contact had told her. Not sure if she could trust him, she had him do a sleep study on his children before giving it to her to give to Taki. She laughed to herself how she had to remind him who she was.

Taki noticed the menacing smile on M's face. "You sure this shit won't kill me? I'm so not feeling the way you're looking at me right now.", she said with a skeptical look.

"Just make sure you take the amount I told you. Too much could have bad side effects. Have you reached out to this friend you spoke of so fondly?"

Taki's eyes sparkled. "Yes. He hasn't returned my call. Almost called him today, but then Michi called, and I got distracted."

M didn't know the boy, but she remembered that Taki said she couldn't go to him before leaving. Even while she was away in Japan, she would see the way Taki's eyes lit up when she spoke of her past with him. *The reminder of the days when she felt the sense of...*

Immediately snapping out of those very long-ago thoughts, she spoke once more.

"Well, make sure you talk to him. You've been waiting ten years to speak. Don't let fear get in the way now." M got up to leave. "Look, there's been some information going around about your parents. As soon as I get the specifics, I will get back to you. Get some rest and keep in touch. You should stop by the dojo to train. Haven't seen you there in a while."

Not sure of the questions or reaction that would come next, M continued down the hallway and out the door to the chilly NYC streets. *I feel it. Something is coming. She better not be involved. I am in no mood.* M looked up at the night sky as she walked away.

"Did she just say what I think she just said? What the hell? Why? What the fuck? Like I care.", Taki whispered unconvincingly. Taki looked at the time. Not in the gaming mood anymore, she decided to get dressed and go out. "Can't stay in this house. Definitely not after evil queen came in here and made it creepy as all hell.", she muttered to herself. "She knows damn well I don't speak about them people or about what happened. Shit, do I know what happened?" She asked herself, feeling slightly lost at the lack of memory.

She walked to her closet and found a pair of black skinny jeans and a black and red sweater with a picture of her favorite rapper and threw on a couple of black and red Jordan 9 sneakers. Taki always had a sneaker fetish. Since she'd been able to take care of herself, she regularly made sure she looked up to par. Now considered a shopaholic, she was making up for the times she didn't have and couldn't take care of herself. Walking out into the brisk night, she grabbed her cell to call her boyfriend. She stopped just at the curb, noticing the white BMW, and met the driver's gaze.

****

After leaving Mikael's and speaking with him, Adam's mind was spinning. "Demons?! Demons?!", he repeated to himself. "Uncle Mike bugging. Powers, demons. This old dude done went on a vacation to the fucking looney bin.", he said, thinking back to what Mikael had told him.

"For some reason, you're special; you were given gifts beyond your understanding. As they manifest, others from that world will be looking for you. Tonight, was just the beginning." Adam remembered what his godfather told him.

What does he want me to do with this information? Am I an alien? Do I turn into a superhero? Fuck that cape shit. I don't know what to do with this. Shit got me tripping. He pulled over to ponder on what Mikael discussed with him. *Do I tell my moms? I have to call Kisha back. What the fuck? How am I thinking about her at a time like this? It wouldn't be a good time anyway. Can't get her involved in whatever it is that's going on.* Rubbing his hands on his face, shaking his head, he looked to his right and into the eyes of the person he had been searching for.

As Taki stood at a halt, looking like a deer shined with headlights, Adam hopped out of his vehicle. He stood at the curb with a stunned look on his face, immediately pulling her into a giant bear hug. "KISH, KISH, WOW, WOW!" He stepped back to assess the individual in front of him, making sure it wasn't his mind playing tricks on him again, still holding her hand.

"Damn, Ma. You were always fine as hell, but damn. You're going to make a motherfucker want to marry you. But um, what you doing out here Ma?", he asked excitedly, not letting her hand go.

Taki stood speechless for a moment as Adam stood right in front of her before she spoke, slightly stuttering. "I live over here. What are you doing here? Are you stalking me? I did call you, but I don't remember giving out my address.", she added.

Adam, staring at her with hunger in his eyes, said, "Mama, I will stalk you to the ends of this Earth. I can't believe you left me all those damn years ago. What's up with that? Had me looking for you and shit. Now I fucking know why. Taki Mashiro? What kind of name is that? Where did you go baby girl? I still feel some kind of way that you disappeared on me like that."

Surprised at his revelation, Taki answered shyly, "A, I didn't know what to say. I mean, what the fuck could I have said? I'm confused by everything that happened. I mean—", Adam, grabbing her face and pulled her body into his, kissing her and interrupting her.

"You don't know how long I've been waiting to do that. I said if I ever saw you again, I wasn't letting you get away from me."

Feeling a spark of electricity flowing throughout her body from his lips, she spoke, "Whoooaaa, wow. Um. Um. Did not expect that, A ." Tilting her head to the side, she looked up at him. "Wow. Um. We definitely have some things to discuss. I was completely unaware of these, um, feelings." Taki was damn near about to explode while she looked at him.

"Come on.", he said, grabbing her hand and opening his passenger door. "You're not going nowhere without me tonight!" Adam stated playfully. Taki grasped his hand and allowed him to lead her to his passenger seat. She watched as he closed the door behind her and then rushed to the driver's side of his car. Adam jumped in and turned to Kisha.

"Girl, where you been? Son?! I missed you. Come on. We going to the diner to get some food and drinks. Catch up and shit. Your ass not too bougie for that, are you?", he asked smiling, showing his perfect white teeth. "Regardless, you stuck with me tonight,", he said as he pulled off into the night.

Riding down the busy streets of NYC, the night air was a little chilly for the top to be down, so they rode in silence for a few minutes. Adam started, "So what's up? Don't get mute on me now, Lil Mama. We have a lot to talk about. It's me, A. Don't be shy."

"Not shy, just in awe. I can't believe I'm seeing you right now. I missed you too. Making me regret leaving you,". Taki said hesitantly. She smiled at him as he drove. "Nice wheels. Don't tell me you still playing bad boy out here?", she said with a side-eye.

"Kish, come on. Don't insult me like that. Too old for that shit now. Your boy is legit. Sneaker store, investments, and some reality show checks. Ya boy is doing good and grinding hard out here. No bullshit for me. Unless you count the strip club,", Adam chuckled.

She was thoroughly impressed with his response. "That's what's up, A! I'm happy for you. I'm a Japanese translator for the UN office downtown. My teacher back in Japan had a plug for me when I decided to come back, so that's where I've been working since, I got back here about six months ago.", she said sheepishly.

"SIX MONTHS AGO?!" he said, turning to Taki as he drove. "You just calling me?! I feel insulted." Placing his hand over his heart, he playfully continued, "Baby girl, your boy is hurt."

"I don't know, scared, nervous? I don't know." Taki stared out the passenger window.

"Nah, on some serious shit, what took you so long to call me?", Adam asked, staring at her while they were at a red light.

Taki turned to stare back at those beautiful brown eyes. "It's a green light,", she said as she laughed at him gawking at her.

"So what? Don't think you're going to get out of answering all my questions tonight either. I've been waiting for this." Adam said sharply, pulling off from the red light.

Noticing that they were almost to the diner, Taki spoke softly, "Real talk. Before we go inside, let me just say this. You were my best friend. Hopefully, you can be my best friend again. I just didn't know how to handle what happened and got scared. I know. I should have stayed to understand what happened. I should have spoken to you before I left, but—", Looking up at him, she watched him stare at her with his eyes almost the color of the sun.

"Adam, your eyes.", she said, searching his features.

"Baby girl, I don't want to talk about that." He said, grabbing her hand. She noticed his eyes were their regular brown color again. She blinked twice. It was almost like it was an illusion.

"A, maybe I should go home. Believe me, I'm glad I saw you, but um, I have a boyfriend.", she hurriedly stated, believing a "fit" was about to come on.

He laughed, still holding her hand, he brought it up to his face, planting soft kisses on it. "Good, I have some competition. Now get your sexy ass out of my car." Adam let her go and stepped out of the luxurious vehicle.

Taki stared at him in disbelief. She watched him walk over to the passenger side and open the door. "Pulling out all the stops tonight, aren't we?". Taki said, smiling.

"Come on, my Amazon Queen." Adam laughed at the nickname he used for her. He reached for her hand again.

"Whatever, A. Don't play. I'll have you ready to beg for mercy under my reign. Stop playing.", Taki nudged Adam aside playfully. She missed his banter and the playfulness he brought out of her. Taki grabbed his arm as they walked towards the diner. "I don't have to worry about a girlfriend, side chick, or wife, or all three, do I? I am so not in the mood to fight tonight.", Taki said seriously.

"Nah, we good, Ma. I don't do those. I was waiting on you." He said, the tone just as severe.

As they waited to be seated, Adam scanned around the area for anything suspicious since he knew things were not regular at the moment. He doubted what Mikael told him, but at the same time, he couldn't forget about what happened ten years ago and what happened the other night. Since he was a usual there, the hostess sat them at his favorite booth off in the corner by themselves.

Nervously, Taki sat down. She thought Adam would sit across from her. Boldly, he parked himself right next to her and put his arm around her. "You not getting away from me tonight, Kish. When I tell you I've been waiting on this, girl. You don't know." Adam stared at her with that longing look in his eyes.

"Okay, well, do you remember my usual? And I'll add a shot of Patrón on the side with a glass of water with lemon.", Taki questioned, coming out of her little shell.

"Girl, don't threaten me with a good time. I got this. Patrón? Good choice. It looks like I'll join you." Adam said, smiling as the waitress walked up to the table. "Let me get two cheeseburgers with fries, no onions, well done, four shots of Patrón and two glasses of water with lemon on the side." He gazed at Taki the whole time as he gave the order. "Anything else, beautiful?" Before she could answer, he spoke again. "Oh, and an order of mozzarella sticks for just in case she's hungry while we wait. Don't rush the food. We chilling."

Taki interrupted Adam, "Sorry, cancel the sticks and make that one cheeseburger and fries, and can you tell me if you have any vegan options?". Taki looked at the waitress curiously.

"I hear the tofu burger and the apple sesame salad is good."

Taki immediately responded. "I'll try the tofu burger with fries, thank you. So you did remember. I'm somewhat impressed. Wouldn't have expected you to remember that."

"How could I forget? That's all your ass ordered for like three years straight. Wow, vegan now. Really?", he asked as Adam stared at her curves lustily.

"Haha, funny. It used to be my favorite food from here, man. Don't judge me." Taki pointed her finger in his face playfully. She changed back to a more serious tone. "First, I want to say I'm sorry for just leaving the way I did. We won't speak on that yet, but I am sorry for taking off the way I did." Taki nervously looked up at him.

He placed his hand on her thigh. "Go ahead. I want to hear you all the way out." Adam stared at her with those mesmerizing eyes.

"Remember Ms. Brown from the child protective agency? The one that used to help me out?" Taki waited for him to answer.

"I think so. I remember you talking about that lady.", Adam answered hesitantly.

"Well, she got me into a foreign exchange program back in eleventh grade. I was supposed to go then but chose not to. After the 'incident'.", Taki put up air quotation marks, "I chose to leave because I was scared, and I figured I could run away from it all while I had the opportunity." She looked down at her fidgeting hands.

Adam placed his left hand over both of hers, lifting her chin using his right hand. "Baby girl, don't apologize. I can only imagine what you were going through at that time. I just wish you allowed me to be there for you. I was always so used to being there for you that it hurt me that you shut me out like that. I didn't know what to do. I asked the principal and the guidance counselor you were cool with what happened to you, and they said you got accepted to a program somewhere. That's all they would tell me." He stared at her with that yearning look. "Again, I don't want an apology. Just tell me, how was Japan? What city did you live in? Shit, you always loved anime, karate flicks, and video games. Perfect place for you, in my opinion.", he said, laughing.

Taki laughed with him. "I loved it, man. It was awesome. I got introduced to an awesome family that took me in for the program. Ms. Brown, if you remember, had the dojo in the Bronx that I was forced to go to when I got into that last fight with that girl.", she scowled.

Adam thanked the waitress for their drinks. "Yea, I remember that they had to use damn near the whole security team in the school to get you off that girl. I remember my sister coming to get me, and it was me that made you stop. My crazy Amazon.", he said jokingly.

Taki rolled her eyes. "Anyway, she had a plug for a great dojo out there to continue my training. Instead of me coming back for graduation, she got it to where I could stay and graduate there and go to college. So that's what I did. I went to school for Anthropology with a minor in African Studies. Had a cool job working as a senior research analyst for a data company. No kids, no husband, just a quirky best friend and a few other people I got close to while there. Never stopped thinking about you, though."

He was awestruck by what he heard. "Wow! Lil Mama been busy. I'm impressed. Anthropology? What the hell is that? African Studies, I can see that. That's what's up. I'm proud of you. Congratulations." Adam said with that perfect white smile. "When my sister told me she spoke to you, I was in shock. I know that Facebook shit is a small world, but damn. So, I'm going to thank the internet and the Facebook gods for bringing you back to me."

Blushing, Taki continued, "I loved it. Did not want to come back at all. Still wondering why, I did," she said, drinking her last shot of Patrón.

Moving closer to whisper in her ear, Adam said, "Stop frontin'! You came back for me. You were missing me too much. Couldn't take it anymore. Had to come home to Daddy."

Taki felt like she could feel the heat coming off of him. "Whatever, A. I'm not playing this game with you. Order me another drink, Mr. McFlirt." She said, putting some distance between them. "True shit, I'm still trying to figure it out. Ms. Brown and my sensei felt it would be good for me to come back and make sure all chapters from the past are closed."

Calling the waitress over to order more drinks, Adam responded, "All chapters closing, huh? Sounds like you doing some soul-searching girl. Well, just as long as you don't disappear on me again, I don't care what you searching for. Even though I think you found what you were looking for."

There goes that beautiful smile again. "I'm not searching for anything, thank you very much.", Taki said sarcastically. "I am very much happy with my little life. I have a good man that treats me well. I make great money and look good as hell with my best friend that I get to talk to all the time. So, I'm not complaining.", she said snippily. "I guess I have to close that chapter that neither one of us wants to deal with right now. Ms. Brown told me she received some information on that night." Sensing Adam tense up, she placed her hand on his forearm. "I still haven't told anyone what we saw that night. I barely remember it, to be honest." She spoke barely in a whisper.

Feeling a sense of calm coming from her, Adam answered, "It's all good, Lil Mama. We'll get to that eventually. I don't want to mess up my first time seeing you in years. Just know we'll discuss that later." Adam had to adjust himself to where he was still close but left enough space for them to have a face-to-face conversation. "Well, great update, Ma. Glad to hear you're doing so well, except for the boyfriend part." Adam said, smiling. "I had a girl. Things didn't work out. You know me, Kish. I can be a little distant sometimes, and I see that doesn't work for a relationship and causes issues. So, I'm chilling until my future wife finishes playing with her boy toy." He laughed as he ended his sentence.

Taki looked at him as he took his shot. "Well, I always told you it's okay to let people in, A. You're not by yourself. Just open up. So, besides being an entrepreneur, what else have you been up to? How's your family? Your sister Tay gave me a little update. My condolences about your father, and send my love to your mom. Your family was always good to me. I can't imagine how you all feel about losing him.", she said, remembering the good times she spent upstairs in their building with his family.

"They moved out to Jersey. Pops bought him and Mom a house out there about seven years ago before he passed away. Mom is doing good, though, enjoying Erica and Denise's kids. Tay and I are still going strong with holding off on the grandkids." Adam chuckled. "Everybody good, though. Thank you. We still holding firm for Ma. You know Pops built us Ford tough. I really haven't been up to much. You know he made sure I wasn't going to stay a knucklehead."

"I went to Morgan State University, the HBCU in Baltimore, graduated from there, and started working with a marketing company in downtown Baltimore for a few years. Got into the nightlife there but missed home and made a plan for me to come back to NYC. I was able to network with a lot of people in that area and got into stock investments while at MSU, which helped. Opened up a sneaker store and bought me a penthouse downtown here in the city. With my networking skills, I got my sneaker store featured on those reality shows about rappers and their lives. Been back here in the city for about three years now." Adam stared at Taki as she listened closely to his words. "I was hoping you would have been here when I got back. But nope.", he said, taking another shot of alcohol. "It's all good. I found you now." He turned back to look directly at her with a smirk.

Taki was impressed with his life update. "Wow, A, that's what's up. I'm happy for you. Sounds like you living your best life out here. I'm definitely going to have to check out that store you got. You know I love me a good pair of kicks." Taki said, smiling ear-to-ear.

"Don't think I didn't peep the black and red Nines you got on your feet right now. I see you, fly girl.", Adam said teasingly. Noticing how neither one of them barely touched the food, Adam asked, "Want anything else? You sure you good?"

Taki answered, a little tipsy, "I'm straight, maybe one more shot and some water for me. I'm actually enjoying myself." She picked up her phone to check the time. "Oh shit, it's like one in the morning. Damn.", she said, wiping her face.

"Have somewhere to be? Boyfriend will be looking for you?", Adam questioned.

"FYI, Mr. Nosey, my boyfriend does not live with me, and I do what I want. So, don't go being funny."

"If you're ready to go, let me know. I can bring you home. You're going to have to give me your address, though. Believe it or not, I just randomly pulled over, coming from my godfather's house, to, um... I mean, from talking to him," Adam said nervously, bringing up the memory of what Mikael was talking to him about.

"We can go now. Haven't been getting much sleep, so I need to get some rest while I can.", Taki said, yawning and regretting that last shot.

"Got you. Same here. I have to go to the store tomorrow too. Some celebrity clients are coming in to shop before regular business hours, so I have to be there. Come on." Adam placed two hundred-dollar bills on the table as they got up to leave.

****

As he drove back towards the upper west side of Manhattan, the area where Taki lived, Adam glanced over and to see Taki fast asleep in his passenger seat. Adam turned the heat up a bit and laid the chair back so she could be more comfortable. "Shit, she didn't give me her address. Kish," he called to her, slightly raising his voice. "Kish, Kish," nudging her, "Yo, you forgot to give me your address. I don't know where you live. Kish."

Slightly waking up, she responded, confused, "Huh? Doko ni ikimasu (Where we are going)?"

"What the fuck did you just say?". Adam snickered. "Kish, what's your address? I don't know where you live." He pulled over on a block he thought he was on earlier. "Kish, Takisha, Takisha! Wake up. Give me your address.", he said, nudging Taki as he spoke.

"Huh, wah? San-Shi-Go Tōri, Hachi Ju Hachi (speaking her address)."

As soon as she finished speaking, she fell back to sleep. Laughing at her response, Adam continued trying to wake Taki for her address so he could get her home safely. After going back and forth in English and Japanese with Taki for about another fifteen minutes, Adam gave up and decided to head home.

"Fuck it. I'll carry her ass to the elevator if I have to. Make a mental note, no more tequila for Kisha. She starts speaking in tongues and shit ." He glanced over at her sleeping while he drove to his penthouse.

Parking in his reserved spot, Adam decided to give it one more try to see if she really was sleeping.

"Kish, Kish. We at my crib. I'm taking you upstairs. We at my house. You're going upstairs with me."

"Atchi e itte kudasai, kuso (Please go away, fuck)!" Taki responded, aggravated.

"Okay. Let's do this!" Adam said, laughing. "How this brings back memories." He remembered the times they both would be so wasted walking from the house parties in their building. Holding her as if he were carrying her on their wedding day, he stepped onto the elevator and pressed the code for the top floor as he watched her beautiful face snug against his chest as if that was where she belonged. Enjoying the sight in front of him, he walked off the elevator towards the guest bedroom since his new bed hadn't come in yet and placed Taki on the king-sized bed. Taking her shoes off and putting the comforter over her, he chose to stay up.

Adam sat at his desk near where Taki was sleeping to do some paperwork. After about an hour, he started to feel sleep coming. Grabbing a pillow from the bed and a blanket from the linen closet in the hallway, he laid down on the carpeted floor, next to a sleeping Taki, thinking, *I'm only going to lay down for a little while. I won't sleep long.* He set his smartwatch for a six-a.m. alarm. As his head touched the pillow, he immediately drifted off to sleep.

SPRINGTIME

Taki jumped out of a drunken stupor. "Oh shit, my head. What the fuck?! Koko wa doko (Where am I)?" She rubbed her eyes, looking around to find a bottle of water and some aspirin sitting on a nightstand next to her. Checking her cell for the time, she saw a text from Adam that read, HEY LIL MAMA. I HAD TO GO TO THE STORE THIS AM. YOU WERE SLEEPING SO PEACEFULLY. I FIGURED YOU'D GET UP ON YOUR OWN. THERE'S A DRIVER DOWNSTAIRS WAITING TO TAKE YOU HOME SINCE YOU FORGOT OR WON'T GIVE ME YOUR ADDRESS. I'M HAPPY I RAN INTO YOU LAST NIGHT. MAKE SURE YOU DON'T DISAPPEAR ON ME AGAIN. LATER." As soon as she finished reading it, her phone died.

Taking a sip of the bottle of water, getting up to look around for a bathroom, Taki was surprised at where she ended up. She tried to remember last night's events. "How the hell?", she asked herself as she walked around looking for signs of a female or roommate. Taking a small tour of his penthouse, except for the locked door, most likely the master bedroom, Taki observed the area, impressed with what she saw.

The living room had a lovely earth-tone color scheme, next to an open kitchen with stainless steel appliances and French doors leading to a balcony with a beautiful sitting area. There was no sign of a woman, but she knew that he most likely paid a designer or told the realtor to keep it exactly like he bought it. Checking the time, "Nanda Ittai (What the fuck)! I slept that long?! Two o'clock?!" She grabbed her sneakers, feeling unusually well-rested as she left.

****

"What's up, my guy? How you doing?" Adam asked his customer that just walked in, giving him a brother-like hug. As scheduled, Jadakiss, one-third of the legendary rap group the Lox, walked in to make a few purchases. Adam was still ecstatic from last night, even though he was a little tired and hungover and was even running late this morning.

"What's going on, my man? Know what you're looking for?"

"Nah, not really."

"I got the new shipment already laid out for you in the back. Come with me," he said, motioning the rapper and his entourage towards the back of the store.

Adam's vision of a sneaker store was a boutique for Nike, Adidas, and other popular street brands. It was very chic and welcoming, with a sport-like feel that made his store famous in the busy NYC fashion market. With a gaming area, small basketball court upstairs, and on-site DJ at all times, walking into Just Kickin' It felt as though you were walking into a party to shop.

"Man, you definitely stepped your game up since the last time I was here. Basketball court? Seriously, my G?!" Jadakiss said jokingly. "I'm digging it, though, digging it. Show me what you got," he said, walking slightly behind Adam towards the room for VIP shoppers.

"Derrick, make sure the floor is stocked well. Sade, get on the displays. Peggy, you can come with me."

A good friend of Adam's and his business partner, Peggy met Adam while attending MSU. She had hazelnut-colored skin. She was thicker than a snicker, as the men would say. This week's hair color was a blue and black mix. Peggy was an Atlanta chick that ended up in Baltimore stripping to go to college. She had graduated with a degree in Economics the same year as Adam. They both kept in touch with different business ventures and investments. She was great at networking and finding numerous ways to make money. She was the true definition of a hustler. They never had an intimate relationship even though she was sexy as hell. Peggy reminded Adam of one of his sisters and always treated her as such from the time they met.

"What up, what ya need me fo'? I already ordered the desk," she said in her sweet voice with a southern twang, staring at him sharply.

"Not gon' speak on it while we got company," he said, smiling. "I need you to keep Jada and his people busy and happy. See if they want any refreshments and let me know if you need me. Have to make a few calls real quick." Adam rushed off and jogged down the hallway to his office. "Don't worry, I'll pay for the desk with my own money!" he laughed as he continued down the hallway.

Peggy retorted back before he could disappear from her sight. "Do I look like your motherfucking assistant? It's done already. The store wasn't payin' fo' yo' shit!" She then walked towards the VIP shopping area to assist the rapper.

Adam closed his office door to sit at his desk. He pulled his cell phone out of his pocket, calling a number saved in his phone. "What's up, my friend? She left? Word? Where you drop her at? Message for me? Huh? She said that? Damn, always so stubborn," he said, chuckling. "Aight, thanks, my man. I'm good. I'm driving today. If I go out later, I'll call you." *End call.*

Scrolling to his favorite person in the world, he pressed the call button. "Hey, beautiful. Love and miss you. How are you today, Ma?" he said, waiting for an answer on the other end.

"Hey, baby," Valerie replied. "I'm good. Too blessed to be stressed. How are you? How have you really been?" she asked curiously. "I was on the phone with Tay, but I told her I would call her back since I saw you calling me."

"Is she good, Ma? Trouble with her?" he asked, raising his eyebrow.

"Boy, don't ignore me. How have you been?" Valerie said in her motherly voice.

"I'm good, Ma. Like you say, too blessed to be stressed, right?" Adam answered hesitantly. "I do have some good news to share with you, though. One, I saw Uncle Mike. He's back around. Went to see him yesterday, and then guess who I ran into?"

"Who? In that damn store, I can only imagine who you see," Valerie answered.

"Kish, Ma. I ran into her on the Upper West Side, driving back from Mike's crib. Word, it was crazy," he said, drifting off to the thoughts of talking and then carrying her to his apartment.

Snapping out of it, Adam listened to his mother speak. "Well, that's definitely a surprise. How is she? Tay told me she spoke to her a while ago on that internet, but I didn't know she was here in the city," she said.

"To my understanding, she's been back here for a while. About six months. She works down at the UN office. She was in Japan all these years."

"Oh wow, Japan. That's far away. Interesting. Did you ask her why she didn't keep in touch and why she never called you? And did y'all really talk?" she asked, remembering her son's pain when Taki left.

"Yes, Ma. We spoke about that a little bit," he replied in his low voice. Adam always had a great relationship with his parents, so they knew about the "incident" that he never spoke of. "You know I'm not ready to speak on that, so no, if that's what you were looking for," he stated, somewhat aggravated.

"Look, I just want to know if you're good. It's weird all this shit going on, and she suddenly pops up. I'm glad to hear Mikael is back around. He called me to check in."

"I dig it, Ma. You're looking out for your baby boy, but I'm good. No harm, no foul. We kicked it, and that was it. Word up. You always liked Kish, so don't go acting funny now," he said, cheering the conversation back up.

"Never said I don't I just find it strange that you ran into Takisha like that. Anyway, let me call your sister back. It was nice talking to you, son. Love you always. Call me if you need me."

"Love you too, Ma. Tell Tay to check her phone in a few minutes." Hanging up and going to the money transfer application on his phone, Adam sent his sister $500. "That's my good deed for the day," he mumbled to himself.

Now, let's see if she read my message. He checked his texts and saw that Taki had read his message but hadn't responded.

"Let's see if her funny acting ass answers the phone," he said, pressing the call button. "Hello, you have reached Taki Mashiro. I am un—" *End call.* "Well damn, Kish." Fantasizing about seeing her, being around her, her voice, smell, chocolate brown eyes, and feeling the fire coming from within him, Adam closed his eyes, slowly breathing. "Play hard to get if you want to. I like a good challenge." Smiling, he rose from his office chair to continue his workday.

****

Walking down her block, Taki made the driver drop her off a couple of blocks away to make sure he didn't tell Adam exactly where she lived. Remembering the message, she told the driver, "Tell A I said thanks, and maybe I'll let him know where I live next time," laughing at the thought of him popping up on her anytime.

"I need to brush my teeth and shower. What the hell? When was the last time I stayed out all night?" Walking into her apartment, she remembered her phone was dead. "Damn, that's what I get for never charging it," she grumbled to herself. Placing the cell phone on the wireless charger, Taki walked to the kitchen to see if she had any leftovers from dinner yesterday. She settled on grabbing the bowl of strawberries and blueberries that she had after M left. "Fuck it. It's Saturday. I'll find something to do today."

After going to her bedroom to shower and get dressed, there was a sudden knock on her door.

"Y'all motherfuckers are definitely O.D.in'. Just coming to my door without announcing you're coming. Better be the fucking lottery or Publishers Clearing House." She snatched the door open to see who was disturbing her late afternoon start, only to be faced with a bouquet of assorted flowers and a tall, dark chocolate, handsome man that would make any woman melt.

Mark, standing six feet tall, had skin the color of a Hershey kiss that glistened in the sun, bright dark brown eyes, and dark eyebrows that you swore he got waxed; they were so perfect. He had the prettiest white teeth that shined against his dark skin. His features reminded her so much of Adam. Those dark eyes and eyebrows made her think of the fire yellow color she had seen in Adam's eyes last night. Snapping out of her thoughts, she spoke.

"Hey baby, what are you doing here? Why didn't you call me? You know I don't like unannounced visitors," she said, staring at him in disbelief.

Mark moved in to give her a hug and kiss, with flowers still in hand. "Good afternoon, beautiful. I was hoping you were home. I know you don't like surprises, but I wanted to spend this afternoon with you."

Returning his kiss and hug, Taki began motioning him inside, following him down the hall. "Oh, wow. Well, you caught me about to get in the shower. I didn't have plans, but why didn't you call?" She grabbed the flowers to place them in a vase. "These are beautiful, handsome. Smells wonderful. Thank you very much," she said, smelling the flowers as she walked to the kitchen.

"You're welcome, beautiful. I figured I could come put a smile on your face. Michelle told me you looked upset before you left work yesterday. I tried calling you earlier today since I didn't hear from you since we last spoke. And today, I kept getting your voicemail."

After placing the flowers in a vase with water, Taki walked back to the sitting area where Mark was seated. "Like I told you yesterday, I had some things to do with Michi, then Ms. Brown came over here last night. After she left, I went out for a little bit and ran into an old friend from school." She still struggled to remember what had happened last night. "My phone did die. You know I never charge it," she said, chuckling.

"I know, that's why I just came over." He smiled. Moving closer to her, placing his hands on her hips to draw her in, he kissed her on her neck and said, "I missed you."

Kissing him back on the cheek, Taki moved back and stood up. "Hey, I'm going to get in the shower. Give me a sec. I'll be out in a bit, and we can figure out what we're going to get into," Taki said, walking towards the bedroom to go shower and get dressed.

Disgruntled, Mark pulled out his cell phone to send a text message and turned on the TV for background noise as he waited for Taki. "Damn, she still won't let me hit?"

As Taki showered, her thoughts wandered to why she hadn't slept with Mark yet. She thought she liked him. He was attractive, but she couldn't bring herself to go all the way with him for some reason. He was the guy Taki met when she returned to the U.S. They worked in the same building, knew mutual associates, and decided to go on a few dates. The next thing she knew, they were an item. He never pressured her for sex, even though he always let it be known that he was sexually attracted to her and wanted to have sex with her every chance he got. At first, she desired to go there with him, but for some reason, as time went on, she never could bring herself to go all the way with Mark.

"It's sad. I rather let go with my toys than add him to my list of suitors." She chuckled out loud at her thoughts. Michi used to tease her all the time. "You don't have a boyfriend; you have a toyfriend."

They always went out to expensive restaurants, theaters, movies, a couple of work functions, but she still didn't want to sleep with him. Mark made her feel comfortable. He gave her beautiful gifts, but she was not sexually attracted to him enough to sleep with him, nor did she have strong feelings for him. They had been dating for about four months now. She hadn't felt a touch of wanting someone in a long time, then she thought of how she had felt when Adam kissed her.

"Why him?" she asked herself. "Of course, him."

Getting out of those feelings and finishing up her shower, Taki called out to Mark. She wrapped her extra-large towel around her naked body as she stepped out of the steamy bathroom.

"Hey, where are we going? Anywhere I have to dress up?"

Seeing Taki walk to her bedroom, Mark got up from the couch and followed her. "Well, I do have reservations for us at City Island. Afterward, I was thinking of going to see that new exhibit at the museum, and then it's up to you." He stared at her as she went through her closet trying to decide what to wear.

Hearing him in her bedroom, she turned around. "Oh, I didn't know you came back here," she said, peeved.

"I'm sorry, I wanted to make sure I could hear you. Taki," he said sensually, "you are so beautiful to me." Walking towards her, he grabbed her waist with his left hand and her chin in his right. "I want you."

He pressed his lips against hers firmly. After she kissed him back, he began to place kisses down the outline of her cheekbone to her neck. Rubbing her upper thigh, he whispered, "I want you so bad, Taki. You are so lovely, all for me."

It's been so long, and he's supposed to be turning me on, but it feels so bland. I'm not really feeling his kisses or touches. Too often, she attempted to make herself feel something for Mark to sleep with him. Snapping out of her thoughts of the first base attempt at love-making due to her feeling him tug on her towel to move to second base, she hesitantly said, "I'm not ready, Mark. I like you, I do, but I'm not ready to give myself up yet. It's been a long time, and I want to make sure it's real."

Slightly angry, heavily breathing through clenched teeth, he responded, "Baby, come on, we are as real as it gets. I want you so bad." He grabbed her waist once more to pull her back closer. "You are everything I have ever wanted," he said, kissing her again.

"I like you too, Mark. I'm not ready. I'm sorry." She kissed him softly and then started to walk away.

Mark stood there, obviously frustrated. "I'm sorry too, beautiful. I just want to make you happy. I want to show you how I feel about you." He grabbed her hand and caressed her arm.

She grabbed his face and spoke slowly. "You do show me. Us having sex has nothing to do with that. When I am ready, I will let you know." She kissed him on the cheek and walked back to her closet. Taki turned around to face Mark. "You know you don't have to do this. I know it's probably difficult for you, but I made a promise to myself, and I am sticking to it," she said, turning back around to find something to wear.

"It's okay, Taki. I understand. Just know, I love you. I want this. I will be here for you for however long you allow me." Mark spoke confidently. "I'll be out here if you need me. It's going to be chilly later, so keep that in mind when you pick out something to wear," he said as he walked back into the living room.

Just like that, they were back to normal. Mark would try, get denied, and then they would go about the day as if nothing happened. Finding a nice pair of hip-hugging, blue skinny jeans paired with a light multi-colored off-the-shoulder sweater with tan ankle booties, Taki finished getting dressed. Brushing her hair into a bun, Taki walked from her bedroom entirely dressed. She added gold hoop earrings and gold hoop bracelets with a gold and diamond heart pendant necklace that she had for ages right before she walked into the living room.

"Hey, you ready? Sorry it took me so long," she said excitedly. "It's a beautiful day! I can't wait to eat. I'm starved."

"I'm hungry too. I figure we can Uber. I wanted to have a few drinks and not worry about parking.

"I couldn't agree with you more."

"They'll be here in fifteen minutes. Come on, beautiful, let's go enjoy our day."

He reached out for Taki's hand. Grabbing her phone and keys and throwing them in her purse, Taki placed her hand in Mark's, and they proceeded outside to wait for their ride.

****

Riding in the Uber with Mark, watching his lovely smile as he was texting, Taki pulled out her phone to send a text to Michi. HEY BOO, HOW DID THE TOURNAMENT GO? CALL ME WHEN YOU GET A CHANCE. YOU WOULDN'T BELIEVE WHAT HAPPENED TO ME YESTERDAY.

While she waited on Michi to respond, she figured now was as good a time as any to text Adam back. HEY, WHAT'S UP, THANKS FOR BEING A GENTLEMAN LAST NIGHT. WE WILL KEEP IN TOUCH. TAKE IT EASY. She placed the heart on his message for good measure.

Mark grabbed her hand as she placed her phone back in her purse. "So, tell me, what's been going on? We haven't got together in a few weeks. Don't tell me that it's work," he said, searching her face for answers.

She looked at him sheepishly. "Honestly, it has been the office. So much BS goes on there, and I haven't been sleeping. I can be cranky when I don't sleep." She turned to look out the window, still holding his hand.

"I know, Taki. I just want to spend more time with you. I really enjoy your company," he said, squeezing her hand as he spoke.

"I know, handsome. We will. I'll get better at balancing work and us. Cool?" she said, giving him a gleaming smile.

"Yes, beautiful. I would love that."

They got out of the Uber and walked toward City Island Lobster House. Mark got them reservations on the water for the afternoon. As always, he pulled out the stops. Going to their reserved table, Mark pulled out Taki's chair and then sat across from her. Taki giggled at the thought of the boldness Adam showed when he sat right next to her.

"So, what do you want to order, beautiful? What's on the mind that's making you smile? I hope I'm included in those thoughts," Mark said, smiling back at Taki.

"Well, I'm thinking about how I am happy that you came to check on me and how we are going to have a wonderful afternoon."

"That's all I want, beautiful," Mark replied as the waitress walked to the table to take their orders.

MIKAEL

Pacing back and forth in the living room of one of his many apartments throughout NYC, Mikael began thinking. *What in the heavens is going on? What is he? Obviously, he's spilling out energy that they can sense.* For all the years Mikael has known Adam, he never could figure out what kind of creature he was and chose to stick around to try and find out. Being a science experiment for Mikael, he developed a closeness to the young boy and his family. He decided to train, protect, and assist his parents in raising him with the issues Adam had.

Initially, Adam's father, Senior, was a possible recruit in their early years of the security firm. Mikael was a partner. During one of Mikael's numerous visits to the Moore household, he came across a young Adam and witnessed one of the "issues" he still had to this day. Due to the established relationship with Adam's father, it made it much easier for Mikael to keep his eye on the boy.

Adam's parents were good people, and Mikael made sure he helped them without directly interfering with their lives. Since the passing of Senior, Mikael had become even closer to Adam, assisting the family in all aspects of their lives. Unsure of what Adam was, he made sure he helped him control his fire sensations and energy with yoga and meditation teachings.

From a little boy, Adam would produce mass surges of power and fire in his sleep. He also showed signs of being more robust, faster, and more intelligent than average humans throughout his childhood to adulthood. Although Mikael understood that there were such phenomena globally, he could not pinpoint what exactly Adam was, which kept him intrigued with the boy all of these years. Unfortunately, Adam was getting stronger and had been having more fits of fire lately.

Remembering why he left five months ago, he got a tip on a young woman in the Far East having similar issues. He went to see if one of his contacts could get him in touch with her to see if their problems were related. Resulting in a dead-end when he went to Japan, Mikael met with an associate of his to assist in finding the young woman. Knowing the associate was not trustworthy, Mikael began to search for his own answers to assist Adam in his plight. "If I just knew what he was, then maybe I could help him."

Mikael considered a mythical being himself, had a significant problem that needed some sorting that had nothing to do with Adam. He couldn't keep ignoring the fact that they were losing this war, a war that had taken its toll on him and continued to defeat his cause.

"I have to figure out something before this gets any worse." He looked up to the sky. "Can I get a break?"

He pulled out his cell phone and placed a call. "Hey, the boy was attacked yesterday. Don't know how he isn't dead right now, but something is up." Listening to the reply on the line, he became concerned. "WHAT?!!!! I'm on my way." Mikael rushed out of the door as soon as he ended the call.

While walking down the street, Mikael realized he had to place another call.

"Have you thought about our conversation, and are you being safe?" he asked in a severe tone, skipping all the pleasantries.

"I wish you would stop it, man. You dead ass making me think I should have you committed," Adam answered just as fiercely. "Look, Uncle Mike, I'm at work right now. How about we link up later so we can have a real conversation?".

"Not sure what I'll be doing later, Adam, but you need to take this situation seriously. We will talk," Mikael said, hanging up the phone. "That boy is going to make me very angry," he said as he thought about his location and where he was going. Tired of traveling as a human, Mikael transferred to Otherside to remain unseen. He unleashed those gigantic wings and rushed to the sky, off to meet with his friend of many ages.

****

"Xeno, what is this you were saying on the phone? Did they take over another den? How?" Mikael asked, pacing in front of a bleeding Xeno on a rooftop building just outside of White Plains, NY. "What in damnation are you doing?"

Xeno, one of Mikael's friends and soldiers, was a guardian of Mikael's area in Upstate New York. Being one of Mikael's most trusted friends, Xeno stood at six feet, six inches tall. His skin was the color of an almond, eyes the color of snow, hair black as night worn in a low, curly afro, with a thick and jagged scar that went down the left side of his face. Barely missing the corner of his mouth.

"Look, don't piss me off more! I had no choice but to let them take it over. Would have been too many casualties to defeat them. We can get it back," Xeno said, doubled over, trying to catch his breath. "Where the fuck was you?!!! Chasing that fucking boy again? Shit, if he's as powerful as you say he is, have him join us. We need the assistance. We lost about twenty today, including Lieutenant Zel," Xeno said, staring coldly.

Mikael and Xeno stood eye-to-eye glaring at each other, with Xeno slightly larger in size.

Mikael yelled, "Don't tell me what it would have taken to defend and keep this place. You were responsible for keeping this place under us. You failed!" he said, staring back just as coldly. "Far as pissing off, your incompetence is pissing ME off!" Mikael stepped away from Xeno to contemplate their current state of affairs.

Xeno yelled back, "You're the one playing fucking human daddy and shit while we continue to fight this war and die! Your fucking fancy suits and shoes won't change the fact that we're losing and dying! So, I can give two fucks about how pissed you are. I had to watch twenty of the people that I considered friends die, so, fuck you, prick!"

Mikael stepped closer to Xeno's face to confront the anger that he felt due to the loss of his friends as well. "Let me tell you som—" Mikael was interrupted by a hand on his shoulder.

Dillon interrupted the two men. "Look, he is not the enemy here. We have better things to do than argue like children." Dillon, the leader out of the three men, said in a low flat tone as he stepped in-between Mikael and Xeno.

Dillon stood a few inches shorter than the two men and had dark terracotta skin, green eyes and long, sandy brown hair pulled back into a sleek ponytail that went past his shoulders. He was just as annoyed at the events that Xeno laid out to Mikael. "Now Xeno," one of the few people that could get away with calling him that, "please explain to me how this transpired. I am interested to learn how these demons have come to take over the last of the dens in this area," Dillon said, his glare cold.

"Look, D, I think somebody betrayed us. I was out checking up on the information you sent to me last night. When I came back, there were multiple hordes of mid-level demons attacking the den, and most of the other guards had fled to Otherside or were dead. I killed the ones I could before retreating. There was nothing else I could do but collect what I could and flee. I figured once I regrouped with one of you, we could reclaim the den," Xeno answered, lowering his head as he finished.

"Mikael, as Xeno has asked, where were you?" Dillon pondered on what could have kept Mikael occupied. "Xeno could have used your help, and then maybe we would not be in this predicament right now." He stared at Mikael with a menacing smile.

"Dillon, while you've been off doing whatever it is that you do, Xeno and I have been stuck here training and protecting these soldiers as we figure out our next move. For some reason, the demons are running amok, and we are losing," Mikael said, staring back at Dillon with anger in his eyes.

Dillon nonchalantly replied, "Don't be mad at me, brother, for the foul deeds that those vile creatures have done. I told you. I am in search of getting rid of all our problems for good. To my understanding, you were off doing what it is you do as well, true? Now, if I thought you were not competent enough to handle the army and dens, I wouldn't have left you in control."

He turned to Xeno. "Well, we have some cleaning up to do, Xeno. I am relatively fond of this area and would rather our use of this den continue. So, this is the plan, Mikael. You continue to figure out why there is an increase in demon activity in your area. Xeno, you're going to come with me. It is too soon for them to have sent their cleanup crew to claim the den officially, so that's what we will do since some of our safeguards are still in place. I feel some of the wards are still standing, so the demons have not claimed the area. Make a few calls for mid-level warriors—about ten. We'll take this area back and make sure we don't have this kind of issue again."

"Dillon, I didn't call for reinforcements due to the casualty rate for the humans. The area is busy this afternoon, so by the time we can attempt to reclaim the den, the demon wards will be active," Xeno spoke hesitantly.

Dillon glared back at Xeno. "Then how do you suppose we reclaim the area if you feel the human death toll will be too high? Is this the answer you would give to all that returned to the light?" He stared at Xeno in disbelief then added, "How about this? Make the call as I stated. We will reactivate the wards before they return to the area to claim it. I have a feeling they won't rush since they think there was a full retreat order. Especially since you stated that there were hordes of demons. Why now? They have been bold as of late. Any ideas, Mikael?" He turned his head to Mikael, who was staring blankly over the town.

"We had powerful wards around that den. Even small, the people there weren't a threat—new recruits. I believe something else is at play here. I am not eliminating a traitor amongst us. How would demons get through our wards so fast, and who ordered a full retreat? I did not, and by the look on both your faces, neither one of you did either. So why did the guards retreat? My other question is, what would be the point of taking over this den? There are at least ten other dens in this state that they could have attacked, so why this one? I don't think it was a coincidence. Maybe the attack on Adam is related to this as well," Mikael said, contemplating.

"Ahh, Adam, your young charge. How is he lately? Has he gotten stronger yet?" Dillon asked, eyes gleaming with wonder. "We could use him in this fight."

"He is not ready, Dillon. I attempted to explain to him what was going on, and he dismissed me as one of those mentally challenged humans. I find it preposterous that I have to continue with this charade. If I didn't respect his father, I would have ended Adam years ago since we don't know what he is. I could just tell him the whole truth, so we can figure out what kind of creature he is," Mikael answered Dillon.

"I can clearly sense his blood is of Other. Due to the underdevelopment of these so-called powers, I cannot tell what the Other is exactly. I'm working on that as we speak," Dillon said.

"What is that supposed to mean, Dillon? I trust that Adam will follow any directions or advice I give him to remain normal in his little human life," Mikael sighed rubbing his face.

"Regardless, I do not trust this unknown. We do not have time for anything that would foil our plans to win this war. After Xeno and I clean up this mess with this den and area, I will continue to work on the revelation of this young charge of yours, Mikael. Until then, keep a close eye on him. He isn't trustworthy enough to tell him everything."

"I don't need you to explain what it is we have time for, Dillon. I will make sure to keep an eye on the boy and any other instances that involve those filthy creatures. There has definitely been a spike in their presence in the city. Anything else, sir?" Mikael stated, knowing it would annoy Dillon.

"Well, let's hope your incompetence does not show in the next set of events," Dillon responded blandly. "Let's go, Xeno; we have some evil to vanquish." Dillon laughed as he and Xeno released their beautiful wings and set off for their mission.

****

Standing at the top of the building, looking over the city, still visibly annoyed by the recent events, Mikael contemplated his next series of moves. "I can't afford another defeat." Pulling out his cell phone, Mikael sent a text. HEY, MY HARD-HEADED GODSON. MEET ME AT THE DINER YOU ATTEND ALL THE TIME AT NINE TONIGHT. WE HAVE TO SPEAK.

Placing his cell phone in his pocket, he looked up to the sky and shouted, "What do you want from me? Just give us the strength we need to end this." He unleashed his wings to fly off to one more place before he met with Adam.

THE RISING SUN

Adam walked around the store to make sure everything was okay before closing. He received a text from Mikael and replied. OKAY, MAYBE AROUND NINE-THIRTY. I'M GONNA HELP WITH CLOSING TODAY. HIT YOU WHEN I'M ON MY WAY. He placed his phone back in his pocket.

"Hey Sade, who's closing tonight?" Adam raised his low deep voice to make sure she could hear him at the register over the music.

"I am. Derrick is off at nine. Is there something wrong?"

"Nope, I'm leaving around the same time, so just close at nine. Go ahead and start cleaning up so you can leave too. I'll help you lock up."

He headed back to his office to check the rest of his texts and saw Taki's name come up as he scrolled through the list of new messages. He stopped at her text and read it immediately, which brought an instant smile to his face. Adam responded with his own message. MY APOLOGIES, BEAUTIFUL, I'M AT WORK. BEEN BUSY ALL DAY. I HOPE YOU'RE ENJOYING YOUR DAY. TTYL.

"Alright! A couple of hours before I get out of here. What is my Saturday going to look like?" He scrolled through the messages to see if he could find any plans for his Saturday night after meeting with Mikael.

A knock on his office door snapped him out of his thoughts. "Hey boss, somebody is out here asking for you," Sade shouted through the closed door.

Adam rose from his chair. "I'm coming now. Give me a second." He went to the door and quickly scanned the store to meet with the customer. He strolled toward the man dressed in a navy blue and white pinstripe three-piece suit, matched with expensive navy blue and gold loafers, smiling at Adam as if they had a business meeting scheduled. Adam felt underdressed for this unplanned meeting. He reached out his right hand to shake the gentleman's.

"Hello, my name is Adam. I'm the owner. Is there something I can help you with?" he asked curiously.

"Well, hello, very nice to meet you." He shook hands with Adam. A small electrical shock amongst the two caused their eyes to widen slightly. "My name is Dillon. I think we need to have a conversation about a mutual friend of ours. Is there somewhere we can speak in private?" Dillon asked boldly.

Adam was unsettled at the revelation that some expensive suit-wearing dude wanted to speak with him about someone he knew. "I probably don't know who you're talking about, so is there anything business-related that I can assist you with?" Adam asked cautiously.

"Well, I think the name Mikael will ring a bell, which will remind you of the acquaintance that you know. I believe you know him very well," Dillon said with a smug look on his face. "Now, is there somewhere we can speak in private?" he asked, leaning to the side.

"Uncle Mike?" Adam spoke out. "Um, okay, let's step into my office. Come this way." He motioned for Dillon to follow him.

As they walked down the hallway, Dillon looked around. "This is an interesting choice of business here. I am confused at the point. Is this place for shopping or attending an event? What is the purpose?" he asked blandly.

"Well, I wanted to create an environment for people to feel like they're at an event while they are shopping. You can enjoy video games, basketball, and music. At the same time, you search for your favorite brand name clothes and shoes," Adam replied confidently.

"Great sales pitch. Overload the humans' senses with worthless noise to get them to spend all their money. Great. I knew we were going to be great friends," Dillon mocked with a joyful clap of his hands.

Adam ignored the stranger's antics. As both men began to settle down, Adam was still curious about the stranger sitting in front of him. His whole body was tingling, which was making him extremely hot and aggravated. He was interested in what this "Dillon" wanted with his godfather.

"So, what can I do to help you? You spoke about a family member. What's up with Uncle Mike?" Adam asked as he rested back in his chair.

Dillon sat back in the chair as he played with his fingernails. "I believe he has been trying to enlighten you about some worries of his concerning your health. I came to tell you that you need to believe him. Everything he states is true." He smiled as he spoke.

Stunned at what he heard, Adam hesitantly asked, "Excuse me? What are you talking about?"

Dillon stood up and leaned over on the desk. "I have no time for coddling today. So, I will leave you with this. Everything Mikael speaks is the truth. If you don't listen, you will die." Then he transferred to Otherside, naked to the human eye, and walked out of the office to leave.

"What the FUCK?!?!" Adam yelped, frozen at his desk as he watched the silhouette of "something" wander out of his office door. "Did I just see a motherfucker fade? That motherfucker just vanished?!" He began to rub his eyes. "Uncle Mike, what the fuck have you gotten me into?"

He immediately picked up his phone to call his godfather. Adam disconnected from the voicemail recording. "Oh, don't go missing now, motherfucker." He redialed the number. "Yo, Mike, what the fuck is going on? Some fancy motherfucker came in here asking about you and vanished in my fucking face, my G! The motherfucker faded into thin air!" *He better call me the fuck back ASAP!*

Suddenly, he felt the burning sensation in his body. The feel of the pain in his head and all over his body caused Adam to double over. He grunted through clenched teeth and clicked the automatic lock button under his desk that controlled the office door. Same as his penthouse, his office was soundproof and had its own sprinkler system just in case he had an uncontrollable issue at work.

Adam screamed in pain, and his veins felt like they were being singed on the inside. He fell to the floor in a fetal position. *WHY? WHY? WHY ME? FIRE, FIRE, HOT, HOT, HOT, SUN, SUN.* He snapped out of the spasmatic thoughts at the sound of his cell phone on his desk.

"Come on, A, get up," he said through the pain and clenched his teeth. He grabbed the phone with the bit of strength he had left. "Hello, hello, help me. Help me." He pushed past the anguish of the pain.

"ADAM?!! ADAM!!" Taki yelled through the phone. "What's wrong?!!" she yelled again.

No response.

"Shit, what's wrong? Where are you? Answer me, damn it." Clearly worried, she began to feel as if one of her own fits was about to start. Taki ignored her own body's signals. She hung up and quickly remembered he was at work. "Fuck, I don't remember what the name of his store is."

Taki was worried about Adam. She quickly sent an instant message to Tay, Adam's sister. HEY, WHAT'S THE NAME OF YOUR BROTHER'S STORE? PUTTING SOME PEOPLE ON TO SOME KICKS, Taki lied, as she didn't want to worry Tay.

The reply bubble instantly popped up with a reply, JUST KICKIN' IT, TELL MY BIG HEAD BROTHER I SAID THANK YOU AND LOVE HIM! Relieved at Tay's quick response, Taki pulled up the Uber app to go see about Adam.

****

She stood in front of her apartment as the Uber pulled up and immediately got in. She pulled out her cell to call Adam back. *Pick up, pick up, pick up!* Taki glanced at the approximate time they should arrive at his store and yelled into the phone, "Oh my God, are you okay? No, you're not okay. Don't lie to me! I'm on my way!" She put her head back on the headrest and her body started to ache. She began to get lost in the thoughts of her past.

This reminds me of that night. Taki shook her head to make sure those memories didn't resurface. "Hurry!" she yelled at the driver as he made a right onto the block of the store. She rushed out of the car, running into the store, and picked up her phone to call Adam.

She continued to ignore her body's warning signs. Taki walked toward the lady at the register.

"Hello, my name is Taki Mashiro. I have a meeting with Mr. Moore. Is he available?" She prayed that her hasty thinking worked.

"Yeah, he's in the back. Follow me," Sade said, fed up with the busy day and ready to close as a customer walked up to the register requesting assistance.

"Don't worry, hun. Go ahead. I got it. This isn't my first time," Taki lied to rush through the needless conversation.

"Okay, I'm sorry. I have to help this customer. Go ahead back there. He's available," Sade replied as she headed over to the customer.

Taki rushed to the back. Since the layout was simple, she navigated relatively quickly to the manager's office. She pulled out her cell and waited for an answer.

"Adam, please answer. I'm at your office door," she spoke at the door and heard a clicking sound. Taki grabbed the doorknob and flung it open. Unable to see Adam, she yelled, "A, A, A, where are you?" She looked around the luxurious office space.

Taki noticed an oversized black and white sneaker peeking from the corner of the desk. She rushed to the other side of the desk and saw Adam lying on the carpet with small burnt spots around him. She dropped down to her knees and grabbed his head. "A, A, wake up, wake up. I'm calling an ambulance," she said as she pulled her cell phone from her back pocket and felt a soft mental nudge that begged her to not call them.

"Why not?" Taki said out loud, confused as she placed her phone back in her pocket. She rubbed his head and felt his body was hot.

At the immediate feel of Taki's touch, Adam's thoughts began to clear, and his body calmed. He stared at the chocolate beauty in front of him. "What the hell? Why and how are you here?" he asked in a faint breath.

"What the hell is wrong with you? Are you a diabetic?" Taki asked in a worried tone as she laid his head on her lap while she kneeled on the floor.

"Nah, Mama. I'm good. I didn't eat today," Adam lied. "We were swamped, so I forgot. But I'm good now, though." He stood up, unsure of why he felt better all of a sudden. "Are you okay? You stop by here for something?" Adam reached for her hand to assist her.

"I'm great. I wanted to come cop some kicks and forgot the name of your store."

She looked up and caught eye contact with blazing fiery eyes as she saw remanences of the sun. "A, your eyes, they're—" She was cut off by him kissing her luscious lips. After a few seconds, she continued to allow him to kiss her and felt that electric spark flow through her veins. Taki felt she was about to explode.

"Hey, hey. You're going to have to stop just putting your mouth on me," Taki panted as she stepped away.

He moved back into her personal space and replied, "You like me putting my mouth on you," as he used his index finger to caress her exposed shoulder. He stared at her with that hungry look.

"Look, I didn't come here for this. I thought there was something wrong with you. I was calling you for information. So, now that I know that you are good, I can be on my way." Taki turned around to leave.

Adam took her left hand to stop her from leaving. "Kish, don't go," he said hesitantly.

She allowed him to hold her hand. She turned around and met his eyes and saw that they were back to their regular color. "Look, A, you're my friend. I already told you I have a boyfriend. Don't do this." Taki shook her head and turned away to leave. The fear that one of her own issues was happening began to grow as she rushed out the door to head home.

Damn it, A. What the fuck is going on with you? Why did she come here? How did she get in? I locked the door. He was clearly unable to remember anything that happened after he fell over in pain. He checked his phone and noticed that Taki did call first. Confused about the events of the day, Adam looked at the time. He noticed it was about a half-hour before closing. "Okay. I most definitely have to see Uncle Mike. Shit is getting out of control. Who the fuck was that guy?!" He remembered the conversation with Dillon before his recent episode.

As he shook his head, he looked down at his burnt carpet and began to walk to the front to check on the store. Derrick was cleaning up while Sade was at the register closing out all but one. Adam began to feel a tingling sensation throughout his body, similar to the one he felt when this "Dillon" came around.

Adam noticed a young male with dark stringy hair, blue eyes, and piercings all over his face and ears. The stranger was dressed as if he lived on the street. He approached Adam and stared in wonder. "Hello you." He reached up to touch Adam's face.

Adam swatted the young man's hand away. "Excuse me, how can I help you? Is there something you need?" He glared back at the individual in front of him.

"So shiny!" The homeless-looking man clapped his hands together in a trance-like voice that sounded as if he saw something else while he spoke.

"Do you want to make a purchase? If not, I suggest you leave, or I will call the cops." Adam got a nervous feeling about the young man.

"I want to know," the pierced man clapped in awe as he began to back away from Adam, "when can I see you again?" He sang in the tone of the popular R&B song from the nineties.

"My man, it's been a long day. I suggest you leave." Adam began to stalk the young man with a menacing look.

"Now, now. Be nice. I will see you again." He finished the end off in song as if he really meant it as he walked out of the store.

"Hey, boss man, who you talking to? Come help me with the rest of the count so we can get out of here," Sade shouted at Adam.

Adam turned to look at Sade as he spoke. "You didn't see that crazy motherfucker that just came in here?"

"I don't know what you are talking about over there. I see my big-ass boss standing there being weird and shit. Don't make me quit," she replied jokingly.

"What?!" Adam said in a low tone. He didn't want Sade to hear him. "I'm coming. I'm ready to get the fuck out of here, too." He headed toward the register to assist Sade in closing. Adam mumbled, "What the fuck kind of night is this going to be?"

DEVIL'S ADVOCATE

Dillon walked out of Just Kickin' It, still on Otherside, and said, "Xeno, my friend, did you feel that? That boy is stronger than what we originally took him for. I see why our Mikael is so intrigued. Just by touching him, I felt his powerful energy. I'm very interested to know what this boy is. Come on, we have work to do now. I really didn't want to do that. Maybe we can figure out what else he attracts, leading to the possible revelation of what sort of creature he is." He smiled as he turned the corner with Xeno in tow.

"Dillon, why won't you just let Mikael handle the boy? This is a waste of our time. The demon wards could be up by now." Xeno stopped abruptly. "I don't see how this boy is more important than our mission at hand. You're losing sight just like Mikael," Xeno stated brashly.

Dillon stopped walking as well, never turning to look at Xeno. "I find your breathing a waste of time, but I tolerate that, don't I? Don't dare compare me to Mikael. My interest in this Adam is what and who he is. To see if he will be an advantage or harm. Now, let's continue with the real problems at hand—getting rid of demons," he said, finally turning to Xeno. They both released their wings to leave. Dillon felt something, something he hadn't felt in a long, long time. *So, you came out to play? That's interesting,* he thought as he flew away while looking down at Adam's store. Then, he and Xeno headed to reclaim the den.

THE SUN RISES

Finishing up locking the metal gates to the store, Adam said to Sade, "Yo, my day has been crazy. Hopefully, it ends better." He shook his head as he placed his keys in his pocket.

"For real, the vibes have been off all day today. I might bring some sage and incense tomorrow. Bad mojo in that building. What's up with you, though? Were you over in the corner talking to yourself?" Sade asked as she and Adam walked towards the train station as they waved goodbye to Derrick.

Embarrassed that she would even think that, he replied, "Nah, just was thinking out loud. Lot of shit on my mind, you know?" Adam stopped at the train station entrance. "You have a good one, Ma. Get home safe." He gave Sade a hug and peck on the cheek.

"Later, A. Hold ya head!" Sade replied.

Adam usually walked his female associates to the train or paid for their ride home if the store closed too late. He wanted to make sure his employees were safe when they left his place of business. Walking up a side block from dropping Sade off at the train station, Adam pulled out his phone to dial his godfather.

"Why didn't you call me back? I left you a message. You wouldn't believe my fucking day, Unc. Who the fuck is Dillon? I'm on my way to the diner now. I told you I had to close. Whatever, man. I'm on the way," A said in an exasperated tone, hanging up as he reached his car.

Pulling off to head to the diner, Adam made a call on his Bluetooth.

"Ma, sorry to call so late. I'm about to go meet Uncle Mike. Some shit is going on, and I don't like it." He thought before speaking again. "Okay. Well, I'll sort it out. Don't worry, Ma. I'm fine. No, I haven't had an episode," Adam lied. "I gotta go. Pulling up to see Uncle Mike now. Love you and talk to you later." He disconnected the call as he continued to drive.

Once he reached the diner and parked, Adam proceeded to walk to the entranceway of the restaurant. Still frustrated by the day's events, eyesight instantly went black and unable to move, Adam quickly passed out.

****

Awakened by the feel of cold air and wind that whipped against his body, Adam began to open his eyes and saw nothing but black. It was as if a cloth was placed over his head. He immediately panicked at his inability to see and feel as if he was in the air. "WHAT THE FUCK?!" Adam squirmed and kicked his feet in a panic, unsure of where he was.

"You idiot. You're going to fall. Don't do that. Stop!" Adam heard a muffled voice.

"Get the fuck off me!" Adam pushed away from whatever was holding on to him, freeing himself from the individual to find himself falling into thin air. "AAHHHHHHHHHHHH!!!! WHAT THEEEEE—" Adam screamed at the top of his lungs.

"You're going to get yourself killed. Keep it up!", Adam heard still unsure of what he was feeling. The blood began to rush to his head. Adam figured he was being carried upside down. He was unsure of why he was in the air upside down. *This day just gets better and better.* Suddenly, Adam felt his ankle being let go.

"What the?! Ouch!" he hollered as he landed on hard concrete. "Get this shit off my head!" Adam exclaimed, tugging at the cloth that was forbidding him to see.

"Calm down. Let me take it off. You won't be able to," the muffled voice said to Adam.

Still struggling to get the headcloth off of him, Adam yelled, "Get this shit off me so I can fuck you up! You don't know who you're fucking with, homie," Adam said angrily.

"Oh really, you think so?" the muffled voice replied.

"Take it off and find out!" Adam said, standing in a defensive stance. *Oomph.* Adam doubled over in pain as he took a punch to the gut and jaw before being swept off of his feet. "Oh, shit!" he said as he hit the floor.

"Waste of talent, boy!" the voice stated coldly.

"Uncle Mike?" Adam said, cocking his head to the side.

Mikael, walking up to Adam, pulled the cloth off his head, extending his hand to assist him in getting up. "Thought you were being kidnapped for ransom? You're not that rich, boy." Mikael laughed at the way Adam was staring at him. "Cat got your tongue?" Mikael asked.

Adam rushed towards Mikael, grabbing his suit jacket. They stared at each other eye-to-eye. "What the fuck is wrong with you?! Why did you have me hanging upside down in the air?" He looked around at the empty warehouse space they were standing in. "How the fuck did you have me upside down in the air? Why the FUCK couldn't we just meet in the diner?"

"I will advise you to take your hands off of my clothes, my wonderful godson. I love you, but I am having a terrible day and will probably hurt you," Mikael answered coldly.

Feeling the fear as it entered his mind, Adam let Mikael go, staring at him in disbelief. Adam shook his head. "Fuck that! Shitty day?! My day has been royally fucked. For some reason, my day was fucked up because of you!" He pointed his long index finger at Mikael's face. "Some stupid motherfucker name Dillon came to the store. Had me feeling all kinds of weird. Then he does some fucking vanishing act, but it looked like I could still see him."

Adam continued, "On top of that, some weirdo came in trying to touch me and was singing and shit. Supposedly, I was the only one in the store that had seen him since Sade didn't see the bum. So, fuck you and your shitty day!" Adam was breathing heavily after giving up all of that information at once.

"What? Dillon? You saw him on Otherside? How is this possible?" Mikael hurriedly asked.

"I don't know. What the fuck did I see? Who is he?" Adam asked Mikael.

Mikael walked closer to Adam. "What did he say to you? Did he do anything to you?" Mikael checked Adam for any marks or anything that Dillon could have done.

"Chill. Don't go all godfather-like on me now. I'm in all this weird shit because of you. Shit was alright before you brought your ass back here," Adam said, aggravated.

"Adam, don't piss me off tonight. Please," Mikael said, putting his head down as he thought about Dillon visiting Adam. Speaking through clenched teeth and a menacing look, Mikael spoke again. "What did he want, and what did he say?"

"Uncle Mike, don't look at me like that. All he said to me was I should believe you or I would die. Then he disappeared in front of my face. You may think I'm crazy for saying this, but when he vanished, I could still see a silhouette of a figure walking out of my office. Like I said, Uncle Mike, it has been one helluva day," Adam said in a defeated tone, leaning on one of the many columns in the empty warehouse.

"You can see through the veil? Whatever is happening to you, you're getting stronger. Humans shouldn't be able to see anything once we transfer to Otherside," Mikael said, looking at Adam with a confused look. Adam stared blankly as Mikael continued. "Otherside is the other realm connected to Earth Realm, where I told you those like myself and other creatures can live without the eyes of humans."

Adam immediately responded, "And what the fuck am I supposed to do with that information?"

Mikael shook his head in disbelief. "What else happened tonight?" he asked with a long sigh.

Adam answered him gravely, "After that, I flipped. The shit that happens in my sleep happened at work. I gotta replace my fucking carpet now. On top of that, Kisha came and seen me like that." He put his head down as he spoke.

"Who is KI-SHA?" Mikael asked, trying to repeat what Adam said. "What does she have to do with this?" Mikael questioned, wondering who Adam was speaking of.

"You remember the girl I used to be around all through late middle and high school? She used to live in the same building as me," Adam answered with a gleam in his eyes.

"Ahh, the girl you refused to tell me how you really felt about. And the young lady that was there that night, correct?" Mikael asked.

"Yea, Unc. Fuck that. She is not involved. I'm just glad she didn't see that nut job of a friend of yours. Don't think I haven't been paying attention. You still haven't told me about this Dillon. Asking me questions and shit, and you still haven't told me about that stupid motherfucker that came to my shop." He walked towards Mikael with his fists clenched.

"Boy, come over here and get beat up!" Mikael posted up to meet Adam eye-to-eye. "I am not in the mood. You're not the only one with things going on! Now tell me what else happened so I can figure out what the HELL is going on!" he shouted in Adam's face, releasing some power.

As Adam's body reacted to the slight breeze, he knew Mikael was right. He needed to calm down, get the facts straight, and determine his next move. "After Kisha and Dillon left, I went to check on the store. That weird dude I mentioned had a bunch of piercings on his face. The dude with the chains in his face gave me the same eerie feeling your Dillon gave me. He was just talking stupid. That's not the shit. Sade really didn't see him. Afterward, walking with her to the train, she asked me why I was talking to myself. I don't know, Unc. This shit got me baffled right now," he said as he wiped his face.

"Okay, well, we will get more in-depth about Dillon in a second. The young man you saw trying to touch you. Did he have any tattoos? Chains on his wrist?" Mikael searched Adam's face for clues.

"I didn't see all of that. Chain Face dude was dirty, short, and dingy. Didn't get a good look at him. I just wanted him out of my store without touching shit," Adam stated.

Looking around, thinking, Mikael replied, "I told you it was just the beginning. All kinds of creatures are going to come looking for you. For what, I don't know. I advise you to stay low until we can figure this out."

"I have a business to run and money to make, Uncle Mike. I don't have time for the little escapades and bullshit you talking about. Whatever you got going on, leave me out of it. That motherfucker Dillon did something to me that made me have an episode. I don't need shit or people like that in my life right now. Bad enough I have to deal with this freaky shit on my own, let alone deal with whatever freaky, weirdo shit you got going on." Adam vented with a fiery blaze in his eyes.

"What part of 'you are Other and other creatures similar or hateful of you will start to come for you,' don't you understand? Then you won't have that precious little store or your life! You better listen to me or find yourself in some mess you can't get out of. Heavens, I'm still trying to figure out what you are," Mikael said with a hard stare at Adam. "If you would just stop and think for a minute, you would have noticed all this weird crap started when your episodes got more substantial and more frequent. Why do you think I left? I had some connections that said someone else was going through similar symptoms and gave me a lead on contacting them. By the time I got there, the information had gone cold. I've been gone for five long months trying to find you a solution and not even handling my own business. You could at least give me some respect and listen to what I have to say!"

Mikael slightly raised his voice. "I'm actually tired of pretending and babying you. Maybe Dillon had the right idea. Your parents knew more than you, and you're so damn hardheaded," he said, unleashing his wings as he spoke. "Never want to listen, always have to do things Adam's way. Well, now look." He shouted and paced as he stared at a shocked Adam. "You have no choice but to dive in headfirst so you can really understand the danger that you are in. You're not a regular human, and until we find out what you are, your life is in danger." Mikael stood in his full Angel Army garments. There were massive, translucent wings highlighted with cobalt blue that spanned about twelve feet wide.

Mikael's look and exuberating power knocked Adam to his knees. Black leather combat boots, black cargo pants with an opened leather vest, black, long-sleeved shirt with an emblem of an angel crown and an ax, highlighted in purple and gold, with what looked like twin metal katanas sheathed on his back. There were metallic-looking things on the front of the vest, along with leather wristbands with what looked like small knives attached to them. Standing in front of Adam as if he was ready to take on an army, Mikael stopped ranting. "Anything to say?"

"What, what the fuck are you?!" Adam pushed to get up, frozen on his knees. He felt a strong presence in front of him and was unable to comprehend what was going on. The air began to feel heavy. His body felt hot, causing him to pant uncontrollably. Soon, Adam's body began to shake, and his eyes turned a bright yellowish color.

"Oh!" Mikael jumped back and upward as the surge of energy began to leak from Adam's body, causing the air around them to sizzle.

Adam began to scream. "Uncle Mike, HELP ME. HELP ME. IT HURTS. IT HURTS SO BAD. AHHHHHH, I'M BUR—" Adam went silent as his body became engulfed in a cylindric flame.

Mikael, unable to see Adam anymore between the flames, had to apply more energy because he felt the barrier around the area weakening. As he continued to watch the fire consume Adam, and feeling his power, Mikael thought to himself, *what in all heavens is he?*

Slowly moving towards the circle of fire to see if he could search for Adam, Mikael walked closer, feeling a few of his feathers being burned the closer he got. "He better be lucky they will grow back," he said, looking at the areas on both of his wings where the energy was singeing the feathers. *I haven't felt power like this in a few millennia. Someone or something is bound to feel this.*

"A, you have to stop. You can't keep doing this. You're going to cause this whole place to blow!" Mikael yelled as he tried to get through the wall of fire around Adam.

Reaching, taking hold of what felt like Adam's shoulder, a flood of erratic thoughts came flooding into Mikael's mind. *FIRE, FIRE, FIRE, FIRE, HEAT, HEAT, HEAT.* He instantly snatched his hand away

"What was that? A, you have to calm down, now!" Mikael yelled as he looked down at his right hand and saw it was almost burnt to a crisp. *What did I do? This barrier is not going to hold all of this energy much longer. I have to get him calm before he turns into a nuke.*

Fully tapping into his own set of concealed powers, Mikael reached out to touch Adam again, using his power of persuasion to invade Adam's mind.

"A, calm down. It's okay. Calm down. It's okay. I am here for you. You don't have to be frightened. Calm down, and let's talk."

"I'm not scared. I'm just waking up. I have to do some stretches first," Adam's voice playfully responded as it pushed against Mikael's mental strength. "Now leave!" Mikael was instantly kicked out of Adam's head.

"WHAT IN HEAVENLY SKIES, BOY?! This is going to get interesting," Mikael said as he picked the naked Adam up, throwing his large frame over his shoulder.

HER

The Uber ride home sucked. As Taki sat in the four-door sedan's back seat, she laid her head on the headrest, pulling out her cell to send a text. HEY GIRL, CALL ME. I DON'T CARE WHAT TIME IT IS.

What happened back there? I felt it. I felt it coming on. Then it suddenly stopped. Putting her head in her hands, she fell deeper into her thoughts. *What is wrong with me?*

Interrupted by her cell phone ringing, she pulled it back out of her pocket. "Hey, Mama! Oh, it's you." She huffed and puffed her disappointment. "I'm fine, M, really. What? Huh? I felt one coming on, then it stopped. Never fully started. I'm actually feeling great. No, I haven't used the serum yet. May use it tonight, though. It'll be good to get another night of sleep. Okay, I'll call you if I need you. Thanks." *End call.*

Reaching her destination and thanking the driver as she exited the vehicle, Taki stopped by the store to grab some snacks then walked down to her place. Entering her apartment with thoughts scattered all over, she decided to try to eat some of the leftovers from her outing with Mark. As Taki was in the kitchen heating up her food and snacking on the bag of mixed nuts, her cell phone rang. Seeing the picture, she became excited. "Chick! Yo! You wouldn't freaking believe the last couple of days I've had. I called you back! What's up??" Taki asked as she placed Michi on speaker.

"Yea, I was sleep earlier. You're going to have to get used to our thirteen-hour difference, young lady!" she responded playfully.

"Whatever. I told you to bring your ass over here, and there won't be a difference," Taki said jokingly but seriously. "Anyway, guess who I ran into last night? You wouldn't believe it," she said, teasing.

"Girl, stop it with the dramatics and get to the juicy part. Bad enough you got me up early on the weekend," Michi replied, laughing.

"Shut up before I don't tell you shit. I saw Adam, the guy I went to school with here," Taki said.

"You mean the sexy piece of chocolate you showed me pics of? Girl, do tell," Michi said excitedly.

"Well, first, Ms. M came over last night with her stuffy ass. FYI, you know when I opened the door, this meinu (bitch) had her fucking swords out, ready to chop my head off? Talking about she heard a threat," Taki said seriously.

"I always told you that bitch was freaky and crazy. I don't even know how the hell my parents know that Kuso henjin (fucking weirdo). Get to the good part, fuck her."

Taki laughed "I decided to go outside, and look who I see parked outside my crib? Adam."

Michi interrupted, "Whoa, whoa. The Nanda Ittai (What the fuck)?"

"Damatte Watashi o shūryō sa se (Shut up and let me finish). I actually noticed him first. I was too shocked to say anything, and then he noticed me staring at him and then hopped out of his car and hugged and kissed me," Taki said, enjoying her memories.

"Hey now! You cheating on your toyfriend? That's not nice," Michi replied, busting out laughing.

"First of all, I'm not the whore in this family, and no, I am not cheating on my man. I like Mark. Far as Adam kissing me, that kiss was a surprise. Mich, that boy knows he can flirt. I had to tell him to cut it out. We went to the diner and had some drinks and shit. Let's just say, the night did not end how I expected it to," Taki said softly, still sitting at her counter in the kitchen.

"Oh shit," Taki yelped as she felt a sharp pain to her head and chest simultaneously. Her whole body started to shake. "Not now, not now. Shit, not now. Don't pass out! Call Ms. M! Hurry!"

"Taki, what's wrong? Taki? Can you hear me?"

Unable to respond to Michi due to the massive pain throughout her body, her thoughts jumped to loud screams. "FIRE, FIRE. HELP ME. IT BURNS. Michi! HELP ME, IT HURTS!! IT HURTS!!" She was writhing in pain. "OUCCHHHHHH!!! IT BURNS!!! STOP IT! IT HURTS!" Taki then passed out on the floor.

****

Looking down at the device making that annoying noise, M saw Michiko Tanaka's name on the screen. "Yes, Ms. Young Tanaka, how can I be of assistance? WHAT?!?" She was not known for yelling, but she did then. "I will be right there. I am in her area," she lied to Michi before disconnecting the call. *What now?*

With no time to humanly travel back to Taki in time, M transferred to Otherside. "This is more like it," she said, missing the use of her powers. She instantly transmitted herself in front of Taki's apartment that was located in the basement of a brownstone. Unable to transport inside due to her strategically placed barriers to make sure that Others could not get in, M began checking Taki's basement apartment's front area for bystanders while returning to her human form, smoothing out her clothes as she stood in the corner. She released her left-hand twin blade to rid the lock on the apartment door.

Hearing Taki's screams before she completely opened the door, M ran down the hall towards the loud cries in the kitchen, finding Taki on the floor, thrashing in pain, screaming, "IT BURNS. IT BURNS. SOMEBODY HELP ME."

Clearly seeing no sign of a fire, M fell to the floor to hold a screaming Taki. "Shh, child," she said, beginning to rock her. "Takisha, breathe, breathe. It's all in your mind. Let's clear your mind. Picture the sun, pic—"

Screaming in agony, Taki yelled, "WHY? WHO ARE YOU? WHAT DO YOU WANT FROM ME?"

Looking around at who she could be talking to, M responded, "What do you see, child? Who are you talking to?" She continued to rock her as Taki continued screaming in pain. Closing her eyes, she said, "I'm unsure if this buried power will work."

M placed her hand on Taki's head to enter her thoughts. Immediately, she saw a fire-like being shouting at and reaching for a screaming Taki. Unable to hear the being's voice or see its face, M grabbed the mental version of Taki screaming and held her, blocking the being from Taki's sight.

M rocked Taki. "Shh, Takisha, calm down, calm down. I am here. It is okay. It is all in your mind. Let it go."

Instantly, awaking from their mental adventure, M looked down at a sleeping Taki, confused at the events that just took place. Standing up, picking up Taki, she thought, *What was that? Is there some sort of being trying to possess her? Don't tell me that's been the cause of our troubles this whole time.*

"I told her to take the serum. Now I am going to have to stay in this damn, excuse me, place until I find out what's going on," M said to a sleeping Taki as she placed her gently on the bed.

OTHERSIDE

Mikael laid Adam on the couch in the den of the apartment in the Bronx. He looked down at the young man. "Wow, Adam, we have to find out what you are before you blow us all to kingdom come."

Mikael called out for his maid, "Elise, get some blankets, water, and a change of clothes for Adam here. Also, please have the others assist you in placing more power in the barriers here. I am unsure of what my young charge will attract here. I will return very soon."

He pulled out his cell phone to call Dillon and heard an unexplainable noise on the other end. "WHAT DID YOU DO? Why did you make contact with the boy? I told you I had him handled," he yelled into the phone.

"I am swamped right now, Mikael. Did you call me to complain like a woman?" Dillon flatly raised his voice at something in the background. "Die, you mongrel!" A sound of hacking flesh came from Dillon's end of the line. "I figured the boy could use some enthusiasm for our cause. We know the boy is of Other. From my short assessment, at least, he is not a demon. Xeno, behind you, hold on a second, Mikael."

There was the sound of fighting in the background. "Yes, it's Mikael. He didn't like my visit with Adam." Mikael listened in on Dillon's conversation. At the same time, he overheard the fighting going on. "Okay, I am back. Well, while you're over there coddling the boy, Xeno and I are handling real business. So, what did you find out, Mikael?" Dillon asked while still fighting.

"Well, you are right. Adam is not a demon. His power is incredible, though. We will speak more when I see you both," Mikael replied.

"Let Xeno and I finish up here. We may have another player on the board here that I noticed earlier. Where are you?" Dillon asked.

"I'm in the Bronx. Won't be here long. I still feel the energy on him, so we have to move soon. Just waiting for him to wake up," Mikael said in a confused tone.

"Bring him to Otherside. Until we figure out what he is, he can't be let out of our sight," Dillon said in a heavy breath.

"Getting your ass kicked over there? Need some help?" Mikael said with a chuckle.

"Actually, I am taking a break. Xeno here is getting the job done. They sent some formidable opponents for mid-level demons. Still, they are no match for Xeno here." He yelled towards Xeno as he was fighting at least five scaly demons. "No worries, we should have this den back in no time. XENO!!! I have blood on my shoes!! These are Gucci! Mikael, I have to go now. Meet us Upstate at the house in the woods. We will discuss the rest," Dillon said, aggravated, and disconnected the call.

"This guy is worried about some stupid shoes." Mikael shook his head as he walked back into the den area where a naked Adam was still lying passed out. Calling out to Elise, he asked, "Were you able to do what I asked?"

Elise replied in her heavy French accent, "Oui, monsieur. We strengthened the barriers, and I have laid out some clothes for Monsieur Adam. Is there anything else?" she asked, smiling as she looked at Mikael.

"One more thing, did you get any information on my Japan trip?"

She answered hesitantly, knowing he would not like the answer. "No, it seems as if someone is purposely blocking our attempts at getting any information from other means. Some of my colleagues have stated that some trouble in the Far East is unrelated that could cause our connections in the area to go dark. We will continue to monitor the status over there," Elise said gravely.

"Great, thank you, Elise. Let's hope their issues over there don't mix with ours over here," Mikael said with a smirk. "Now, only if my godson will awaken," he said as he looked at a sleeping Adam.

He walked over to him and felt his head. "He is scorching. Never knew how that boy walked around with a fever all the time. How the hell did he wake up so fast? The powder in the cloth should have had him out for hours, let alone fifteen minutes. What in the heavens name is he?" he said, irritated as his body began to feel a familiar feeling. "Not now!" Mikael knew this was not good news.

Rushing to the dining area, he met Elise. "What is it?"

"I think it's a horde of demons, monsieur. We put stronger barriers up, but I believe they still feel Monsieur Adam," she said.

"I brought him here thinking we would be safe. Elise, leave. You and the others go back to Otherside. I am meeting Dillon there later. Meet us at the castle. Stay there and get the army assembled. We have to figure out what these demons are doing. All of this activity is not a coincidence." He rushed around to get prepared for the upcoming fight.

"Take Adam with you as well. We have to get him away from here while we have the chance. I will hold off the demons to give you the time you will need to get out of here with Adam." Looking out the window, he saw the hordes of demons that had accumulated around the area. "What is all of this?" he asked, watching the hordes beat against the barrier.

Elise and the other maids gathered up their items and put a robe on Adam as he lay sleeping on the couch. Mikael sent a text message to Dillon and Xeno. SAFEHOUSE IN THE BRONX IS BEING ATTACKED. NOT SURE HOW IT IS COMPROMISED, BUT IT IS. MEET ME AT THE CASTLE. He placed his phone back in his pocket.

Mikael yelled towards Elise and the other three maids, "GET OUT OF HERE NOW! The barrier is about to come down." He kept an eye on the horde flying right through the window he was standing in front of. "Leave now!!" he shouted just as the first demon broke through the glass of the window, attacking Mikael with its sharp teeth.

Mikael used his hands to catch the demon's snapping teeth, pulling its head apart like an orange, and drew his sword, splitting the demon that was jumping towards him as the first one's limp body fell to the floor. Immediately killing the first two demons, the next two from the flying horde came at Mikael from both sides in his apartment's den area. Ducking to his left to deflect the bite from the demon on the right, he used his left wrist knife to cut its stomach open as he dodged it, grabbing the neck of the demon, charging him from his left, and stabbing its throat with his right wrist blade. Mikael watched as the bodies fell to the ground, disintegrating to dust.

Sensing and hearing more demons trying to get through the wards at the bottom of the building and through the other doors, Mikael unsheathed his katanas from his back, revealing two beautifully sculpted swords. Standing with his back at the wall near the shattered window of the den, he looked at the hordes of demons coming to the area. "Ready to die!" he screamed and then released his full strength to fight off his enemies as he calculated an escape route.

MOONRISES DURING THE SUN

"Watashi no atama (my head). My body." Taki slowly began to sit up. She looked around, noticing she was in her bedroom. She searched for her nightstand lamp in the dark. Clicking on the light and seeing the time on her wall clock, she reacted. "NO, NO, that can't be right." The time was nine o'clock. "What happened?" She was desperately trying to remember. Rubbing her head, she sat up on the bed.

"Michi! I was talking to Michi. Where's my phone?"

She jumped up to search for it and fell over, still feeling weak. "Damn, that episode was bad." She held on to the side of the bed. Using her bedroom furniture to walk to the door, she walked to the living area to cut off the TV. "Oh shit!" She was startled when she saw M sitting on the couch.

Turning to Taki, getting up to assist her, she said, "What are you doing out of bed? Come on." M motioned for Taki to return to her bedroom.

"When did you get here? What happened?" Taki asked, leaning on the arm of the couch as she rubbed her head.

Noticing Taki was not returning to the room, M began to gesture Taki towards the couch to sit down. Assisting as much as Taki would allow, M went and grabbed the blanket from Taki's bedroom, laying it on her.

"How are you feeling?"

"I've been better," Taki responded in a low, raspy voice. "This was bad, M. I've never felt like this before. I feel like I was being burned on the inside. This shit, I mean, this stuff is scaring me." She pulled the blanket up to snuggle into the couch.

Sitting at her feet, M responded, "Ms. Tanaka called me, and I let myself in. You were passed out on the floor in the kitchen, and I helped you to bed," leaving out the more essential details.

"Have you spoken to Jade? I need her help. I don't see why me coming here is going to help," Taki said, tearing up. "It seems like it has gotten worse since I been here. I can't take this anymore. I want to go home."

"I know being out of your element is going to be hard, Takisha. You are a strong woman. You will get through this," M stated confidently, trying to convince herself as well. "You just need some food and rest, and then you will feel a lot better," M said, trying to calm Taki.

"I'm tired of being strong. I'm tired of saying it's going to be alright. I am so fucking TIRED of being TIRED!" Taki said, raising her voice at the end to a scream. Rising from the couch, she continued, "I can't continue to live like this. I can't. What the fuck am I supposed to do? I have to find out what is wrong with me. I feel like a prisoner inside. Obviously, no got damn doctors can help me." She paced back and forth in front of the couch. "I have to figure this shit out on my own. There is no way in hell I will go another day with having one of the episodes. That shit felt like my life was being sucked out of me. Something was coming for me."

She looked at a staring M. "Don't think I am losing my mind but believe me, something is messing with me or coming for me. In the episode yesterday, I had these weird visions as if I could see something pulling at me." Taki continued her pacing with a determined look.

M watched in awe as Taki reminded her of her young self. *My young self. Wow. When was the last time I thought of those times?*

"Takisha, calm down. I know that look. What makes you think after all this time, you are going to find out what is wrong with you? We took you to the best doctors in Japan. There is nothing medically wrong with you."

"I know that, M. That's why I said I will find out on my own. No doctors. At least no medical doctors. Where's my phone?" she asked, looking around for it. Finding her phone still sitting on the kitchen counter where she left it, she grabbed it to make a call. M interrupted her at the kitchen and living area doorway.

"Takisha, sit down. You're not well. First, let's get some food. You slept for almost twenty-four hours. You need to eat. I will make you a cup of tea, and we will sit and discuss our food options," M stated, unsure of what was going through Taki's mind.

"I don't want to rest. I don't want to eat. I feel like a fucking prisoner in my own body. Do you really know how it feels? I can't take this shit anymore!" Taki responded, slightly raising her voice at the end.

Following Taki to her bedroom, M called out to her, "Takisha, where are you going?"

"I don't know. I just don't want to be here," Taki replied quickly. "I have to get the fuck out of here before I lose it. So, if you don't mind, I need to get dressed. I am not in the mood for your kumbaya shit tonight," Taki said with a stern look.

M was ready to smack Taki for her insult. "Little girl, I doubt very much your eyes have experienced more than mine. So, I don't give a damn about how you feel about my kumbaya shit, as you put it so bluntly. We will go out to retrieve some food, and after that, you will just take the serum until we can figure out what is our next course of action about these episodes."

Taki replied in an aggravated tone, "Look, M, I know you feel as if you have some right to me since you always helped me along the way, but don't ever get it twisted. I do what the fuck I want to do. I allow you to stay around due to the assistance you do give me with this situation. But don't think for one second I won't say fuck you and deal with this shit on my own. I'm grown now, and technically, I don't have to deal with you anymore as far as me being your ward or whatever."

Stepping in real close to Taki, speaking through clenched teeth, M looked up. "Takisha, I will take your insolent tone as the aftereffects of your worse episode yet. But, if you dare speak to me in that manner again, the pain from last night will be the least of your worries. Now hurry up and put something decent on. None of that hip-hop stuff you wear either." M turned away, walking into the sitting area before Taki could say another word.

Feeling as if she was just scolded by her mother, Taki said, "Fuck you," in a low tone.

"Did you say something, Takisha?"

"No," she said, calling to M. She plopped down on the bed. "Damn. Now what the fuck am I going to do? I can't take another night like that. What the hell did I see?" Taki tried to remember the bits and pieces of her episode.

Having slept the day away, Taki knew work was not in her plans for tomorrow, especially after her day today. "I'll just call out," she said to herself as she pulled out a white, mid-length, sleeveless, body-hugging dress with lime green flowers on it. She paired it with some brown and gold wedges, gold bracelets, gold door-knocker earrings, and her favorite gold necklace. She called out to M as she walked down the hallway.

"Come on, we going to Brooklyn. I want some cheesecake." Taki grabbed her purse, keys, a white sweater, and her phone to walk out the door.

Following Taki to get into a blue sedan, M was puzzled about what Taki was thinking. Having a clear understanding of the Others in the world, M was still confused about the cause of Taki's issues. After the episode yesterday, possession could have been in play. *But if it was possession, the being would have already possessed her, correct? Or, maybe whatever underlining issues she is going through could have made her more susceptible to possession.*

Sitting in the back seat, lost in her thoughts, she was interrupted by Taki. "Do you think I'm crazy?" she asked, looking at M sincerely.

"No child, you are not mentally ill. We spoke of this plenty of times before."

"I feel like it, especially with this crap going on. What if I told you I remember something from my episode?" Taki said, laying her head back on the headrest as she spoke.

"Remember what, Takisha?"

"I think I felt this before. It was so familiar. I don't know. I don't understand. I don't," Taki said, waving it off.

"Takisha, talk to me. I can only help you if you tell me what it is. That is something new compared to the prior episodes. You usually don't have a memory of anything. So, if you think it may help in finding out what is wrong, speak up," M said with a concerned look.

"It's nothing, M, really. If I remember more, I'll let you know," Taki replied, continuing their ride to the restaurant in silence.

Sitting at the table as she ate, Taki began to wander in her thoughts. *Why is all of this happening to me? I never could understand why my life just can't be normal.*

"Takisha, care to share your thoughts this evening?" M asked softly.

"I'm just wondering if I will get my peace," Taki replied, picking at her salad on her plate. "M, I know I asked this before, but why are you here? I know I am a bit much to deal with." She looked up at M, placing her fork on the table. "I'm in my favorite place to get some cheesecake and can't have any. I'm sorry for the way I spoke to you earlier. I was out of line and—"

M interrupted her. "Takisha, I really empathize with you more than you know. I can't even understand the stress that you are going through right now. I accept your apology. Now make sure you eat well here. You need your strength. I also believe you need to start training again. I have a bad feeling about what is yet to come," M said firmly. "Now eat up. It may be a long night. You don't need any cheesecake," she said, smiling but feeling a sense of terror in the air.

HIM

Adam began to open his eyes, seeing a concrete ceiling as he laid in an unfamiliar place. He was unable to move due to the heaviness his body felt. "What the fuck? I can't move." Calming himself, taking a slow breath, Adam sat up slowly. "Where the hell am I?" He looked around, seeing what reminded him of the medieval castles he used to see on television. Still feeling the heaviness of his body, he moved a lot slower than usual. It was as if the gravity was different.

Adam moved slowly towards what looked like an entryway, pulling at the heavy wooden door to open it. Leading to a corridor area consisting of two walkways, he heard sounds coming from the left. He proceeded down the hall to get closer to the commotion.

At first, Adam thought he heard arguing, but the closer he got, he heard laughs and pounding sounds as if something was going on. Unsure of what to think, Adam continued to walk towards the area where the loud conversation was coming from. Entering the room, he found himself staring at a pair of green eyes, a couple of white eyes, and a pair of brown eyes that were all too familiar.

"Uncle Mike, where are we? Why do I feel like this?" He was slowly moving to find somewhere to sit down. He settled in a seat next to the guy with the white eyes, trying not to stare at them and his scar. "Hey, what's up?" he asked, nodding his head towards him.

"What's up, Adam. I'm X," Xeno introduced himself. "Have a seat. You the man of the hour anyway." He laughed at his own statement.

"Adam, we have much to discuss. I was going to come to wake you soon if you didn't get up. You must have really exerted yourself with that stunt you pulled," Mikael said. "First, let me introduce you to someone." Pointing to the guy with the green eyes, he said, "This is Dillon. I am officially introducing you two, so there are no hard feelings. Cool?" He looked back and forth at both men.

Adam was still unsure of what was going on and a little pissed at his godfather's light mood. "YOU! You're the reason I feel this way. What the fuck did you do to me?" He got up quickly, jumping across the table and grabbing Dillon by his suit jacket.

Surges of energy crackled in the air between the two men. Mikael pulled Adam off Dillon. "Hey, Adam, you don't want to do that today, my boy. We all had one hell of a day. So, please calm down so I can speak to you like a grown-up." Mikael was aggravated by his godson's reaction to Dillon.

"Fuck that, Unc. This bitch ass ni—" Adam said, interrupted by an unknown force causing him the inability to move or speak.

"I told you to be careful, my hardheaded godson. This one's temper is worse than mine," Mikael said to a frozen Adam.

Dillon walked straight to Adam to let him know it was his doing. "See, young man, I have been around a lot longer than you have. I did not choose my appearance, and I will not allow you to use such language in describing me. You see, your so-called godfather here loves you. Me? I don't know you, so I could care less if you live or die," he said, squeezing his left hand tightly.

Adam felt as if his entire body was being squeezed. "AHHHHHHH!!! WHAT THE FUCK?" His eyes were burning as bright as the sun, and his body was getting hotter. "Get the fuck off of me!" Adam replied with a determined growl.

"YO!!! This motherfucker got balls," Xeno said, laughing loudly. Adam broke free of the hold and jumped towards Dillon again.

Mikael got between the two men before Adam could reach Dillon. "Now, now, boys. We are on the same side," he said, placing his hand on Adam's chest. "Adam, calm down and sit. You don't need to have another episode. We need you at your full strength." He pushed Adam towards a chair at the table. "Now sit!" He put a little more force in his voice for Adam to sit down in the chair.

Dillon, walking back towards the table, brushed his clothes off. "Are we sure he is not of demon species? He acts just like those mongrels. What have you been teaching him, Mikael?" Dillon asked, disgusted. "I believe your parents taught you better manners than that, especially having grown up with both. Isn't that right?" he asked, smirking.

"Hey, Dillon. Shut up. Don't do that. Sit your Cinnamon Toast Crunch-looking ass down and shut up, too. You're supposed to be the elder here," Xeno said while glancing at Dillon amused.

"He started it!" Dillon replied, aggravated by the events that had just played out.

Mikael looked back and forth between both men. "Are we good?"

"Yes," they said in unison, both staring at each other coldly, as all four men were seated back at the table.

"Great. Now on to more important things. As I was trying to explain to you earlier, Adam, Dillon is a long-time, um, work associate. As you know, I have the security firm, and we procure wonderful talent to fulfill our ranks," Mikael said calmly. "For the years I have known you and your family, I have known about your issues, but we just can't seem to grasp exactly what you are. Now, whatever you are, your energy signature attracts Others for reasons we have yet to understand. So, until we figure out what you are," he said, standing up to slam his hands on the table, "be prepared to be my right hip. Now you have no choice but to stay here under our protection until we find out why the demons want you." Mikael shifted his gaze to Adam as he sat back down.

Staring at Mikael with an unbelievable look, Adam replied through clenched teeth, "You're out of your fucking mind if you think I am staying here. Don't think I forgot about the shit that happened earlier. WHAT THE FUCK ARE YOU, AND WHY THE FUCK AM I HERE?" Adam snarled, eyes turning yellow, body starting to feel hot. "Yo, I can't breathe. This shit feels like I have asthma here. Where are we?" He placed his head on the table from the heavy feeling.

"Adam, calm your nerves. Breathe slowly. Clear your head," Mikael replied. "You are not used to this place. If you calm down, you will get used to it. Just breathe."

Adam panted and felt his body begin to shake and the fire sensation in his veins again. "I can't stop it. Mike, help me!" Adam said wearily.

After sitting next to Adam, Xeno grabbed Adam's forearm and started squeezing down hard on it, almost breaking it, causing Adam to scream at the top of his lungs.

"WHAT THE FUCK ARE YOU DOING, Xeno?" Mikael shouted across the table, getting up to walk towards Xeno.

"Um, no, I am rather enjoying this. Have a seat." Dillon interrupted Mikael's attempt at releasing Adam from Xeno's grasp.

Staring at Dillon with a menacing glare, Mikael responded, "I am in no mood for your games, Dillon."

"I am not in the mood for yours either, Mikael, so sit down before I put a little more force in the next one," Dillon said with a smile, not meeting his eyes.

Sitting down and watching to his right, he saw a screaming Adam glowing like the sun under the robe. "STOP IT, Xeno!!! You're going to kill him!" Mikael said, shouting from his seat.

Adam felt as if his body wasn't his anymore. *What the fuck? Why can't I stop this shit? What the fuck is wrong with me? Am I killing myself?* He felt helpless with the pain and sensations he was feeling. "*I don't know what's worse, this Scarface-looking motherfucker breaking my arm or my body feeling like it's sunburnt,*" he said to himself. Feeling the heat of the sun, the warmth of a fire, and pure energy, Adam felt like he was in Heaven. "I've never felt anything like this before. So bright, so strong. The fire, it's so beautiful, so—" Adam said to himself before he was interrupted by water.

Feeling himself underwater, Adam flayed his arms up and down. "What the fuck?!? I can't swim! I can't swim!" He continued to shout and scream in a panic, crying out and thrashing his arms and feet around against what felt like air. When he opened his eyes, he found himself sitting in a fountain as the three large men standing over him burst out laughing.

Xeno spoke first. "Your ass is too fucking big to be talking about," in high pitch voice, "I can't swim, I can't swim!" He mimicked a drowning person as he bent over laughing.

"I am intrigued as to how Mr. Adam almost caused a nuclear explosion here. Any hotter in here, and we all would have received a serious sunburn," Dillon interjected, staring at Adam speculatively.

Laughing at Xeno and Adam, then turning somber, Mikael said, "Boy, I don't know what you are, but we better find out before you do some serious damage. If you were home or at your little store, you would have destroyed a whole block. The energy you exert is incredible." He reached out to help Adam up. "Come on, son, we got stuff to do. Don't worry, I will answer a few of your questions. I didn't forget," Mikael said, still chuckling as they walked away from what looked like a garden area.

Adam responded to Mikael. "Where the fuck are we is my first question. Looks like I fell in an episode of Game of Thrones or some shit," he said, looking around. "What in all fashion hell do you have me dressed in?" Adam looked down, pulling at the brown robe his large frame was dressed in, getting used to the breeze.

"Well, if it wasn't for you burning all of your clothes off, you would have your own clothes to wear. So, for now, this is what you got."

Adam pulled at the robe as he answered, "Whatever. Finding me some threads, answering my questions, and getting me the fuck out of here should be your main list of priorities right now, Uncle Mike. You know damn well I'm not staying here. You definitely got me fucked up if you—" Adam immediately fell down like a large timber to the concrete ground.

"Ouch! That's going to hurt later!" Xeno exclaimed, looking down at the unconscious Adam.

Dillon interjected, "His mouth is quite irritating. Fools, that's their problem. Humans are so arrogant and fragile at the same time. They will be the end of us all," he said grimly.

"You didn't have to do that. We still don't know what he is, and that could have triggered him. We need to understand what we are dealing with to plan for what is to come. We also need to find out why the demons are so attracted to his energy signature. It makes no sense," Mikael said, rubbing his head as they all stood in the garden.

"So many questions and no answers, Mikael. I truly loathe when you speak," Dillon interrupted. "If you all were paying attention, Adam here was syncing with his untapped powers—the glow, the energy, and the daze as if he wasn't here. This boy here is something else. We must figure out what he is to make sure he is with us, not against us. Either way, he will be dealt with," Dillon said as he looked down at a sprawled-out Adam.

"What do you mean 'dealt with?' There is no reason to harm him. He doesn't even know what he is. He is not a threat," Mikael said as he assessed the look on Dillon's face.

"We don't know if he is a threat or not. He just proved to us that he is not in control of this power he wields. If need be, he will be put down if he becomes a danger to us and our plans," Dillon immediately responded.

"You both are idiots. This boy is more than something else. I felt it. He is of us. It is our job to protect him. You both are too blind for your own selfish reasons. Adam is more. Maybe even more powerful than us. I don't know. What I do know is I felt the purity of his powers. I felt it," Xeno said.

"That's preposterous," Dillon said, appalled. "I felt nothing of the sort. There is no way a mongrel like this is touched. His power is incredible. But without proper training, using it would be disastrous for us to try to incorporate him with our plans." Dillon followed behind Xeno as they walked through the garden to go back into the castle.

Mikael shouted at their backs, "So, I just get left out now, huh? Boy puts on a light show, and now all of a sudden he's important." He shook his head as he caught up with the other two.

As Xeno laid Adam down on the bed in the room he was in earlier, he said to a staring Mikael and Dillon, "You guys can act coy if you want. I know what I felt. You both can't tell me it hasn't been a few millennia since we felt power like that. It's incredible. I would think he was a god if I didn't know any better."

"Xeno, my friend, you really should stop talking this blasphemy. This boy is no such thing. We will get to the bottom of these powers of his," Dillon scoffed and hurried off to his own quarters of the castle.

"What is his problem?" Mikael asked.

"You know he's sensitive when this topic comes up. I'm going to check on something. I'll hit you if I need you," Xeno responded as he walked out the door, lost in his thoughts. "I can't wait to go see her!"

MEETING NEW FRIENDS

Stepping out into the late-night chill, Taki and M left the restaurant in Brooklyn. After dinner, Taki convinced M to walk with her, not wanting to go straight back home. As they walked the still busy streets, M asked, "Takisha, before the past few nights, when was the last time you slept through the night?"

"Honestly, M, I don't remember."

"The episodes in Japan were not this powerful. I truly wish to help you. Do you—?"

"Wait, I did have a few drinks with a friend very recently and ended up sleeping for a long while. But that could have been because I had too many shots of tequila." Taki looked at M with a smile.

M scowled at Taki's sudden mood change, curious as to why. "When did this happen? What friend do you speak of? I know Mr. Reign is not the cause of this flushed look you have." M was interested in her sudden glow.

Resuming her walk, Taki replied, "Friday night, when you left my house from dropping that stuff off. You made it a little creepy as always when you bring that up. So, I decided to go take a walk and ran into A. I mean, Adam. Weird, right?" She continued walking with a smile.

Shocked at the revelation she just heard, M wondered where he may fit into the recent events. "You mean the young man you were involved in the incident with?"

"Crazy M, he was just in front of my apartment sitting in his car. He didn't know that's where I lived because he was just as shocked to see me as I was him. I still say what a crazy coincidence."

"Well, that is a fascinating coincidence, if I must say so myself. Was Adam around for any of these episodes you had the past few days?" she asked inquisitively. *Could he be the cause of the issues that Takisha is having?*

Immediately replying as she heard the disapproving tone in M's voice, Taki said, "What are you thinking? Because he is not the bad guy. Actually, the only night I didn't have an episode was when I saw him, including running into him yesterday for a few minutes. I really don't remember when I fell asleep since it was late, but I slept until about two yesterday afternoon. Crazy how I've slept more in the past forty-eight hours than I slept in six months." Taki continued their stroll as she enjoyed the cool air.

"Are you sure he didn't put anything in the food or drinks you ingested the first night you saw each other?" M asked, now more interested in Adam. Before, M just wanted Taki to have someone from her past to be around to help her get through the tragic events of long ago. Now, the interest had grown to suspicion. *Could he be the troublemaker all this time? I do remember after that night, the episodes got worse, and after the information I received—I-?* Taki pulled at her arm.

"Come on, M. Look, it's a psychic place that's still open. Maybe they can help me. You said there was nothing medically wrong with me. Maybe I need an exorcism." Taki laughed at her own joke.

"Child, what is wrong with you? Do not play with things that you don't understand. This is probably a fraud as usual anyway," M replied as they walked into the storefront.

Both women stopped a few feet from the entrance, looking around at the small area in front of them, decorated with orange and brown curtains with candles, incense, and light spiritual music playing on a loudspeaker. A few aisles of what looked like a shopping area for witches included oils, powders, boxes, pitchers, and glasses that were filled with things that you could hardly pronounce. There was a counter with a large crystal ball sitting on top filled with smoke that was moving around like a small thunderstorm, surrounded by trinkets that looked like they came out of a Harry Potter movie. "What the fuck did I just walk into?" Taki spoke out, feeling a tingling sensation throughout her body.

M, very uncomfortable, felt a burning in her lungs and throat. "Let's go. I can't. I have to leave." She coughed.

"Welcome. Please, don't leave. I was about to close and felt the pull of someone needing my help." A beautiful, heavily Spanish accented voice came from behind the curtain area of the store. Lucia, a psychic, looked like a twenty-two-year-old. Average height, curvaceous, beautiful sun-kissed olive skin tone with long, curly, jet-black hair that reached just above her waist. "Hello, my name is Lucia. I am going to tell you your future." Lucia moved from behind the counter to introduce herself to Taki and M with a wide smile.

Taki hesitantly reached out her hand to reply. "Hello, my name is Taki Mashiro. I just stopped to look around. No need to bother you." She felt chills down her spine as she held Lucia's hand.

Lucia, not wanting to let go, felt the warmth and energy that came from Taki. "You are an interesting one. You already found what you are searching for. You will help each other help us all. Come, let me give you a reading." She let go and began to walk off. Stopping in her tracks, she turned around and said, "You! What are you doing here?" Lucia spoke directly to M, disgusted.

Uncomfortable with the being in front of her, sensing this Lucia was of Other, M replied, "Takisha, let's go. This fraud is just trying to take your money." She reached for Taki's other hand.

"I do no such thing," Lucia quickly rebuffed. "Why are you here? I can't put my hands on it, but you should not be here!" She grabbed for Taki. "Come, let me help you get rid of this darkness."

"Hey, lady, I don't know what the hell is wrong with you, but I need you to calm down—" Taki snatched her hand away from Lucia. "Shit!!!" Taki screamed, falling to her knees, "NO! NO! NO! STOP!" She felt the pain throughout her body. "M! Make it stop! Please! Make it stop! It hurts so bad!" Taki yelled, writhing in pain.

Both Lucia and M stared and yelled at each other. "What did you do?!" Both women fell to the floor to the crying and screaming Taki. M grabbed Taki's head and laid it on her lap, trying to comfort her sweating head. "She is burning up. Like she is being burned on the inside!" M said to Lucia through clenched teeth. "What did you do?" she asked, wanting to rip the kneeling woman's throat out.

Lucia responded in fear as she felt the darkness coming off of M. "I didn't do anything. I felt her energy outside. She is incredible. I never felt energy like hers before."

"HELP HER! I WILL KILL YOU IF YOU DO NOT FIX THIS!" M stated with a deadly glare.

Lucia stared at the scary-looking, brown, petite woman holding the screaming Taki. She reached out to touch Taki's arm to get a reading. "Oh my God! Oh my God! Oh my God! WHAT IN GOD'S NAME?!!" Lucia screamed, letting go of Taki immediately. She fell to the ground, drawing her knees to her chest, rocking back and forth, stuttering, "This can't be. This can't be."

"WHAT DID YOU SEE?!" yelled M, perturbed at the look on Lucia's face when she touched Taki. M knew she saw something.

Lucia stumbled over her words, scared of the woman in front of her with darkness pouring off her. "I, I, I, I don't know what I saw. The power, the pain, it was unbelievable." She tried to decipher the energy signature she sensed, scared and intrigued at the same time. She could not pinpoint the energy due to the mixture of the two women in her store and the chaos that it was causing.

M held a suddenly limp Taki, feeling the after-effects of all the energy that just surged inside of Taki and this area. "What in this world is going on? Why is this happening? What does she have to do with all of this?" M asked sadly peering down at a passed-out Taki.

Taki opened her eyes and stared at a pair of red ones, startled. "What the?" Immediately sitting up, rubbing her head and seeing M, Taki plopped down next to M with a worried look. "M, your eyes. Never mind," Taki said as she rubbed her head. "I feel like I was hit by a fucking truck! I'm sick of this shit!" she exclaimed.

"Takisha, are you okay?" M asked, staring at Taki, searching for injuries and answers.

"NO, I AM NOT OKAY!" Taki shouted staggering up from the floor. She looked towards Lucia. "So, you think you can help me now, lady?" She stared at the woman, remembering her touch while she was in pain.

Lucia, still sitting on the floor of her shop, considered what she just saw. "I, I really don't know what to say? Taki, right? Baby girl," Lucia said in her heavy accent, "you are special. Like I told you. You found what you're looking for. Just have to face it. Watch the people closest to you. Soon a lot of their secrets will be revealed." She got up and walked towards the back of her store. "Now, if you will excuse me, ladies, I have to sit down for a bit." Lucia disappeared behind the curtains.

Taki, still weak, watched as the curtains closed, and leaned on the counter. "Now I'm ready to go home. Should have just gone home like you said earlier. I'm sorry I didn't listen. Didn't expect to have a fit," Taki said gravely.

"You have nothing to apologize for. This is none of your doing. We will get to the bottom of this," M replied as she walked up to Taki to assist her in standing. "Come on. We will go to your place and get you into bed." M helped Taki towards the front of the store. They heard the doorbells chime and looked up to see a tall, dark man with a black hoodie knock on the counter. Ignoring the man, the two women ambled to the door. M held it open as they walked out of the store to the now late-night NYC streets.

REVEALS

Pushing the door open, Xeno felt a significant amount of energy lingering in the air. *What's this? Playing with the humans too much, Lucy.* He watched two well-dressed women walk towards him. Something was off as Xeno approached the counter. Looking back at the women before they left, his thoughts were broken up by the beautiful voice he liked to hear.

"Hey, Papi. What are you doing here?" Lucia asked playfully as she walked out from the back.

"What's going on? Too much partying with the humans, Lucy?" Xeno asked, chuckling.

"No, you know me. Just work, baby. What brings your fine ass by here? Definitely wasn't expecting to see you today," Lucia said, smiling as she hid her true feelings from the events that just happened.

"No crystal ball searching for me today? Come on, sexy, I thought we had a better relationship than that. You always supposed to be ready to see me," Xeno replied while he stared at her with those beautiful, clear white eyes.

Getting lost in those eyes of his, she immediately snapped out of it. "Welp, sorry handsome, you gotta go. You feel that. I don't want no parts. I've had enough weird shit for one day," Lucia said hurriedly, pushing Xeno towards the exit.

"I need to speak with you, Lucy. I need your opinion and possible help," Xeno replied, walking towards the door from her small shoves.

"Come back another time. Adios," Lucia said, immediately closing and locking the door.

"What the hell was all of that about? Just a few lonesome demons out as usual. I know that wouldn't scare Lucia," Xeno said to himself as he began to feel the sensations in the air. "What the hell? Someone's fighting them. Let me join the party!" he said excitedly as he felt the energy surges of a small battle going on not too far from where he was.

Xeno unleashed his wings and flew straight to the area he felt the most potent of energy. He detected low-level demons' presence along with something dark and sinister mixed with an unknown energy signature he'd never felt before. "Let's see what this is all about," Xeno said as he flew lower. He landed on one of the side blocks in downtown Brooklyn, where all the lovely brownstones are. Xeno saw a small, well-dressed woman fighting two demons as five others surrounded her and what looked like another woman lying on the ground behind her.

He recognized the women's clothing from the shop. Xeno watched as the petite woman looked like she grabbed the demon in front of her in the throat and turned around, holding the other one. Watching still at a short distance as both demons immediately fell, Xeno realized the woman had stabbed both demons in their throats, instantly killing them. After directly going into battle mode, Xeno drew his battle-ax from behind his back, flying straight to the first demon that hovered over the fallen woman as the petite woman battled with another demon.

Xeno sliced open the demon immediately to his left with his ax using his left hand. He used his right to throw a small knife from his vest towards another demon to his right. He looked around at the battlefield, sensing more demons approach the area. Xeno yelled towards the petite woman. "Get your friend out of here, lady! You don't want to involve yourself. Get to safety!" he said as he grabbed at the other demon that was snapping its teeth at Xeno

M watched the tall warrior fight the demons, immediately recognizing the insignia on the back of his hoodie. "Mind your business! I don't need your help!" she yelled as she ducked a swing from the demon in front of her and came up with a left uppercut, using her left wrist blade to stab the demon through the chin. M watched the demon fall and disintegrate. She then rushed over to a passed-out Taki, stunned at the scene and individual in front of her. "XENO?! WHAT ARE YOU DOING HERE?" M said, shocked.

X broke fighting concentration from hearing her voice. "Mel?" he said, surprised at who he was looking at. "What the fuck are you doing here? SHIT!" Xeno exclaimed as he reacted to a demon latching onto his left forearm with its sharp teeth. He switched hands to place his ax in his right hand, chopping the demon's head off of its body. Xeno left a blood-dripping demon's head attached to his arm. "AAHHH!" Xeno shouted, ripping the demon's head and teeth off of his arm. "Little motherfucker, that shit hurt!" He threw the demon head on the ground and stomped on it with his large combat boot, making a crunchy sound from the squish.

"Ew. You are still a grotesque beast," M said, repulsed, still leaning over Taki.

"You know you missed me. For real, Mel. What are you doing here? Where have you been?" Xeno replied gravely.

"Right now, your questions are irrelevant. I must get my young charge out of here. I believe it is Takisha they are after," M replied as she stood up to assess her situation. "The only reason those mongrels were getting the best of me was that I had to keep an eye on her." M pointed to a passed-out Taki. "Otherwise, I wouldn't have needed your help." M scoffed at Xeno as he loomed over her and Taki.

"Who is she? Got damn. She's fine as hell!" Xeno exclaimed, staring at Taki. "Thick as hell, too. She got a man?" he asked curiously.

"Uncivilized, Xeno. You're old enough to be her ancestor. You and your misfit friends must fit in very well with these ill-mannered men nowadays." M immediately replied to his advances at Taki.

"Hey, the women today are more liberal and freer! Don't hate, Mel. I remember a time when—" Xeno was instantly cut off by a punch to the gut by M and then a knee to the face. "Shit, what the fuck was that for? I was just—" X caught her knee, then stood up to grab her hand. "I'm not the young recruit you, remember, Mel. Can't just go hitting me like that anymore," Xeno said sternly.

M used her right foot to walk up to Xeno's left leg while he continued to hold her right hand, crossed her left leg over her right leg, kneeing Xeno straight in the head, causing him to fall to his knees. "WHAT THE FUCK, MEL?!" Xeno exclaimed as he knelt down, still taller than her, with him on his knees.

"Don't you dare speak of the past!" M shouted at Xen. "Don't!" The pain she remembered so long ago was trying to resurface. She felt her dark powers manifesting; she tapped into energy she hadn't had to in a long time, eyes widening. "XENO? Do you feel that?" she asked, looking around for the result of the sudden power surge.

Xeno, feeling insulted from being knocked to his knees, replied, "We have to go. Neither one of us is in any condition to go up against that right now. Let's get your charge to safety and then assess what this new threat is."

Unsure if she should trust the individual in front of her, Mel hesitated. "I can get her to her home safely. I do not need you or your friends' assistance!" she said with her voice filled with uncertainty.

"Look, Mel, I don't know what the hell your problem is or why those demons are attacking you. Right now, we have to go! Two of our safe houses here have been attacked in the last couple of days. We lost a large number of troops, including one of our lieutenants. These demons are getting organized and more powerful. From what we both feel right now and the look on your face, we know some real shit is about to go down. Mikael and Dillon have been working on trying to figure out who and why," Xeno explained seriously.

M was skeptical about receiving help but didn't want to risk Taki in another battle. She sensed the power that continued to get closer. "We have been surviving for a long time. I am aware of the war that still rages on, but this has nothing to do with me and my charge. We just want to be left alone until we figure out what is wrong with her," she said, looking down at Taki still laid out on the ground.

Xeno bent down to pick up Taki and laid her in his arms, looking straight at M. "Mel, look, just let me help you and her. Get away from here. Come to the castle, so we can think and put together our resources so we can find out what is really going on," he said in his most charming voice.

M felt the massive power getting closer; the air sizzled by power growth. "Look, just because I know I can't fight at one hundred percent with Takisha hurt is the only reason why I am letting you assist me. Let's go, Xeno. You better not tell him you saw me after my charge, and I leave the castle," M replied and transferred to Otherside to use her full powers.

Xeno joined M on Otherside, feeling the powers that M possessed. "I forgot how powerful you were, goddamn! We could have used you these past few thousand years, woman! We are losing this war," he said grimly.

M walked up to Xeno, reaching just above his elbows, pointing her finger at him, and replied, "FUCK YOU AND THIS WAR! I'm not—" and was interrupted by Taki.

"Such language for a beautiful woman as yourself," Taki said sarcastically in Xeno's arms. "Where am I?" She looked up at a pair of the most beautiful clear white eyes she had ever seen. "Who are you?" Taki reached her hand up to touch the left side of his face. Startled by the scar she felt, she then laid her hand on his face getting lost in his eyes.

"What are you?" Xeno replied, getting lost in the enchanting brown eyes that were staring at him in awe. He felt the purity of the energy coming off of her. *She feels incredible.* He was unsure of why he was feeling a pull to the young woman he was holding.

M cleared her throat to interrupt Xeno's flirting and spoke to Taki. "How do you feel? Are you okay, Takisha?"

Taki answered, "Besides my head and body feeling a little heavy, I actually feel okay. That episode took a bit out of me, but I'm starting to feel somewhat normal. Um," she looked up at Xeno, "can you put me down now, big guy?" Taki asked shyly.

"Oh, my bad," Xeno said, gently placing Taki on her feet, catching her as she swayed slightly and fell into him. "Oops, maybe not now, beautiful. How about I hold you until we get to where we going?" Xeno said, feeling as if he was falling under some spell by staring at her.

Taki shyly said, "Okay," holding on to his neck, so she was more comfortable as he held her.

"Enough with flirting with my charge, you filthy dirtbag," M said intensely. "We have to go. They had to have felt us leave Earth's realm. They will come to Otherside to search for us soon. We have to go." She glared at Xeno, understanding the fascination with his eyes.

"You travel much faster than me. So how about you get us near the castle like I said, and I will take it from there," Xeno said confidently.

"I told you, I don't need you or your band of misfit friends to help me!" M replied, aggravated.

X immediately recognized the presence of the same dark and evil energy they just escaped from. "MEL!! LET'S GO!!" he shouted.

She understood the urgency in his tone. M knew precisely where that immense power was coming from. M grabbed Xeno's forearm as he held Taki and instantly transported them to a densely wooded forest much different from Downtown Brooklyn where they just were.

THE BAD GUYS

Trystan paced back and forth. "You told me you had this under control!" he growled at the lower-level demon, backhanding him. "How could you lose them at a time like this?! If my ass is on the line, so is yours!" He unleashed his sword, instantly slitting the throat of the demon in front of him. Trystan watched as the body fell and began to disintegrate. He said again, "Does anyone want to tell me what really happened?" He growled with an angry vein pulsing on his face as he stared at the others that stood around him.

Zale, the youngest of the troops, stepped forward. "One of those bastard angels came, and they disappeared before we were able to link up with the others. She used her full powers to conceal them when they left," he said before he stepped back in line.

Deuce stepped forward. "THAT BITCH must die! She killed Tre," he said coldly.

"We have to find her first, idiots! Now, stake out the apartments and the boyfriend. Check-in with the woman to see if the boyfriend has any more information. I WANT THAT POWER NOW!" Trystan yelled furiously as his cell phone rang. "Sire," he replied nervously. "Yes, sir. Yes, sir. We are on our way." He disconnected the call as he received the last of his orders. "Let's go. We have work to do. This is not done!" Trystan yelled as his squad followed.

WHAT A SURPRISE

"M, what the hell? I feel...put me down!" Taki exclaimed, jumping down out of Xeno's arms on her own to throw up. She bent over, wrenching up the food they ate at the restaurant. "What the hell was that?" she asked in between hurls of spit coming out of her mouth. "What did you just do?" Taki breathed out as she was leaned over from the queasy feeling she had.

"You are repulsive, Takisha," M replied to Taki's stomach letting go of dinner. "I am appalled at your behavior. I do understand that this is all new to you but goodness gracious young lady, have some dignity." She walked past Taki with disdain on her face.

"ANATA YAKKAI MEINU (YOU MOTHERFUCKING BITCH!)! Don't you dare—" Her sentence was broken up by Xeno's robust and commanding voice.

"I see the bitch in you hasn't changed! You know I won't bring it up, but I'm being honest, I miss the real Melchorde." Xeno reached out to Taki. "Come on, follow me; stay close," he said protectively.

M spoke low. "Is he here, Xeno? If he is here by the power—" Before she could even utter another word, they arrived in front of the castle.

M was always intrigued at the view of their headquarters. The Great Castle of the Army of Angels, as it was called. The stones and columns were created by the god of gold, as it would be explained to the new recruits when they began their training for the angel soldier's duties. Just as she remembered from long ago.

"I can't do this," M exclaimed. "Takisha, let's go. We will find our own way of dealing with these savages." She looked at Taki and reached out her hand to lead her away from the castle.

"No," Taki replied, "I am not taking orders from you. I am tired and want to sit down. Tired of waking up in weird places. Let me go to this weird place be my choice."

M, unsure of Xeno's intentions, said, "Xeno, do not ever make me come out of character again in front of Takisha. Next time, it won't be vulgar words that attack you," she said with a killer glare. "Now, lead us to a place where none of your friends will know where we are. I am in no mood to deal with any more of you today," M said coldly.

"With your attitude, I doubt very much anybody wants to see you either," X mumbled.

Taki stopped, staring between M and the tall, handsome chocolate man standing in front of her. "Um, why do I get a feeling you two know each other?" she asked curiously. "Ex-lovers, with the disdain in your voices and all," Taki said again, wondering why these two were staring at each other like they were ready to kill one another.

"Don't ever insult me that way. I just know Xeno here from my way, DISTANT," M said, exaggerating her words, "past. Don't worry. You rest. I'll gather some information. You won't ever have to worry about seeing him again," M replied to Taki sharply.

"You know this is going to be a fucking day," Xeno said. "Let's go, Your Highness." He called her the one thing he knew she hated, knowing she wouldn't do anything about it. Xeno led M and Taki through the castle's back entrance, closer to his quarters, avoiding Dillon or Mikael.

"How come you didn't want to come here. It's beautiful!" Taki said as she looked around at the wonderfully arranged grounds that covered most of the area. "I can't imagine living here. This is amazing." She enjoyed the smell of the flowers in the air. "But I might as well ask, where are we? This definitely doesn't look like any part of Brooklyn I have ever been to." Taki was curious as to where Xeno was leading them. "Xeno, is that your name? I keep hearing M say it to you," Taki said to the large man's back. "Oops, I'm sorry!" Taki yelped, bumping into Xeno as he instantly stopped walking.

"Unfortunately, that is the name that was given to me. I do not allow most individuals to call me that. Most are dead that know me by that name," Xeno said. He turned around to face Taki and M and replied coldly, "There are a select few, I mean select beings, that are still alive that call me by my full name." He reached out his hand to Taki, "But you, good-looking, can call me X," he added with a big smile.

"Oh! I'm sorry. I know how that feels. I keep telling this one here to call me by my nickname, Taki, but she chooses to call me by my full name as well. So, you are not alone," Taki said, extending her hand to shake his large one.

M disrupted the official introductions. "Enough with the pleasantries. Get us out of the open, so we can regroup, and I can get my charge out of here before I have to dispose of one of you," M said as she walked away, remembering an area that she and Taki could rest at from her time here in the past.

Taki followed M and whispered, "Anata wa, kono yōna meinudesu (You are such a bitch)," as she shook her head.

"Watashi ga shitte iru, anata wa sore ni tsuite nani mo dekimasen (I know, and you can't do anything about it)," M answered harshly with a gleaming smile.

Taki's eyes widened. She was unaware of M's ability to speak Japanese, no matter how many times she saw M with Jade or anyone else when M visited her in Tokyo.

Taki's thoughts were interrupted by X's voice. "She wasn't always like this. Don't let the tough act fool you." He stopped in his tracks. "Your Highness, I suggest you rethink going to the old area you're thinking of. That area is now included in his quarters. So, if you're so keen on not seeing him, I suggest you follow me," X said, enjoying the fact that he knew she was eager to see him anyway.

Uncomfortable even being back in the one place she hated, M snapped. "Just lead the way, you feathered bird brain."

X led them into the corner of the castle that very few visit, besides earlier when he placed Adam in one of the bedrooms there. It was easier to keep unknown people away from the vital part of their headquarters. He unlocked a pair of double doors in what looked like a short tower of the castle from the outside, leading to a large sitting area with glass doors on the opposite wall that led to another garden area with a sitting area to the left with a pair of double doors to the right. Speaking to both women, he said, "I will have some food brought over for you. This door here," he indicated to his right, "leads to a bedroom with a master bath to get yourselves together." X pointed to a single closed door. "Do not go in there. One of Mikael's recruits is having some trouble. So, for both of your safety, stay away. I locked the door both ways, so there is no reason to be alarmed," X said protectively. "I can also have the maid bring some clothes from Earth Realm for the both of you."

"That won't be necessary. I am going to let Takisha rest for a bit, and we will get going. I will not burden you with our dilemma," M said, returning to her calculating and calm demeanor.

"It's okay. It's what families do, right? I'll be back," X said as he left.

"Okay, so now that the sexy man is gone, I can officially freak the FUCK OUT! M, WHAT THE FUCK IS GOING ON, AND WHERE THE FUCK ARE WE?" Taki asked worriedly. "I feel really weird being here. My body is tingling like I am feeling electric sensations through my veins," she said as she sat down on the extra-large, golden-colored cushioned couch.

M sat down next to Taki and placed her hand on one of Taki's legs, looking at her sincerely. "Look, child, I have tried to always protect you from the things that you did not understand. Right now, we are in a place that your mind can't comprehend at this moment. I will tell you everything when the time is right. I need you to trust me and believe that I will get us out of whatever is going on," M said confidently.

"You know I'm not an idiot. You can tell me what's really going on," Taki replied instantly. "I rather you be honest with me and help me understand what's going on so we both can defeat it together." She continued, "So, what is it, M?"

She has the right to know and understand the kind of danger she is in. M replied with great hesitation, "I really do not think you are ready for what is going to be heard. To be honest, I don't think you would believe it. That is why I chose to protect you myself," M said.

"Try me. I've been feeling and seeing some pretty weird shit throughout my life. How about for once, you trust me?" Taki asked with a determined look.

In a huff, M said, "Takisha, what I am going to explain to you is a summary of what I believe is going on here. I truly do not know your involvement and how your episodes tie to any of this. What I can tell you is the bits of pieces of what I have seen for the past few days."

"Okay, I'm listening," Taki said with a raised brow.

Sometime later, Taki sat with a dazed look on her face. Taki exaggerated her words. "Oh-kay. You're telling me that demons and angels have been at war for thousands of years. Somehow, I produce energy that attracts demons to me, and the big sexy guy we were just with is an angel that fights them?" She was unable to fathom everything M just said but getting the gist of it.

M replied, impressed with the way Taki summed up what she told her. "I said a great deal more than that, but you get the point. Now we are at one of their headquarters, where they plan and train their recruits to attack demons that try to feed off humans." She mistakenly used the word humans, hoping Taki wouldn't catch it.

Taki's mind still reeled from the information that she received. "Well, where is this power coming from? Am I a demon too? Is that why they are after me?" Taki asked anxiously.

M moved closer to Taki to place her arm around her. "No, no child, you are no demon. Do not ever think you are one of those vile creatures. You are human. I do not know the cause of why this power comes from you." She looked away, not wanting to reveal everything. "I am certain that something or someone wants you for this unknown power. I have to figure out why. For the time being, Takisha, I am confident you are safe here. I have to gather some information from the resources that I have to see if they have any information as to why you are even on these demons' radar," M said.

"How do you fit into all of this? Are you an angel? Why did X call you Your Highness?" Taki asked, curious as to why he said it more than once.

"My dear, that conversation is for another day. We will discuss it in all due time. I have to go. Stay away from the men in this house. They are disgusting, as you've seen from Xeno. Don't let their charm fool you," M said in a motherly tone.

"If I didn't know any better, I'd think you are giving me motherly advice. So, you do care?" Taki asked playfully.

M got ready to leave the compound. "Just be careful. Call me on that annoying device," she pulled her cell phone out of her suit jacket pocket, "if you need me. Here." She gave Taki a small knife from out of her stiletto boot. "Just in case one of them gets stupid. I trained you for the very things we may have to face soon. Get some rest. Their maids cook the best foods; order whatever you want," M said as she walked out the same way X did.

UNDERSTANDING

Sitting straight up, waking from being passed out, Adam looked around. "That stupid, mother—ouch! What the hell?!" He felt the pain as it coursed from his head. "Why am I back in here?" he asked, looking around at the bedroom he woke up in earlier. "They still haven't found me any clothes yet. This monk robe is pissing me off," Adam said, annoyed.

Getting up to leave the bedroom once again, Adam began to hear voices on the other side of the room coming from a single metallic-like door. Reaching the doorknob to open it, he received an electrical shock as he tried to touch the handle. "Ouch! What the?" Adam yelped, stepping back from the weird door. Walking away from the triggered door, Adam proceeded out the door that he went through before, searching for Mikael so he could speak to him. Slowly, walking down the opposite hall from earlier, just strolling around, Adam came across a reading Mikael.

"Unc, what's up?" he asked, walking into a study area filled with books, maps, and mysterious treasures that looked like they were collected from all over the world.

"Ahh, Adam. Risen from your nap?" Mikael asked, amused.

"Look, I'm ready for you. Tell me what the hell is going on," Adam answered, irritated as he walked to sit in a chair.

"I know all of this is new and uncomfortable," he said, looking at Adam's robe, smiling, "but calm down. That's why you and Dillon can't seem to get along," Mikael said, looking up from his book to a now sitting Adam. "Both of your tempers are ridiculous. The level of childishness between you two is astonishing." He chuckled at his own statement.

"I like how you find everything funny. I really don't like that guy. All the way down to my bones," Adam replied to Mikael, sitting back in a comfortable chair.

Mikael immediately replied. "That makes two of us, but he is a good man. Rubs a lot of individuals the wrong way, but he still gets the job done. Believe it or not, he was not always like that." He leaned closer towards Adam over his desk. "Now, it's about time I answer some of your questions. We do not have time for a full Q&A session, so I suggest you think about the most important things you want to know. I will try my best to answer them without making you all confused and disbelieving," Mikael said with his massive arms folded on the desk in front of him as he stared back at Adam.

"Where the fuck are we? What are you? Why do you keep saying I am of 'Other'?" Adam fired out, emphasizing *Other* with air quotation marks.

"Well, straight to it, I see," Mikael said, smiling. "Well, first, you are in Otherside, a parallel world between Heaven and Earth. A place where all nonhuman creation can roam free without the interference of humans," Mikael calmly added. "Next, I am an angel that is part of an army created to stop demons from taking over Earth, and as of now, I don't know what you are." He assessed Adam's face as he paused. "Still with me?" he asked, making sure Adam was still paying attention.

Shocked by the answers he just heard, Adam replied, "What? Heaven and Earth? Demons? You're not a goddamn angel!"

"I guess those wings you saw were not real, or you setting yourself on fire for the past twenty-something years isn't real either," Mikael said, shaking his head. "You know, if I didn't think my powers might trigger an episode for you, I would truly show the full extent of what you're dealing with. I am pure energy created from the most powerful being that ever existed. We all are. My job is to protect people like you from the evil that lurks around. Yours is to be a human and procreate and continue the line of succession then die, and the circle of life continues," Mikael said in a monotone. "Well, at least that's what most humans do. You may not be human," he stated with a chuckle.

What the hell, Uncle Mike? I'm not sure how to respond. Ever since you and I had this conversation the other day, shit has gotten weird. I told you, I'll have you committed if you keep it up with this bullshit you've been kicking," he scoffed. "I'm supposed to believe that you're some type of angel that's in an army, and you've lived on Earth all this time."

"You know, for being so smart, you're stupid. You are asking me all of these questions, but what questions have you asked yourself?" Mikael asked, questioning him. No response. "That's what I thought. Didn't even think about that. What do you think has been happening all this time?" he asked, staring at Adam with a blank look.

Adam, unsure of what to think, finally replied. "I don't know what's been going on. I'm just trying to survive, man. That shit I go through is nothing. I'll be alright. Made it this long. Don't try to make me believe in your little fantasy world. I'm just ready to get some clothes and be out. I have shit to do," Adam said nervously.

Shaking his head, Mikael released some energy so Adam could feel him. "You know, you are so freaking hardheaded. I really thought we could get past all of this and get to the bottom of what is wrong with you. It looks like I am going to have to show you better than I can tell you," Mikael said, standing up from his desk. Unleashing an incredible surge of energy that would blow up a building, Mikael asked, "What do you feel?" while staring at Adam with electricity in his eyes.

Adam fell out of the chair onto his knees. "I can't breathe. I can't breathe, so heavy," he said, holding himself up with both arms.

Mikael, walking from behind his desk, stepped closer to Adam. "Breathe, Adam, breathe. Remember what I taught you. Concentrate on your breathing; clear your mind. What do you see?" He moved towards Adam to place his hand on his shoulder.

Breathing heavily, he panted, "I can't, I feel hot. It's starting to burn!" Adam raised his voice, trying to ignore the pain he was feeling.

"NO! Feel no pain!" Mikael said, holding onto Adam's shoulder, trying to enter his mind to see what Adam saw.

Adam, hearing Mikael and slowly breathing, began to see. "The sun, the rays. It's beautiful. It doesn't hurt. It feels wonderful. The power, the energy."

Mikael watched as he felt the energy permeating off Adam. As the air sizzled from the purity of the power, Adam's body began to glow. The power of the sun started to pour into Mikael's body as his hand was still touching Adam's shoulder.

"This can't be. This can't be." Mikael immediately released his touch. Backing up from the young man that he considered family, he was unsure of the revelation that had just come to him.

Adam, snapping out of the trance he was in, looked at the dumbfounded look on Mikael's face. "Unc, what's wrong, you okay? Why are you looking at me like that? Unc! Talk to me!" he said nervously. "Yo! What happened? It didn't hurt this time! Unc!" Adam was now standing over a fallen Mikael, shaking him for a response. "What was that? Why are you just sitting there? Say something, Mikael! What the fuck!" Adam said, standing straight up, confused.

Mikael, struggling to stand, shaken at the thoughts that plagued his mind, stood up and looked at Adam eye-to-eye. "My apologies, Adam. Your energy is astounding. I'm amazed at you for having this kind of power. I must teach you how to keep your energy in check. I thought our meditation lessons would have helped. Still, the more powerful you get, the harder it is to conceal." He walked over to his desk and sat back down.

"Uncle Mike, I've been around you long enough to know when you're lying to me. WHAT THE FUCK DID YOU FEEL THAT GOT YOU SHOOK LIKE THAT?" he asked, slightly raising his voice as he stood over Mikael on the opposite side of the desk.

Mikael, placing his hands on his head and leaning on top of the desk, tensely said, "Adam, I told you. Once we figure out what you are, I can tell you more."

"Knock, knock." X walked into the study, interrupting the awkward silence between Adam and Mikael. "Yo, Mike, let me holla at you," he said, hinting at not wanting Adam to overhear.

"Adam, are we good? Can we finish this later?" Mikael asked, sighing tiredly.

"We will be good when I get some fucking clothes. I guess we will finish this weird-ass conversation later," Adam replied, aggravated.

"I'll have Elise bring you some clothes and food. Stay in your quarters. No wandering," Mikael stated calmly.

"Whatever, man, just send me some damn clothes," Adam quickly countered, walking past X and out of the study.

"What was that about?" X asked, sitting down in the seat Adam previously occupied.

"Well, what do we expect from a hardheaded Brooklyn kid that has the power of a god?" Mikael replied, slightly angry.

"Oh, so you felt it too?" X asked, sitting back in the chair with an inquisitive look on his face.

"I don't know what I felt, X. We have to get to the bottom of this as soon as possible," Mikael said, snapping out of his own thoughts. Looking at the sitting X, he continued. "What's up with you? Looks like you got some information for me." He pushed back in his chair.

Leaning forward, lowering his voice into a whisper, X replied, "Mike, you wouldn't fucking believe who I ran into and who's in the guest quarters right now."

"Look, we don't have time for your shenanigans, Xeno. We have enough trouble on our hands. Your horde of women trouble is not important."

Laughing at the response from Mikael, X replied, "For once, it's not my woman problems coming into play. You will most definitely be interested in who we have as a visitor right now. At least before he finds out."

"Well, Xeno, you have my attention. Who is in our guest quarters?" Mikael asked, now sitting up in his chair with great interest.

"Melchorde and a sexy chocolate thing! Man, she is sexy as all hell, Mike. Had me damn near drooling and shit," he replied, getting lost in his thoughts of meeting Taki.

"WHAT DID you just say?" Mikael asked, slamming his hands on the table as he stood up in shock.

"Calm down, Mike. I know she is no longer welcomed here but come on. She's still family. Regardless, she needed help. I found her and a young woman named Taki being attacked by a horde of demons. I helped her before some more came for her," X said defensively.

"Mel with a human? What's that about? Out of all the people I thought you could have said, I would not have imagined you saying that name. Why did you bring them here?" Mikael asked curiously.

"Well, after we kicked some demon ass, I felt this strong demon presence. Mel looked shook, Mike. I know we haven't seen her in a few millennia, but I've never seen her nervous like that. I had Mel transport us here. I figured since your safe house was attacked, I would bring them somewhere much safer," X said.

"Are you sure the woman with her was a human? Scared of what? That woman is walking hell fire herself."

"I didn't say scared. I said nervous. I don't know, Mike. I asked her why they were after her. She mentioned something about her charge. Maybe they sensed Mel and decided to attack her. I mean, come on. I know they're still looking for her," X said.

"Hmm, charge? I wonder myself. Well, we better make sure Dillon doesn't find out. I am in no mood to deal with the Adam and Dillon circus right now. Give her what she needs and send her on her way. We can't allow him to get distracted because she popped back up," Mikael replied, hoping that Dillon nor himself ran across M.

X, standing up to leave, said, "I had to tell one of you. I am going to check on them and make sure they're good, so they can be out. I'll keep you posted."

"Hey, before you go, did you talk to Lucia? Maybe she can clarify this Adam puzzle for us," Mikael said.

"Yea, that was weird. I think Lucia was trying to help Taki. Anyway, couldn't get any info out of her. I'll try again later today. I'll let you know when I catch up with her," X said, walking out of the office.

"What else can we add to this equation? Let me go find that boy before he gets us all skinned alive," Mikael said aloud. Thinking of the chaos if Adam ran into M and how she would react to Adam's unpleasant conversational skills.

OLD AND NEW ACQUAINTANCES

Walking straight down the hall he came from. Adam was frustrated at the conversation he had with Mikael. Not understanding what was happening to him, he began to feel the warmth in his body again. "Fuck this. I am not passing out like some bitch again." Slowly breathing and clearing his thoughts, he held onto the wall until he felt the warmth and electrical feeling in his veins decrease. "I'm going to learn to control this shit," he said as he reached the bedroom where he was resting earlier. "I'm not staying in some room like I'm on punishment either." Proceeding to walk out the door, he was interrupted by a heavy French accent.

"Monsieur Adam, here are the clothes your godfather has ready for you. Breakfast will be served in a little while." She placed a bag on the bed and a tray on the desk filled with fruits and water. "This should hold you over until your meal is done," Elise said in a solicitous tone.

"Thanks, Elise. I appreciate it. I'm not all that hungry but thank you," Adam replied, smiling at Elise, feeling something different about her. "Hey, Elise, what's Otherside?" Adam said, searching her face for any shock or discord.

"Monsieur Adam, Mikael will never lie to you. He has helped many like you. Just have a little faith. It goes a long way," Elise said before walking out of the room and closing the heavy door behind her.

"She's no help," Adam said to himself. "Now I can get the hell out of here," he said with a smirk on his face. "Okay, time to blow this joint!" He pulled the oversized jeans, underwear, baggy T-shirt, hoodie, and Timberland boots out of the bag that Elise left.

****

Pacing back and forth in the sitting room of her suite, Taki stopped to see if she could find someone that could give her some more information or something to do. Bored out of her mind with just sitting there, she had combed over the area she was in at least three to four times to see if she could find more information about where and what the hell was going on. After M's conversation, Taki was more curious than ever to figure out what was wrong.

She went outside to the beautiful garden areas, walking through the sliding glass doors that M and X went through. "This is absolutely gorgeous. I would love to live here." She sat down on the metal bench directly in front of a beautiful water fountain.

"I can arrange that," a loud, raspy voice said from behind her.

"X, oh shit!" Taki said, startled by X's sudden appearance.

"My fault, didn't mean to scare you. Are you okay? I see you're enjoying the scenery," X said, sitting down next to Taki, smiling.

She was nervous about the large, handsome stranger and also ready to go home. "Is the time the same? I didn't call out yet?" Taki replied, smiling back.

"I came looking for Mel. Where did she go?" X said, looking around for her.

"Oh, M said she was going to check some resources, and then when she comes back, we'll go," Taki said, looking out at the garden as she twirled her thumbs.

X, excited to not have to see M, playfully said, "Well, would you like a tour? I can show you around. At least until she gets back. I know it can be boring here. This isn't one of our most up-to-date headquarters."

"I think I'm just going to stay here. I don't want M to get worried if I'm not here when she returns," Taki replied hesitantly.

Standing up and offering his large hand to hers, he said, "Come on. It'll be fun." Just then, his cell phone began to ring. "Hold that thought." He answered, "YO! Hey D," he said with a shocked look, stepping away from Taki.

Taki, sitting on the bench, stared at the large, dark-skinned male. *Well damn, he fine! I can stare at him all day.* She was checking X out from afar as he paced on the phone, watching until he walked back and sat next to her.

"Hey, beautiful. I have to give you a raincheck on that tour. Hopefully, this won't be the last time we see each other. The maids will make sure you're good until Mel gets back," X said, leaving Taki in the garden area alone.

Getting lost in her thoughts, Taki began to feel sleepy as she enjoyed the smell of the flowers, the sun's rays, and the flow of the wind. "I'm going to relax and enjoy this break until M gets back." She stood up to walk to the area that X had showed her when they first arrived.

****

Walking outside to the garden, seeming familiar to him, Adam proceeded to walk towards the fountain area. Searching for a way off the property, Adam saw X walking in the opposite direction of him. Going on to walk to the place that X came from, he saw someone by the water fountain. Adam walked closer to the individual and immediately recognized the woman in front of him. Adam walks towards Taki, unbeknownst to her. Grabbing her from behind, he held her and whispered in her ear. "I told you I would follow you to the ends of the Earth."

Taki dropped down to a spin kick towards the knees, turning around to ID her perpetrator face-to-face. Nearly punching him in the face, she instantly recognized the person in pain. "Now you know better than to walk up on me in strange places! What the fuck is wrong with you?" she said, curious as to why Adam was there.

Feeling the pain in his knees, Adam was bending over. "GIRL! What is wrong with you? That is not how I want you touching me!"

Releasing herself from his grasp, Taki responded, "Don't touch me. I didn't even know who you were. I'm in a weird-ass place. You should have announced yourself before you touched me. What are you doing here anyway?"

"This is the third time we've just randomly run into each other," he said, staring into her brown eyes. "What do you have to do with all of this shit going on here?"

"What shit? I'm waiting for Ms. Brown to come back so I can go home. I don't even understand what I am doing here. Some dude brought me and her here," Taki said, annoyed.

Adam grabbed her hand, seeing her mood change. "Hey, hey, don't get upset, Ma. I'm here."

"I'm going to need for you to calm your little boy nerves and tell me why the fuck I am in some place called Otherside and why demons are after me. AND! What the hell do YOU have to do with all of this shit going on?" Taki said, raising her voice with a glare, staring up at Adam.

Perplexed at what he just heard from her, Adam stood frozen, unsure of how to answer the questions she asked. He stepped back from Taki and said in a low voice, "So, they hit you with that shit too. Angels and demons and shit, right?"

Looking at him, ready to hit him again, she said, "Are you dumb? You don't even understand what I've been through the past few hours for this shit to not be real?" She started to feel herself become angrier as she spoke to him.

Adam, feeling a sudden shift in the air, dark and sinister, grabbed Taki by her hand and pulled it up to his chest. "Hey, baby girl." He used his right hand to shift her head to look at him. "I'm here for you. It's so crazy you just said all of that. Uncle Mike told me the same thing about me."

Calming down by his touch, she was confused at his revelation. "Wait, what?" Taki said with a blank look.

Adam led Taki towards the bench, and they both took a seat. "Yo, tell me what's up with you. Maybe we can help each other," Adam replied, ready to hear what she had to say.

Staring at Adam, Taki remembered the psychic's words: *You will help each other, help us all.* She felt a chill go down her spine. "Look A, ever since that night, I've had these bad attacks in my sleep. I can't seem to shake them no matter how far I try to get away. I'm really wondering if all of this is related to my parents' deaths," she said.

Tensing from Taki bringing up the past, he responded to her with clenched teeth, "There is no need to bring that shit up now. Whatever the fuck is going on now is now. True story, Ma. I don't believe none of the shit my uncle tells me. From the look on your face, I see that you've been through some shit and need me right now." He held on to her hands as he spoke. "How about we figure out what the hell is up with us and forget that past shit?" He looked straight into her eyes, avoiding the topic.

Feeling that electrical spark from his touch, Taki snatched her hand away and stood up. "Look, I know that is a sensitive subject for the both of us, shit. You should know I understand. Maybe it's time we deal with it!" She wasn't sure if she was angry at his stubbornness or the fact that he was acting like they were not in the middle of some strange shit.

"Kish, how does what happened ten years ago have to do with today?" Adam immediately asked.

Seeing the conversation going nowhere about the subject, Taki said, "Obviously, genius, all of this shit is related. You're just too fucking stubborn to pay attention." She was getting aggravated by his dismissal of the subject. "I know it's hard for both of us to talk about it, but how else are we involved in this bullshit?"

"Well, for one, supposedly, demons or some creatures he said are after me too. He mentioned that I exert some kind of energy that attracts them. It's not something I tell everyone about, Kish. Since I was a baby, I've been having weird-ass issues from what my parents and Uncle Mike tell me. As long as I can remember, my body and shit have been weird," Adam said with his head down.

Thinking back to that night, Taki replied, "A, you're not weird. You saved us that night. Who knows what would have happened to us?" She reached out to touch his forearm.

His eyes met Taki's. "Baby girl, you don't even know what I've been going through since you been gone. I don't want you involved with this shit. Word up," Adam said stubbornly.

"It can't be a coincidence that your godfather and Ms. Brown are telling us the same thing. It has to be related to that night, A. When I was with her, even though I was a little out of it, I saw her fighting something, and it looked really similar to what we saw that night." She stood up to stare at Adam. "I am not bugging! It has to be related to that night," Taki said, starting to pace in front of Adam.

"Kish, real shit. I don't know what you and that social service lady have to do with all of this. Wait, social services? Aren't you too old for them to still be around?"

"She's always kept in contact since she was the one that got me in the program to go to Japan."

"All I know is my episodes are out of control. My uncle just showed me he got fucking wings on his back. Some dude, Dillon, got some power to make me have an episode, stand still, and cause me pain. I don't know if I'm in a fucking dream or nightmare right now." He looked up, aggravated by Taki's pacing. Adam grabbed her hand. "Hey! Stop that damn pacing. Always hated that shit. Sit down," he said, slightly annoyed.

Taki snatched her hand away from him. "DO NOT touch me! I'm trying to figure out what the hell I have to do with all of this too. You are not the only one here in trouble!" she yelled, still pacing back and forth.

Wanting to calm her down, Adam stood up to try to console her. "Kish, come on. Come here," he said, reaching for her hand. "I know. My bad, Ma." He held her hand and stared into her eyes.

She looked up at the large man in front of her, not understanding the pull she had to him. "A, I'm fine. I don't need you to get all lovey-dovey on me now." Taki looked away, still feeling the electrical spark his hands gave throughout her body, wanting to interrupt the mood. "Well, it sounds like we are in the same boat. So obviously, this angel and demon story is true. Now we have to figure out what they want," Taki said.

Adam turned her head to face him again. "Don't look away from me. I told you, Kish, I am not letting you get away from me this time. I don't give a fuck what is going on," Adam said brazenly, pulling her closer to him.

"Just like you to flirt with me while I'm trying to have a logical conversation. Did you hear what I said?" she asked, staring in his bright eyes that were sparkling like the sun. "A, your eyes, they're turning that color," she said, panting at the power she felt from staring at them.

Adam felt an incredible pull to Taki. Staring at her, he felt his body turn warm. For some reason, this time, the warmth and electrons felt wonderful on his skin. "Kish, what are you doing to me?" Suddenly, he pulled Taki into a passionate kiss.

His lips were hot at first and then fell into a burning electrical sensation throughout her body. Feeling as if she was about to have an orgasm standing outside, Taki stepped away from Adam. She squinted as if she was staring at the sun, unable to fully open her eyes due to the shine from Adam's glistening skin. "A! A! What's wrong?" she yelled, reaching for him.

Confused as to why she was behaving as if she couldn't look at him, he asked, "Kish, come here. What's wrong with you?" and pulled her back into him. "I'm right here. There is nothing wrong," Adam said, hugging Taki as if it was his last time.

"A, you're as bright as the fucking sun!" Taki said, attempting to step back from him, unable to move due to his large frame.

Looking down at Taki, seeing the fear on her face, he looked down at himself, seeing his skin glow as if he was sunburnt. Immediately, he let her go. "Oh shit! Kish! I am so sorry. What the fuck?!" Adam said, placing his hands behind his head, confused at what he was seeing.

Rushing outside at the feel of such power, Mikael said, "What did that boy do now?" He ran his tall, lean frame down the hall towards the garden area. Heading out of the double doors at the back of the castle, Mikael felt the power surge getting more potent. "Adam! What are you doing?!" Mikael yelled, taken aback that there was a young lady out there with him.

Adam replied, "I'm not doing anything! I'm just standing here!" He felt the surge of energy inside him getting overwhelming. It felt great. It felt euphoric, giving Adam a feeling he never felt before.

"Adam!!! You're going to blow this place. Calm down!" Mikael yelled, feeling the power coming from him.

Getting lost in the power that he felt, Adam stood there amazed at what he was feeling and seeing. "This power! This shit feels amazing!" Adam said to an astounded Mikael.

Perplexed as to how this human could be what he was, Mikael began to walk closer towards Adam, thinking, *I have to stop him before he fully awakens his power.*

Taki, seeing the caramel-colored man coming from the fountain area's entryway, watched as he walked towards her and Adam with a scowl. *Is he a demon? Is he coming to hurt us?* Immediately grabbing Adam's arm, Taki began to feel the warmth and electrical feeling in her body. As with Adam, this time, Taki felt that amazing feeling of warmth it gave to Adam. Instantly feeling her body begin to cool and Adam's hand as well, Taki looked over at Adam to see the sunshine from his body start to disappear. "A!! A!!" She immediately let go of his arm to see him start to shine brighter as she let go.

"Touch him now!!!" Mikael shouted at the strange girl, noticing how she dampened the energy surrounding Adam when she touched him. Mikael was a master at deciphering creatures of Other. *Another one I can't read?* He was frustrated as to why he could not read the kind of creature this woman in front of him was. "Touch him, or he will blow!!" Mikael yelled to Taki. Taki stepped in closer to Adam, hugging him as he began to cool off.

Adam dropped to the ground out of Taki's bear hug, exhausted at the exertion of all the energy he used. "YO! That was fucking amazing!" Adam said as if he was high, barely sitting his upper body up.

Taki stared down at Adam, wondering, *What was that? Why did I feel like we were inside of each other?* She was puzzled at the leftover feeling she had from their strange encounter.

Staring up at Taki, panting heavily, Adam said, "You are amazing, girl!" He was struggling to stand up but remembered the feeling of their connection when his powers were manifesting. He did not understand the link but enjoyed it. "Damn, why do I feel so tired now? My body just lit up like a Christmas tree, and now I'm exhausted," Adam said as he began to faint again.

Mikael caught Adam before he could topple over. "Damn, this boy is going to be one hell of a problem." Holding him on his back, Mikael turned to the young woman. "I see you know my godson here. Tell me, who are you? And are you the woman with X?" Mikael asked harshly.

Getting a tingling sensation just from the man standing in front of her, Taki replied, "I am Taki Mashiro, and my mentor and I were brought here by Mr. Xeno. I am unsure why, but it just so happens Adam was here too." Her voice was low, unsure of why she told this man this information. Waiting for Mikael to reply, she stared at the man she swore reminded her of someone that she could not place. She was having a feel of déjà vu.

"Well, Ms. Mashiro, I am Mikael. I'm Adam's godfather. Follow me." He led Taki back inside with Adam sprawled across his back. "I bet X didn't anticipate this," he said, laughing to himself, knowing X would be disappointed when he found out Adam had a connection to the girl.

MEET AND GREET

Laying Adam on the bed, taking the large boots off him, Mikael just stared in wonder at the man sprawled out, thinking, *This can't be. I thought you all were gone.* He quickly dismissed the thoughts, not wanting to dwell on those long-ago memories.

Interrupted by Taki's sweet voice, he looked up. "Is he going to be okay?" she said, concerned.

Mikael, turning to finally get a good look at the young woman, spoke. "Yes, he just needs to learn how to control what this power does to him so he won't hurt those closest to him," he said, still staring at Taki. Checking her out, he noticed the slightly dirty, green and white dress that hugged every curve of her body. She had a few scratches that her caramel-colored legs showed, and her hair was a little disheveled for his taste. Instantly noticing the natural beauty in front of him, he was still considering what she could be. "So, if you don't mind, please tell me how you know Adam and Melchorde?" Mikael asked bluntly, still sitting on the edge of the bed.

Taki stood closer to the doorway, feeling a sense of animosity from his tone. "Ms. Brown is a mentor of mine, and I've known Adam for a long time," she said, not liking the feeling this guy in front of her was giving her.

"I have never heard him speak of a name as yours. It sounds as if you are of Japanese descent," Mikael stated, remembering the name she told him outside.

Surprised that he said that, Taki replied, "Well, A doesn't call me that name. He calls me what everyone in the neighborhood used to call me, Kisha." She sighed deeply, unsure of why this man was nosey, but she wanted to get more information since Adam told her he was an angel. "So, can you tell me why I'm here and what Adam and I have to do with this so-called war that's been going on?" Taki said, agitated at Mikael.

Mikael was unnerved at the revelation of the woman standing in front of him and her sudden boost of confidence. "Well, just like Adam, straight to it," he said lightly. "To be honest, I do not know what you have to do with any of this. I am surprised that this is my first time officially meeting you. I have heard many stories about you," Mikael said, remembering the young woman from Adam's many stories and also the night of the incident. Mikael always wanted to meet the young lady that was there that night to see if Adam harmed her or if she was the cause of the issues he was having. Mikael was back to square one with her standing in front of him, now more unsure than ever.

Taki was clearly not satisfied with the answer. "Well, it really isn't a pleasure to meet you right now, and you didn't answer my questions. While we were outside, you noticed something between Adam and me. I would like for you to share your assessment," she stated boldly.

Stunned at her quick analysis of the event outside, Mikael attempted to use his power of persuasion to deter the conversation until he fully understood what he was dealing with. "Well, very nice of you to notice that. I would like for you to answer a few of my own questions. How long has Melchorde been your mentor? What are you, and did you do this to him?" He added extra force into his last sentence to ensure Taki would answer the questions truthfully.

"She's the social worker that kept Child Protective Services from putting me in a foster home. What do you mean, what am I? I'm a girl from Brooklyn that moved to Japan after seeing her best friend set fire to the things that killed her parents. I didn't do anything to Adam. That night changed our lives, but he saved me," Taki said, dropping to her knees, tears of anger streaming down her face, unsure of why she just told this stranger her life story.

Mikael was apologetic for the amount of force he used on the young woman. Walking towards her, he reached out his hand. "My dear, I am so sorry. Come, let's get you cleaned up," he said, remorsefully standing over Taki.

Sitting on the floor, looking at the man standing over her and feeling an intense sensation to stay away from him, Taki crawled back and stood up on her own. Unable to precisely understand what happened between her and Mikael, Taki knew she did not like him. As she stood there in front of him, she decided to not let herself be provoked. "I'm good, Mikael. That's your name, right? I'd rather stay here with A until he gets up. He'll want someone familiar around," she said in a sarcastically pleasant tone, walking towards the bed to sit near Adam's head, placing his head in her lap.

He was impressed with the power he felt coming from the young woman and her resistance against his power of persuasion in assisting her. "Well, good. I hope we get a chance to speak again." He turned around and walked out of the room, closing the door. "These two are going to get on my nerves," Mikael said as he went off to search for X.

Taki was glad that the creepy godfather of Hell had left her and Adam. She rubbed Adam's head as he laid passed out. Looking down at him, she said, "First family member of yours I do not like. And he's supposed to be an angel? He's a dick." Moving his head back to the pillow, she looked around at her environment. "What the hell is all of this? How old are these people?" She noticed the old medieval-style decorations in the room Adam was in, different from hers.

She pulled out her cell phone, wondering if it worked due to her seeing X use his cell. Noticing she had two bars in the little corner, she immediately called Michi. Listening for the rings, there was nothing but air. Taki looked at the screen, still seeing the two bars. "Come on, don't get funky on me now," she said, banging the phone with her left hand. Again, trying to dial Michi's number to no avail, she was interrupted by the low, deep voice coming from the bed.

"It doesn't work. I tried. Hella times," Adam said, slowly sitting up, noticing it was much easier for him to breathe. "What are you still doing here? I didn't hurt you, did I?" Adam asked, remembering the fear on her face when he hugged her.

"What? No, you just fell asleep after showing off your power, I guess. At least that's what Mikael thought," Taki replied, sitting down in the wooden chair across from the bed.

"Where is he? We need to talk," Adam said, turning to sit on the side of the bed.

"He left to go somewhere." Taki waved her hand towards the door.

Adam noticed the tension in the air. "What's up, Kish? What happened while I was knocked out?" he asked, walking towards Taki, crouching down to look at her face. "Just, FYI, I am sick of fucking passing out like some bitch. I definitely have to talk to Mikael about us doing something about that," Adam said playfully, holding Taki's hands.

Taki chuckled at his banter. "Stop passing out like a little bitch, and you won't feel that way." She raised her head to meet his eyes, seeing the color of the sun. "You mean fainted, anyway. I like your eyes this color," she said, reaching out to touch his face.

What color?" Adam stood up to search for a mirror.

Taki stood up, pulling up the video messaging app on her phone to use for a mirror. She faced it to Adam for him to see. "Look!"

Looking at himself on Taki's phone, Adam noticed the fire-burning sun in his eyes. "What the hell?! I can't go to work like this!" he said, troubled.

Taki, moving the phone from Adam's face, was astonished at what he just said. "Your eyes turn a freaky color, and you got demons chasing you, and you're worried about your store?" she asked unbelievably.

Adam, not amused with her teasing, responded, "Look, I just want to know what the fuck is wrong with me." He began to feel the warmth come over him again.

"Hey! Hey!" Taki replied, grabbing his arm, "Don't start your shit. This room is too small for us to go boom! Okay?" she said as she still held on to him.

Adam sensed the calmness that came over him when Taki touched him. "What do you do to me?" he whispered as he pulled her towards him.

Pushing him away but keeping hold of his hand, she said, "Look, I am so not in the mood for your flirting, A. I am dirty, have on the same clothes since last night, and still have not eaten since I threw up earlier. I am sleepy as all hell!" Taki said, sitting back down in the chair, exhausted from being up all night.

Adam, crouching back down, held Taki's hand. "Look, baby girl, let me get my peoples to get you some clothes and food. You can even rest here. I know my uncle has a better spot than this for you to sleep. But come on." He tugged on her hand, insisting on her to stand up.

Taki, extremely cranky and tired, said, "Look, A, I am going to wait for M to come back from wherever she went. I want all of us to talk to compare notes and shit on what the fuck is going on. Maybe this army of angels can fill in some holes that I don't get." She stood up in front of A, letting his hand go.

Adam was disappointed in the cold feeling he was getting from Taki. "Whatever you want to do, beautiful. We will get to the bottom of this, and I promise it will all work out fine," he said, grabbing her left hand and placing a light kiss on it as he sat back down on the bed to put his boots back on.

Taki was nervous at the feeling she was getting the more she was around A. "I'll come to find you when M comes back," she said as she shuffled out, returning to the quarters that X initially took her to.

QUESTIONS & ANSWERS

Walking from her quarters, M mulled over the events that happened over the last few days. "What is their role in all of this? That Adam must have some answers." She walked towards the entrance of her special place, a place that she found long ago, away from all things and beings from Heaven and Otherside up until about thirty years ago when she was asked to become a guide to specific humans. Unsure if she was doing her job correctly, at the current time, each of them was going through their own issues and causing M to spread herself thin.

As her boss always said, "Do not interfere; they will overcome it all. Just guide and protect." Lately, three of her charges have been directly attacked by something of Other, especially Takisha. M, wanting answers, transported herself to the gates. Knowing she was not welcomed, but out of answers and needing guidance herself, she began to call out, "HEY! ANSWER ME!"

Interrupted by a guard dressed in a robe, a voice said, "Please leave. You do not have permission to come here."

"I am not going anywhere! I need answers now!" she said, aggravated by the rejection.

"YOU ARE NOT WELCOMED," the guard bellowed to M with force so powerful it made her fall to her knees.

Kneeling, feeling the powerful energy coming from the guard, she spoke with her head down, "I need to speak to— The demons are coming for her. I don't know what to do!" She was angry that her plea would most likely be ignored. Lifting her head to see a response from the guard, M saw herself back at her place, kneeling in the entranceway of her tomb-like area. Letting out a loud scream, knowing no one would hear, M walked into the cave area towards her makeshift living quarters.

Frustrated at her inability to understand Takisha's involvement with the demons and her recent encounter with Xeno, M stood in front of the sizeable makeshift mirror she created long ago, looking at the reflection holding back the feelings she pushed away long ago. Talking to the mirror, M said, "You do not have time for this. You have a job to do, and nothing will stop that. I have to find this Adam and see if he has the answers I'm looking for." She then returned to her cold demeanor.

Instantly transporting herself back to NYC, M approached the penthouse door where she was currently staying to get dressed and start her hunt for the day. "I must find more information so I can get Takisha away from that place. If I see him, I just might kill him," she said as she walked through the luxurious space. Going to her bedroom and reaching her walk-in closet to find something to wear, M picked a blood-red skirt and jacket set, pieced it with a white blouse with ruffles and a pair of white, heeled boots with the blood-red bottoms. "Perfect color for today," she said as she began to gather weapons.

After a long bath, M stepped out into her foyer and looked around to make sure she was ready. Looking down at herself, double-checking she was fit for the human world, she made sure her weapons were concealed just in case Others came for trouble. "Well, let the search begin."

She began to walk out the door but was interrupted by her cell that she left on her bedroom table and returned to her bedroom to grab it. *Jade.* "And what do I owe the pleasure of this call?" she answered.

"WHERE IS SHE?"

"She is safe. Why are you asking?"

"Look, I know I promised to stay out of all of this. You need to know they are back looking for you. I received word from the guards that you are now back on the priority capture list," Jade said.

"What does this have to do with Takisha?" M asked, unbothered by the news she just heard.

"One of my men heard about an angel asking about her. Specifically, about her condition," Jade replied, noticing M's disregard for her warning.

"What did they tell them?" M asked menacingly, not liking the conversation.

"They were fed bogus information. Taki's condition is a very well-kept secret around here. Just so happens, they knew where to search. I haven't spoken to her in a while. I have been receiving reports from the New York area about certain activities. I have a feeling my student may be involved from the reports I am getting," Jade replied, concerned.

"I doubt very much Takisha is directly involved in any of this. We have known her long enough. She doesn't even belong in our world, nor does she understand it. I am going to search for the boy that started all of this."

"The boy from the incident? What does he have to do with this?"

"I do not know. I do believe he is a big part of what is going on. Unfortunately, her spasms have been happening more frequently and growing in intensity. Somehow, he popped back up, and now it's worse."

"Well, I can do my part from here. I can gather some information and send it to you," Jade said.

"There is no need to get your people more involved. I had enough of them this past week. You can tell them to stay away from her before I kill more of them," M replied with clenched teeth.

"WHAT?! Look, I don't know what is going on over there. I told you, whatever you're doing caused a little tiff between the armies, so I advise you to crawl back into that cubbyhole you came from before they find you!" Jade said.

"Look, I appreciate the advice, Jade, I do. As I told you a long time ago, I am no longer a part of that anymore. I will continue to do as I wish. Any one of them that comes for me will meet their end. Thanks for the call, little sister," M said, hanging up on Jade before walking out.

EYES & FEELINGS

Walking down the streets of Brooklyn with his large frame, X began to ponder, *I really can't believe it. This shit about to be lit. Damn shame it took for the lieutenant and the others to return to the light before those two got serious about the war. I've been telling them for years that shit is getting more real, and we need to turn it up more.* Reaching the storefront to enter, he felt a surge of energy nearby, disturbing his thoughts.

Transferring to Otherside in a hurry, X unleashed his wings to reach the location he felt the surge coming from. Immediately smelling burnt flesh, X turned the corner to find a lean, average-height man covering himself with a blanket. All X could see was the man's face that was covered with piercings. "Hey! You okay?" X yelled as he transferred back to Earth Realm as he approached, checking to see if the man in front of him was okay. X all of a sudden felt a peculiar energy signature.

The man, sensing X walking towards him, turned around and yelled back to X as he ran, "You have come to play with me? Come on!" he said humorously as he ran full-speed away from X.

"Huh? Wait! I didn't come here to play with you. Come back here," X said as he ran towards the odd man. Stopping after about a five-minute chase, X realized the man wasn't in front of him anymore. Coming to a stop, X looked around the alleyway that he was running down. He was unable to see or sense the man or any other energy signatures in the area. "Who the fuck was that?" he asked himself as he returned to the main street to walk back to his original destination.

Reaching Lucia's shop, X thought, *Am I going to tell Dillon about Mel? I should. Fuck both of them up if they see each other.* He calmly walked inside the store. Always with the incense, sage, and white crystals burning in the shop, X looked around before he did his usual knock on the counter. "What is she into? How did she get her hands on this stuff?" X asked to an empty room as he searched the aisles of products. *This is irresponsible to have in human hands. They don't even know what they're dealing with.*

Coming from the back room, Lucia spoke, "I know, that's why only special clients are allowed to purchase those products. Now, this is two days in a row your sexy self came in here. Let me find out you ready to stop playing with me, Papi," she said as she stood at the counter, placing her hand on her hip.

Enjoying the flirt in Lucia, X replied, "Don't play like that. You'll be begging for mercy," he said, upping the flirting tactics.

Flustered by the hungry look in the beautiful white eyes she was so intrigued by, she changed the subject. "So, what is your pleasure, handsome?" Lucia asked, moving her finger down her shirt, making his eyes flow with her finger to look at her luscious breasts busting out of the tank top shirt she had on.

Enjoying the view, getting distracted for a bit, then returning to his senses, X said, "Look, beautiful, I can stand here all day and suck on them like a baby hungry for titty milk, but I really need you right now. I need you to come back to the castle and check something out for me. It's an emergency."

Seeing the look of dire need on his face, Lucia replied, "Anything for you, Papi, but I can't leave right now. Can you meet me back here in a couple of hours?" she asked, stroking his shoulder. "I have an important client coming by today. I can't miss this appointment, X."

Understanding the seriousness in her tone due to her use of his name, X said, "Okay. I'll come back here by sundown. Be ready," he stated, returning to their flirty banter by winking at her before he turned to go.

"Hey X, I feel something in the air. Mi don't like it. Been having weird vibes since the other night," Lucia called out to X's back as he walked away.

"Me either, beautiful. Stay safe until I return," X said as he left the shop. Confused as to why Lucia was scared, he wondered if she meant the night Taki and M were in her shop. "What is she?" he asked aloud, thinking of Taki.

Leaving Lucia's shop, X thought of what he could get himself into before bringing Lucia back to the castle. As he flew above the city, he began to get lost in his thoughts. *Could it be? Has one of them really returned after all this time?* Starting to remember the Days of Hunts, X was immediately interrupted by the feeling of incredible energy signatures as if a battle was ensuing. Searching around for the action, he realized the fight was coming from Otherside.

He instantly transferred as he continued to fly. He felt the familiarity of the energy signatures. "What the fuck are they doing here?" he asked, getting pissed off at the sight of the Elite Guard Unit (EGU) of the demon army attacking something he could not see yet.

X recognized the clothing and insignia on the uniforms. All black leather pants with matching vests and their symbol of Sai weapons crossed in-between bladed wings. X attacked two of them from behind, directly grabbing one with his left hand. He ripped its throat out from behind and, using his right hand to unleash three small blades, he landed them in both eyes and the forehead of another demon. Looking at the other six surrounding something, X moved closer. He recognized the energy signature and grabbed his battle-ax from his waist.

"Hey Mel, need some help? I don't want to interfere if you got this." He swung to his left, chopping the guard's head off, leaving five left for M.

Looking around at the young ones surrounding her, M briefly felt bad for knowing this is where they would meet their end. Remorse immediately leaving her thoughts, she ran towards the two guards standing closest to each other. Using her petite frame, ducking low, striking the guard's knee with her left stiletto heel, he doubled over in pain. M unleashed her right wrist blade from her sleeve, sliding straight through his skull. Then she used his dying body as it fell as a stepping stool. Stepping on the other demon's shoulder, she used both of her feet to break its neck, landing back on her feet as she backflipped off of the shoulder of the dead demon.

"Damn, she's fast." He watched as M decimated the rest of the guards that were trying to attack her. "Hey, we have to stop meeting like this, Mel." He leaned on a light pole, watching M stab the last of the demons in the throats as their bodies disintegrated into thin air. "I always hated that smell," he added, staring at M with a look of respect.

M stood up from her last kill. "Why are you following me?" she asked, wiping herself off, making sure her clothes were immaculate. "Not a scratch or wrinkle. Better not had. Probably would have had to kill their whole family if that moved happened," she said as she smoothed out her clothes and ponytail.

He chuckled at the familiarity of the behavior in front of him. "So, I see your peoples is back fucking with you. Didn't mean to impose. I thought it was a human getting attacked," X said playfully.

Slightly aggravated by the open attack, M replied, "I am in no way associated with them. Don't make me kill you, Xeno."

Walking past to leave, X grabbed her arm. "Mel, let us help you. Come on. You disappeared on us before and didn't let us help you. We're still family," he said sincerely.

"If you want your arm, I advise you to let me go, Xeno. I'm not dealing with you right now!" M replied though clenched teeth. "You just make sure Takisha is safe for the time being until I find out why they want her and to see what this special friend of hers has to do with this." She pointed her finger at X with a scowl.

Seeing the frustrated look on M's face, X replied, "I got you, Mel. She's fine. Look, I can't keep him at bay about this forever, especially if he finds a human in the castle. I know you don't want to get involved, but Mel, shit is real for us out here. You know I will do what I can to help, but he will find out the longer she stays there. So, if you let me help you, you can basically get away from us faster, so your boy won't find out you're back around."

M listened to what X was saying. "Look, give me a few hours and my charge, and I will be far away from that castle, and you will never see us again. Stay away from her, Xeno. I will hurt you over that one," she said, strutting away as if a battle did not just happen.

"He fucked up with that one. Damn, she bad. What are we going to do now that we know they're in the picture?" He pulled out his cell to call Mikael. "Come on, answer the phone." *No answer.* He quickly redialed the number. "Hey, Mike! What the fuck!" Listening to Mikael's reply, he said, "Oh shit. You got to be fucking kidding me. I just ran into the Royal Elite Guard Unit attacking Mel. They were out in the open attacking her. Full-on battle. I'm about to get Lucy. I'll meet you back at the castle soon," he said, instantly unleashing his wings.

Landing in front of the psychic's store as he transferred himself back to the Earth Realm, X walked in, feeling the overflow of power left in the air. X walked into the shop, looking around for demonic activity, sensing the hair on his body tingle. He stood and looked around the shop, yelling, "Lucy, Lucy, where are you?" as he walked towards the counter. Doing his usual knock on the counter, he looked to his left, seeing the storm cloud in the crystal ball moving out of control as if it would crack the ball.

X stared in amazement, intrigued by the power he felt radiating off the ball.

"Hey Papi, you came back. I was waiting for you," Lucia said, leaning on the counter catching her breath.

Noticing the drained look on Lucia's face, X said, "Hey sexy, what's up with you?" He walked around the counter to hold her.

Using her hand to hold herself against the counter, Lucia replied, "I am good, Papi. Just another day in the office of Lucia!" She chuckled at the end as she slightly swayed. X, seeing her out of it, scooped Lucia up into his arms and proceeded to walk through the purple and gold beaded curtain leading to the back area of the shop. Seeing a couch off to the side, X placed her on the sofa, checking over her body for visible injuries.

Lucia, realizing what X was doing, said, "Hey, I am fine, X. Really. That last reading was a bit much, that's all, and I have had a busy day," she said as she dozed off.

"Come on, beautiful. I'll take you to the castle. Rest there." He knew Lucia was lying, but he did not want to push it. X lifted Lucia up as she laid in his arms, gently placing her head on his chest. "What the hell is going on around here?" he said to himself as he locked up the store before carrying her off to the castle.

FINALLY, SOME ANSWERS

Mikael sat in his study after leaving Adam and his friend to themselves. *I can't believe this. Why now? What is this going to do to help us?* As he continued going through some ancient texts for any mention of his suspicions of Adam, he looked at his watch and saw the time as his cell phone rang. Seeing X's name on the line, he answered.

"Do not yell! I was dealing with Adam and one of his shows. Somehow that Ms. Mashiro is directly involved. Hurry up and get Lucia here now!" Mikael said to an aggravated X, listening to the reply on the other end. "I will see you when you get here," Mikael stated, ending the call with much frustration.

Leaving the study to go to Adam, he began to wonder. *What if both of them are on their radar? Knowing the guards must understand that M is associated with the girl, that's why they would have attacked her in the open like that. I may just have to speak to Melchorde. Help us all if she gets angry.* He continued towards the room Adam was resting in.

Opening the door, he found Adam sitting on the bed, looking like he was lost in thought. "Hey, how are you feeling?" Mikael asked Adam as he sat in the chair previously occupied by Taki.

"Feeling like a pussy with this passing out shit," Adam replied with a light chuckle.

"Technically, you didn't pass out the second time. That was Dillon messing with you," Mikael said.

"I really hate that dude," Adam replied hastily. "So, what's up? This our peace offering? Thanks for the clothes." He looked down at the shirt, jeans, and boots that he had on. "I don't really dress like this anymore."

Mikael was slightly appalled by his godson's lack of appreciation of the particular clothing he had given him. "You should be more grateful that I was able to get that at such short notice. That full outfit is fire-proof. Anytime you wear those, you don't have to worry about burning yourself naked just in case you have an episode," Mikael said matter-of-factly.

Adam was surprised at what Mikael just told him. "OH SHIT! Thanks, Uncle Mike. I can say I got fire-proof draws now!" Adam said playfully.

Mikael shook his head as he watched Adam check out the clothes he had on. "You're an idiot. I didn't say the underwear. Just the shirt, jeans, and boots. This is until I can teach you how to control your power," he said as he stood up to leave.

"Where are you going? I am not staying in here like some kid, and we are not finished talking. I want to get the hell out of here," Adam said, serious as he stood up.

"I have to meet X. He has some information he needs to discuss with me. I will come to check on you in a bit. Get some rest. Have Elise bring you some food. I know you're hungry. The use of that much power should have tired you out by now," Mikael said to Adam as he began to walk out of the room.

"Hell no. I am not tired, and I am not staying in here," Adam said sternly. "Stop treating me like a child. Let me know what the fuck is going on!"

"First, watch your tone. Second, you want to know what's going on so bad? Come on. Let's see what information X has to share," Mikael said, aggravated as he opened the door for Adam to walk past him.

Both men walked down the hall with their tall and large frames looking like two world wrestling champions walking into the foyer, decorated with purple and gold, accented with white furniture. X rushed into the room, coming from one of the many doorways.

"Hey, I don't know what she was doing before I got to her, but whatever it was, it was some powerful shit," X said as he laid Lucia down on the white chaise that was off to the side.

Mikael, looking down at Lucia, said, "She must be exhausted. She is knocked out cold." Mikael called for two guards. "Hey, come place her in the quarters next to Commander X's and stand guard at her door," he said as X fawned over Lucia.

"Nah, I got this. I'll take her there."

"We need to talk. The psychic will be fine, X," Mikael said as he placed his hand on X's shoulder as he stood next to him.

"What's the kid doing here?" X said, pointing his head towards Adam.

"He is eager to learn. Doesn't want to be treated as a child, so he would like to know what is going on as well," Mikael replied.

"Oh really? First, the boy believes you belong in a mental institution. Now he wants to know what's going on?" X teased as he began to walk towards another doorway leading down a long hall.

Mikael, motioning for the guards to leave and for Adam to follow him and X, said, "Well, what do you expect from a so-called human. Maybe he will believe me this time." They both shared a laughed.

Adam, overhearing the commentary, spoke up. "Um, I am right here. I can hear you." He couldn't help but check out the beautiful Latina X was carrying. Adam was staring at her as if he knew her. Sensing a familiarity to her instantly, he felt like it was déjà vu.

X, feeling a tingle of energy rising behind him, stopped and turned. "We're going to have to teach you to control that, Adam. So, Mikael, what do you think of all of this?"

"I do not know. I want to know what the psychic knows before I say what I think I am dealing with."

"I don't know either," X said curiously. Reaching their destination, two guards stood in front of two large double doors.

Motioning to open the room doors, Mikael said, "Hey, let her rest. We won't rush her to get up. These two are going to be here at least for the day." He walked over to lay Lucia down on the humongous bed that sat on a platform in the corner of the room surrounded by beautiful windows and gold and purple decorations.

"Come on, let me tell you what I know," X said to Mikael, leading him and Adam to a sitting area in his quarters.

As the three men sat gathered around the small sitting area, X began. "First, I believe Mel is not telling us everything about her little friend. I have felt and seen an increase in demon activity in our area like never before. But to see the Royal Pussies attacking Mel openly like that is dangerous. I felt the energy in the Earth Realm. That's how serious it got.

"On top of that, some weirdo with power is offing demons. Never seen him before. A slinky-looking motherfucker with a bunch of piercings on his face. He—"

"See, I told you! I'm not crazy. Sounds like the same weirdo that came in the sneaker store the other day!" he said excitedly.

Mikael looked over at Adam. "I never doubted that. You are the one that said you were in the corner talking to yourself," he said.

Adam, not liking Mikael's sarcasm, said, "I technically didn't say that either."

"Can I finish my story, you two?" X said, interrupting their disagreement.

"No need. I already found out that Ms. Mashiro is, in fact, Takisha Williams. The young lady that was involved with Adam's incident long ago and that she somehow dampens this one's out of control urges," Mikael said, pointing towards a listening Adam.

"Wait, what?" X said, staring back and forth at Adam and Mikael, confused at the revelation. Adam looked at X and shrugged his shoulders.

"You hitting that? Don't tell me you hitting that?" X said in a defeated tone.

Mikael was embarrassed by the question X just asked. "What is wrong with you? You're an imbecile."

Adam looked at X with a confused look. "What's up with you, my dude? That's my peoples. I grew up with her. How you know her is the question?" Adam asked, raising his eyebrows.

"Calm down, player. I want to know. She fine as hell. I was trying to get to know her, that's all," X said playfully, lightening up the mood.

Mikael interjected, "I doubt very much you wanted to know anything besides how loud she screams," he said as he got ready to leave.

Adam narrowed his eyes at Mikael's comment, getting up to leave as X stopped them. "Real shit, though. We have to find out why they want these two. I'm not sure, but they coming after Mel, so you know it's real."

"Once we figure out what this one here is, that will give us a clue on how we can suppress or hide his powers. Obviously, he is only targeted when his powers are active. Far as Ms. Mashiro, we will find out how she is connected to this one here," Mikael said, pointing towards Adam. "Until then, she will be safe here. We need to talk to Melchorde to see what it is she knows."

"She would rip your tongue out if she heard you say that. Mel is not a nice person, Mike. Word up. She definitely earned her title," X said.

"I am in no mood for her attitude, X. I just need to know how her charge fits into all of this with Adam. Once we figure that out, we can solve some of our problems and move on so we can continue to concentrate on this war," Mikael stated reasonably.

"Who is Mel? How does she know Kisha?" Adam asked.

"That is a good question, son, that I do not have the answer to. I believe that your friend may know more than she is telling us, or you both have found yourselves in things that you don't understand," Mikael answered firmly.

As the three men continued walking away from X's quarters, Adam interrupted the silence. "Hey, Uncle Mike, you think all of this has anything to do with what happened that night?" He stopped walking as he asked the question that had been plaguing him.

Mikael responded, "Honestly, I do not know. From what you told me, I cannot see how it is tied to now, but then again, I told you I don't believe in mere coincidences." He placed his hand on Adam's shoulder. "But don't worry. I assure you, I will protect you and make sure you get to keep that little store of yours," he said, chuckling and giving Adam a slight nudge.

"Boy, with that power you wield, we're going to be calling you for help in no time. I've already thought of some weapons I can make for you," X said excitedly.

"Hey, don't you think you are going a little too far, Xeno?" Mikael asked as they continued down the hall towards the foyer.

"Man, look, I get this shit is close to you because of who he is, but come on. Regardless of what, there is a war going on. Obviously, these two, have something to do with it as well. If we can get them on our side, that would be even better. You already know we can do the enemy of my enemy is my friend with Mel," X said convincingly.

Mikael contemplated X's words. "He doesn't understand, Xeno. I hear what you are saying, but I do not believe he can do what you expect. I do agree with you on them being involved in this war. I just do not know or see why. Until we figure out how they fit in, we won't be able to develop a strategy to protect them and continue mobilizing in this war," he said with a thoughtful look on his face.

"You two are really talking about me like I'm not standing here right now," Adam said, interjecting in on the conversation.

"We're going to have fun! Leave it to me. I got you!" X said as he began to walk away from their group. "Hey, hit me up when Lucia gets up. I'll be back!"

"What the hell was that about?" Adam asked.

"He always gets excited about making new weapons. It's been a while, but he is what we call our *weaponologist*. He makes all types of weapons and defensive items for the army. He is fascinated with the human world and replicates a lot of our newer weapons from the ones he's seen on those crazy devices that everyone watches," Mikael answered.

"You mean a television?" Adam asked, raising an eyebrow. "Weapons? What does he make weapons for?"

Mikael shook his head at Adam for lacking understanding. "What have you been doing since you got here? Have you been listening? Come on, let's go to my office. The girls should get some rest. It's going to be a long day. You should rest too. Let's just say someone is going to do a read on you. Hopefully, she can tell us what you are," Mikael said, resigned.

"Whatever. Anything to speed the process in getting my ass out of here."

"Look, I already texted Peggy for you. I told her you were passed out drunk and staying home today. So play nice, and after we see how we can suppress this power, I will let you go," Mikael added as they walked into the foyer.

Adam looked around in awe at the decorations and art that surrounded him "This shit is cool as hell. Like I said, whatever I have to do to get the hell out of here."

"Well, go find Elise, get some food, and rest until we are ready. I have some other things to tend to. I do have other pressing concerns besides you, godson," Mikael said as he began to walk off. Calling back to Adam, he spoke again. "Go find that beautiful Taki girl and have some fun." He laughed heartily before walking away.

"Fuck you!" Adam yelled back as he sat down in one of the oversized chairs in the foyer area.

WHAT SHE KNOWS

Sitting on the couch playing the solitaire game on her phone, Taki began to think about the predicament she was in. "Energy, powers, demons, angels, and the strange castle. Takisha, what the fuck in romance novel hell did you get your ass in?" she chuckled.

"Hopefully, we can help you get your *ass* through whatever it is you're involved in," X said, walking through the doorway from the garden area, interrupting Taki.

Slightly startled by his subtle pop-in, Taki responded, "Don't do that. I don't take being snuck up on kindly," as she rolled her eyes.

"You been around Mel too long. What's up, beautiful? You okay? They treating you right? I see you didn't change your clothes yet," X said, looking down at Taki's disheveled bun and slightly dirty clothes.

She felt bad for not accepting the hospitality besides some fruit and some water. "I'm okay. I'm waiting for M to come back, and then she'll take me home. I'll be fine until then," Taki said shyly.

"Look, shorty, don't be shy. You can take a nice bath and get some sleep until Mel comes back. We need to speak with her anyway. I found out you know Adam. Small world, huh?" he said with a smile.

"Oh, you know A too? I mean, Adam. I thought he was oblivious to what is going on," Taki said.

"Just met him. Know of him. What can you tell me about him?" X questioned.

"He's someone I consider a close friend, good guy, and he basically is someone I consider special," Taki said.

X noticed the shift in her mood and sparkle in her eye when she spoke of him. "Special as in friend special or mentally challenged special?" he asked to lighten the mood.

"Don't play like that. I mean special as in friend. Even after all of these years," Taki said, playing on her phone, "I feel closer to him now. Anyway, I don't know why I am telling you all of this."

"Well damn. Wasn't that cute?" X responded, chuckling.

"Hey, can you tell me why you can use your phone here, but I can't? The angels have their own cell service provider or something?" Taki asked, changing the subject.

"Nah, we just have our phones coded to work here. There is an application that extends the service to Otherside," X said. "Basically, the phone reads the towers we are near on Earth Realm."

"Can you add that to my phone? I really need to call my sister," Taki asked slyly.

"I don't see why not. They wouldn't be able to find you if they tried to track the phone," X said to Taki, smiling.

"Wait, what? Why would—"

"Don't worry, just a little precaution for all of our devices. We are fighting a war, remember," he said, reaching his hand out to gesture for Taki's phone.

Taki placed her phone in his large hands and watched him go to the settings. "Don't be trying to look at my pictures either," she said, smiling.

X teased, "Wonder what you got hiding in there." He laughed loudly as he acted as though he was searching through her phone.

"Give me that!" she said.

"Hold on, I'm almost done. I don't want to see no pics. I want to see the real thing," he said, turning to stare at her with those intense, clear white eyes.

"Are you done?" Taki asked with a smile, getting a nervous feeling from X gazing at her.

"Damn, scrrrrrrrr," mimicking screeching tires, "that was a curve for real. Damn. Just go ahead and keep shutting me down. You're going to find out I'm the sexy one in this outfit!" He handed her the phone. "Done! Now, that will be three hundred dollars, please?" He put his hand out, waiting to be paid in full.

"What?!" Taki screeched. "You didn't tell me you were charging me!" she said with a shocked look.

"Oh, you thought because you were pretty, you were going to get this shit done free? Especially after that curve?" X asked, laughing.

Taki sat in silence staring at X, ready to unleash a defined cuss out from A to Z.

"Before you start bugging on me, I'm playing. I hope you can take a joke. Lighten up! I'm just playing!" X said as he stood up from sitting on the couch next to Taki.

"You better have been. You were about to get the cuss out of the century!" Taki said.

"Seriously, get your shit together, Ma. We have to get to the bottom of all of this and soon. Wash, eat, and get some rest. Hopefully, later we will have answers for all of us," X said as he began to walk out. Turning around to face Taki, he spoke again. "True story, we got you. Mel is family to us, even if she doesn't want to admit it. So, with you being under her protection, you're under our protection. Don't worry."

M never spoke of her family, and Taki assumed that she was alone like her. She was curious about how M was associated with the angels and what Taki had to do with all of this.

"Might as well shower and eat. I'm exhausted. I need a comfortable bed and a nap," Taki said as she walked towards the bathroom that X had showed her earlier. Entering the bathroom, in awe of how beautiful but old the decorations looked, Taki began to run her bath since no shower was available. *It's been a while. Let me relax in this big ass tub.* She began to run the water and searched for towels and other toiletries.

Finding everything she needed. Taki undressed and emerged herself in the hot bath water with the lovely smelling oils, soap, and flowers she found. "This is wonderful," she sighed.

****

Adam returned to his temporary room to eat some of Elise's fruit and drink some water. Feeling a sense of calm and relaxation after laying down and closing his eyes to rest, Adam began to see visions of the sun. Staring at the beautiful ball of fire that shined on him, he accepted the warmth and the energizing feeling that the sun's rays gave him. "What is this feeling?"

Seeing a door forming in the sun as he began to walk, Adam was suddenly interrupted by the sound of Mikael's voice. Loud voices surrounded him, and then a sudden jolt of electricity entered his body, causing him pain. Instantly opening his eyes, Adam looked around as he was laid out in the foyer area he had been in earlier. X, Mikael, and the Latina woman Adam saw X carrying earlier were looming over him. At the same time, he heard Kisha's faint voice in the background.

As Adam immediately started to get up to search for her, Mikael interrupted. "Hey, calm down, she's okay. Are you okay? What happened, Adam?" he asked with a confused look.

"Get out my way. Where is she?" Adam said as he tried to get up, searching for Kisha. "KISHA! KISHA!" He could feel her energy inside him, calling for him. Unable to explain the feeling to Mikael, Adam pushed Mikael out of his way to search for the faint voice he heard.

"Calm him down now! I do not know what is going on," Mikael said as he sensed the power radiating off Adam.

Taki, hearing the commotion as she laid down, was unable to move. "Adam! I'm okay. Calm down, calm down. You're going to make it worse. STOP IT NOW!" she said as loud as she could with the bit of energy she had.

Adam responded to her voice, falling to his knees, realizing that she was lying next to him the whole time. Seeing her lying on the ground, he grabbed her hand. "Kish, what's wrong? You okay? What happened?" Adam asked wearily.

"I'm fine, A. Looks like our little episodes coincide. We both just had one at the same time," she said weakly.

Adam stood to pick her up. "Why do they have you in this ugly robe?" he asked, ignoring the fact that they were not in the room alone.

Mikael interrupted Adam and Taki's conversation. "Adam, please, for the power in me, what in all heavens just happened?"

"I think this one went into a fit," X answered, pointing at A, "causing this one to have one too," then pointed at Taki. "It has to be the mix of the energy signatures and the fact that they are here in Otherside."

Adam looked at both men, confused. "I don't know what happened. I laid down for a bit. I took your advice, Uncle Mike, to rest. I remember dreaming about the sun and its rays with a door—weird shit. Next thing I know, I heard you yelling." He looked at Mikael, still holding Taki.

"All I know is I felt you, and then X heard Ms. Mashiro screaming from the bathroom," Mikael said to a muddled Adam.

"How can this be? Why is this happening to us?" Adam asked aloud as he laid his forehead on the top of Taki's resting head. Mikael worried at the revelation that the two so-called humans were possible gods. Turning to Lucia as she stood next to X, he sternly said, "Can you still do a reading on him? We need to know what these two are, and NOW!"

"I think we should stay out here. This is going to get ugly. If he is what you are scared of, I worry we will have no way of stopping his awakening," Lucia said to Mikael and then looked at X worriedly.

"Hey, we will be right here. Don't worry," X said, pulling her closer to him and rubbing her arms.

"Reading? Do y'all really think that we should be messing with me right now after this episode?" Adam asked defensively.

Mikael immediately responded, "We have to find out what you are now! You almost killed her and didn't know it, Adam! For once, stop being a prick and listen to me!" His cell phone rang. Looking down at the annoying sounding device, Mikael saw the name he loathed at the moment.

"What, Dillon? I do not have time for your bull right now. I will call you back. Give me— What did you say? Impossible. They've been gone for almost a few millennia. There is no way a kami is around," Mikael said into the device. Staring at X and Adam with squinting eyes, he continued, "We may have a similar problem. Are you coming back here soon? We have to update you on what's going on here. If what you're saying is true, that means my assessment of Adam is correct. I will let you know when I know more." *End call.*

"We have to do this now. Get it started. X, take Ms. Mashiro here and bring her to your quarters. That should be far enough to make sure she doesn't feel the effects of the reading. Guards, I want two on her door and three at her window with an extra barrier protecting her. Get on it now!" Mikael demanded.

Adam looked around as everyone around him began to move from Mikael's orders. Unsure of what was about to happen, his thoughts were interrupted by X. "Hey, give her to me, my man. I promise I will keep her safe. You need to do this."

Uncertain of what to do, Adam gave the resting Taki to X. "Hey white eyes, nothing better happen to her. Let's do this, Mamacita," he said, looking at Lucia.

Mikael turned to X before he left them. "Hey, I will probably need your help. Come back after you have her settled." He then turned to Lucia and Adam. "Come on, you two. Let's get this done," he said, walking towards the exit of the foyer area.

Adam allowed Lucia to walk ahead of him and then spoke to her. "Hey, what are you?" He was unsure of the uneasy feeling he was getting from the energy he felt from Lucia.

"What would make you ask me that, Papi?" she asked, turning around and giving Adam a wink.

Adam, instantly blushing at Lucia, raised his voice, speaking towards Mikael. "Where are we going, Uncle Mike?"

"We are almost there," Mikael replied just as they walked towards an open field past the pool area. Mikael looked directly at Lucia. "You sure you can do this? I can't seem to get a clear read on the boy, and I've seen his power up close and personal. It's nasty."

Lucia, confident in her skills, answered immediately. "This my job, Papi. I know what I'm doing." She gestured for Adam to hold her hand.

Adam reached for Lucia's hand. "So what do I do?" Adam asked with a questioning look on his face as he looked back and forth between Lucia and Mikael. He looked around and saw more guards in the area than he had seen in the last two days. "What's with the extra security? I have never seen these many extras," he said as he held Lucia's hand.

"Don't worry about them, Adam. They're just for precaution," Mikael answered immediately.

Holding Adam's hand, starting to breathe, Lucia said, "Hey, Adam, don't let go of me, okay. Hold on regardless of the pain or power you may feel. Just to let you know what we are doing, we are fully awakening the powers inside you. To get a clear read of what you are, I have to tap into your powers at their peak to learn the origin of your power. So, please, stay calm, do not let go. Ready?"

"I was born for this!" he said confidently as he moved from side to side, getting himself ready for whatever it was this woman was about to do.

"Now, Adam, I am about to call forth your power. Do not fight, do not get scared, just let the warmth and power take you," Lucia said to Adam as he stood in front of her.

Feeling a breeze brush past his face as he stared into the big brown eyes of the Latina woman that he felt was so familiar, Adam began to get lost in her eyes. A sudden flash of heat and fire came to his mind as he began to feel his body get warm.

"Oh shit. Oh shit," Adam said aloud as he began to feel the power that he fought so hard to keep at bay.

Lucia looked to her right at Mikael.

"NOW!"

Mikael placed the last of the powder-like substance to complete a circle around Adam's immediate area, placing an invisible barrier. "Now, A, this is going to hurt." She began to squeeze Adam's hand as if to not let go. "Okay, Papi, let's see what raw power you got in there." Her hands began to glow as Adam's body began to illuminate as well. "Adam, don't move. Let your mind and body be free. Think of the feeling you get when you have these episodes," Lucia said as she stared at Adam. "What do you feel?"

"I'm getting that hot feeling again. I feel it coming Unc," he said, panicked.

Mikael walked over to Adam and placed his hand on top of Adam's shoulder for support.

"Hey, be careful. Try to hold back your power. If you're going to assist, you might as well feel this shit too," Lucia stated as she watched Mikael. "Now, Adam, it's about to get real in here. Don't fight it. I know it will hurt, but I need you to remain calm, okay? Do you feel that?" she asked as she closed her eyes and her body began to levitate off the ground.

Adam felt pressure as if he would throw up, making it feel like he should ball over in pain, but he could not move. He opened his eyes to look at Lucia to see why he couldn't move. Both of their bodies were in the middle of this cylinder. Adam could still see Mikael and the castle grounds and the guards walking the grounds for some strange reason.

"Uncle Mike, you see that?" he asked as he began to look at the fire closely.

Looking at Lucia to see what she was doing, she started a strange chant as she let Adam go and stepped outside the circle. Adam was confused and feeling the heat and pain from his fits like never before.

"WAIT!! NO!! IT HURTS! IT HURTS!" he screamed as he began to glow and felt the electricity burning through his veins and body from the inside.

"Calm down, Adam, you got this."

Adam felt himself get hotter and hotter like he was going to explode. Then all of a sudden, the vision of the sun returned. He continually saw the great ball of fire in his dreams and fits of rage, feeling a power so thick and hot that he felt as if he were walking on the surface of the sun.

As the door he envisioned before came to fruition a few feet in front of him, Adam began to walk closer to the doorway. Continuing to walk towards the entrance, ignoring the excruciating blazes that surrounded where he was, Adam grabbed the doorknob, feeling his body dissipate from the fire and heat radiating from the door. Screaming in agony as he awakened, he was surrounded by a white mist no longer on fire.

Reaching into her pocket to grab her cell phone, M suddenly felt a tremendous sense of pure power coming from somewhere. Her body began to tingle as she disappeared from where she was directly in front of the large gates she was previously rejected from. As they began to open, M asked, "What is this? Are you here to assist me?" She walked towards a dark figure that was standing far ahead of her.

Sensing nothing but pure energy and power radiating from the being in front of her as she was a good hundred feet away, she could not use her own ability to assist in the suffocating feeling this strange being was creating in the area they were in. Unsure of what and why this was going on, M called out, "HELLO! WHO ARE YOU?"

Adam turned around slightly, startled by the woman's loud voice behind him. "Oh shit?! Who are you? How do I get out of here?" he asked, staring at the petite woman in front of him.

M could not fathom what was going on in front of her. The feeling this "human" was giving her was all wrong. Having not felt this feeling since she as a child in training, she was unable to move her mouth or swallow. Slowly forcing herself to speak, she asked, "Who are you? How did you get here?" She stared at the large man who was now no less than ten feet away from her.

Adam immediately responded, not understanding the hostility in this woman's tone. "Look, calm down, lady. I just want to get back to my uncle's crib. I'm not into this freaky shit that's going on. Can you help me?" he asked, worrying about the look on the petite woman's face, seeing the darkness surrounding her.

M struggled to speak to the young man in front of her. "What are you?" M whispered, almost unable to breathe or speak.

Adam backed away from the woman in front of him. As she moved closer towards him, he began to think of Taki. Feeling a sense of power familiar to him, Adam repeatedly thought of Taki as his body began to dissipate.

"WHAT THE FUCK?!"

Mikael was shocked at Adam standing in front of him. "BOY?! Where in good heavens did you go? Trash the place and just disappear? We had everyone at our disposal looking for you?!"

"Where is Kisha? How did the reading go? What am I, Uncle Mike?" He fired off one question right behind the other, confused at the events that had just taken place.

Mikael was stunned at Adam's casual tone about his abrupt vanishing act. "Do you know for the past six hours we've been out looking for you, and for some reason, we can't seem to get in touch with Mel! All you have to say is how did the reading go?"

Adam was frustrated at losing time. "SIX HOURS?!!! What the fuck?! I've been cooked alive and stuck in some dark place for six fucking hours! How the fuck am I supposed to know? All I remember is—" He fell to the ground, passed out from exhaustion, before he could speak another word.

Mikael yelled, "Hey X, bring some water with you," as X turned back around to go inside the castle. Staring down at Adam with a look of confusion, he thought, *Why now and why him?* Mikael noticed Adam's eyes opening with that burning fire orange and red.

"You okay?" Mikael asked as he watched Adam begin to get up.

"You know, with my powers being all synced and shit, I figured the passing out shit would be over with." Then, he stared at Mikael as if he was seeing him for the first time. "You are pure energy," Adam said, staring at the figure standing in front of him.

Hearing the others come outside, Mikael turned around. "Don't move. I do not know if this being in front of us is still Adam. He passed out and woke up like this," he said, watching the god-like being in front of him.

"What the fuck, Unc? Of course, it's me. I'm just different. You feel it? I can't describe it to you, but I feel amazing." He stared down at himself as he stroked electricity through his veins; the fire was literally at the tips of his fingers.

Lucia walked towards Mikael. "Leave him alone. Don't be so serious. He is finally awakening. His god powers have fully synced with his soul. Now, Ms. Taki here shouldn't have any more issues," she said with a big smile.

X was confused as he stood behind Lucia. "Come again? What the fuck does new god here have to do with sexy chocolate over there?" X asked, pointing towards Taki as she stood in the doorway. Mikael raised a brow with a hard stare, looking for clarification from Lucia.

Lucia stood next to Adam. "This one here has the power of persuasion," she said, pointing at Adam. "His power is so great that his mind was calling out to the person that has the closest bond to him. It was her," she continued, pointing to Taki, "making her feel the awakening of his powers. It's almost as if their souls were awakening at the same time," Lucia said to the group. "Adam, how do you feel?" she asked, staring at him in wonder.

"I feel amazing. I feel like the sun is in the palm of my hands." His eyes began to look like a blaze of fire.

"Hey, hey!" Lucia said. "Calm down, fire Papi. You have to remember, you don't know how to control these newfound powers and gifts." Lucia smiled as she turned around to speak to X. "Okay, handsome, it was nice playing with y'all and all, but I have to get back to my business," she said, laying the heavy Spanish accent on thick.

"Ready to leave already?" X asked with a playful smile as he grabbed her hand, and they began to walk away.

Taki stepped aside as she watched Adam from afar, feeling the intense power radiating off him that made it difficult to breathe. "What about me? I feel weird. I mean, I'm glad to hear I shouldn't have those episodes anymore, but um, that still doesn't answer why the demons are after me. I can see them wanting A, now that he's a god or whatever."

Mikael responded. "One problem at a time. Lucia still didn't do her reading on you to see what you are. It's obvious you're of Other if you were able to survive that whole ordeal." Shaking his head in disbelief at the set of events that just occurred, he pulled out his cell to text X. GET THE WHOLE SPIEL FROM LUCIA BEFORE YOU LET HER GO. I WANT TO KNOW WHAT EXACTLY SHE KNOWS ABOUT ADAM! Looking up to Adam and Taki, Mikael spoke again. "Adam and Ms. Mashiro, please stay here while we try to find Mel. We have to speak with her as soon as possible. She has to know what is going on." He walked past Taki, leaving her and Adam alone.

THE SUN GOD

Standing in shock at the aftermath of power left behind by the being, M looked around at the empty space that she was standing in. "Where am I?" she asked as the man in the robe from before came from the west side of the empty space.

"You now have access to the rest of your mission. The Akashic Records are now accessible. Information needed for your mission can also be found here. No one is to know your true mission or nature. As they begin to awaken, each one will gain access to this place, and when it is complete, you will all learn the true purpose of the awakenings. As the only one who accessed this place, you will only have the information needed for their role," the man concluded before walking away from M.

"Wait, that's all you're going to tell me? I still do not know how to guide and protect!" she yelled across the room as the robed man faded away. Just as M let out a long sigh, a bookcase filled with books formed to her right in the corner of the large, spaced area. Walking to the bookcase and placing her hands on the first book that caught her eye, she read the first page, remembering the stories told to her long ago. Immediately, she slammed the book closed.

"Why the fuck is this being brought up now?" she said through clenched teeth as she stared at the library of books of old. "Get it together, Melchorde, no need to get riled up now. You will get to the bottom of this. I bet those winged perverts have some information to share about this." She thought of speaking to one of the men she despised almost as much as the individuals who created her. Checking herself and her emotions, M decided to return to the Castle of Angels to see if they could gather any other information and check on Takisha. Unsure if she would return to this weird place, she used her power to return to Taki and speak with Mikael.

"Great barriers," M said in a raised voice, from the rejection of being able to transport straight to Taki.

M was immediately surrounded by a dozen or so guards.

"HEY! What are you doing here? Step away from the gate!" one of them yelled at her.

Knowing she could decapitate them in less than five seconds, M spoke, "Call Commander Mikael, tell him Queen Melchorde of the Golden River Realm is here to speak with him. Immediately!"

The angels, shocked at what they heard, immediately surrounded her. "Demon, be gone!" one yelled.

Another spoke. "Mel?! Is that you?! MEN! STAND DOWN NOW!"

Gatekeeper Henry stepped from behind the crowd formed in front of M. He'd been known for the past thousand years. He approached M and bowed in submission as she watched.

"My apologies, Your Highness. We are on high alert in this area, and we were not expecting someone with your stature to just appear at the front gates without notice."

"No need for the formalities, Henry. I appreciate that you are still here. I am glad I did not have to kill the new recruits," M said with a smile.

"Again, my apologies for the disrespect, Your Highness. Your long absence and sudden appearance startled them. I will make sure to not let it happen again," Gatekeeper Henry said, nervous as to why she was here after all this time.

M, killing the tension, reached out her hand for Henry to shake. "It's been a long time, my friend. Great to see you. Really, no need for formalities. I wouldn't have killed them. Maybe hurt them really bad," she said with a laugh as she looked at the group behind the gatekeeper.

Gatekeeper Henry, unsure if she was serious or not, smiled and reached out to shake M's hand. "Your Highness, it is always a pleasure. I will let Commander Mikael know you are on your way to see him. I will have two of my guards escort you to the castle to wait for him." He bowed again to make sure to show the utmost respect.

"It's okay, Henry. I was here earlier. I know where it is. I don't need any escorts if that's okay?" she said with a smile.

"Yes, Your Highness, I apologize. Please let me know if I can be of any assistance." He stepped aside, and the recruits did the same.

"No, I'm fine. I might have Elise make me some banana bread like she used to," M said as she smiled and walked past Henry and the dozen or so guards with death radiating off of her as if they were saved by a needle thread.

M laughed at the commotion she heard as she walked away towards the front doors of the castle. Unsure if it was still the same as when she used to come here, she entered the front to see Mikael walking right past her and then stopping. "Yes, Mikael, it is me," M said as he walked towards her with widening eyes.

"You know, when Xeno told me he saw you, I was shocked, but to have you standing here, using your official title to get in. Interesting. What made you think that would work?" Mikael said, fascinated at the being in front of him.

"Someone would have remembered me, or I would have had to get rid of your whole front line," she replied with a smile, standing in front of the large man.

"My little sister, Melchorde, never changed. Have you?" Mikael said, pulling M into a hug.

M immediately rejected his hug, pushing at the large chest right in front of her. "Move! Get off me! Damn perves!" She shoved Mikael away in a playful way.

Stepping away, Mikael said, "Come on, Mel, you missed us! I do not care what your mouth says. So, you ready to come home? We need you." His tone became serious.

Stepping more into the foyer towards the sitting area, M replied, "Look, I'm only here to get help for my charge and to get information on a possible situation that we are not prepared for."

Mikael sat next to her chair on the couch. "We solved that problem already, but we have a bigger one," he said, sitting back and staring at M.

"What do you mean you solved that already? Solved what?" she asked skeptically.

Mikael replied, "We solved Ms. Mashiro's problems. To my understanding, my godson Adam was the cause of all of that. I do apologize on his behalf. Since he is fully synced with his powers, Ms. Mashiro shouldn't have any more episodes." Mikael repeated Lucia's assessment.

M stared at Mikael in disbelief. "What do the demons have to do with this?" She was unsure if all their problems were solved.

"Now that, we still do not know. What I do know is we have the God of Sun back on Earth Realm, and somehow your charge can dampen his powers," he said as he looked at her.

M was irritated at this revelation. "WHAT?! They are long gone. There aren't any gods left. They were all captured and destroyed," she said, remembering the Days of Hunts.

"I remember," Mikael said, saddened by the sudden memory. "After what I witnessed today, I know that for a fact it is indeed the Sun God that has awakened in my godson Adam," he added, placing his hands on his head.

M remembered the being in front of her at the gates and the robed man's words. "Their awakening," she said to Mikael. "Do you know why or how?"

"I do not. We haven't had any other orders besides keeping the demons away from the humans. For some reason, there has been a rise in the demon attacks," Mikael replied to her question, staring off into space as he spoke.

M was listening but still unconvinced as to how Taki was connected to all of this. "Your godson, Adam, is this the same young man that Takisha is acquaintances with? I have been searching for him for some time now," she said with a calculating look.

Mikael sensed her dark thoughts. "Look, I don't know the nature of your relationship with Ms. Mashiro, but somehow ever since that night of the incident happened, she became involved. Maybe his powers affected her somehow, or maybe she is Other as well, and that's why the demons want both of them. I want answers just like you," he said as he glared at her.

Not liking the situation at hand, M said, "Where are Takisha and Adam? I believe you would not leave him unguarded wielding that kind of power?" She looked back at Mikael with an emotionless face and tone.

"They are both fine. I left them to talk. I believe they needed some privacy," Mikael said smiling, knowing she would hate the fact that he left them alone.

"WHAT?! You left my *human* charge with a newly awakened GOD?! Alone?! Without any protection?! Where is she, Mikael?! So help your Ultimate High, if anything happens to her, Mikael. I will have your head!" She headed down one of many hallways connected to the foyer they were sitting in.

****

Gazing at the being in front of her, Taki stared at him in disbelief. She was thoroughly confused about what she had seen for the past couple of days.

"God? What the fuck kind of shit have you gotten me into, kid?" she asked, shaking her head as she felt the immense pressure pouring off him as she got closer. "Are you always going to feel like this?" She placed her hand on his chest as she reached him, remembering what Mikael said about her dampening his powers. Adam felt amazing as he stared at the beauty walking towards him. He wanted her to be closer to him. He wanted to feel her body and touch her soul. Adam felt a tingle as if Taki entered his body.

"I want you," he said as he grabbed her face and kissed her with so much intensity, his body began to glow.

Adam felt a sense of wonder as he felt himself enter her. He began to see flashes of what looked like memories of Taki, from her fighting with an unknown lady to staring at pictures of him and her. Memories of her laughing with a group of people he didn't recognize. Adam, letting go, stared back at Taki as he watched the tears stream down her face. "I am so sorry. Kish, I am so sorry. I didn't mean to…" Adam said with a hushed tone, still holding onto her as he stared down into her brown eyes.

"How did you do that? What was that? You were kissing me, and next thing I know—" Interrupted by Adam placing his lips on hers again and feeling that pleasing warmth and electrifying feeling, she couldn't finish her sentence.

Taki was lost in his kiss. The sensation he was giving made her feel as though she would orgasm fully clothed standing outside. She soon pulled back from Adam's kiss. "Whoa, whoa. Timeout, playboy. Let me breathe for a second." She stepped out of his arms, knowing if she let that kiss continue, she probably would have given him some right there in the garden.

"Look, A, we have to figure out what's up with us before we think about, *what's up* with us, so stop doing that. You're messing up my thinking," Taki said between panted breaths. "Shit, at least tell me how you feel now." She stared at him, wondering about his newfound power.

Adam, standing there lost in Taki, wanted more of her, wanted to be with her, to smell her, to taste her.

"I want you," is all he could muster from his swirling thoughts. He pulled Taki back close to him. "Please, stay close to me," he said through clenched teeth as he noticed his mind clearer the closer she was to him.

Taki worried about him. She placed her head on his chest. "It's okay. I'm right here. Are you okay?"

"I'm better when I am close to you. For some reason, my thoughts were a little muddy. You being here made it a little better."

"So, how do you feel now, god?" she said, chuckling.

"Haha. Funny. Real fucking comedian now," he replied as he looked down at her. "I feel weird, Kish. I don't know what to call it. All I want to know is how do I go back. I can't live like this. I almost killed you, Kish. As I stand here, my mind is becoming sharper and clearer. From what I just remembered from my last 'attack,' I could have killed you if I didn't let go," he said, thinking of how he survived the incineration.

"Let go? What do you mean?" she said, stepping back to look him in his face, still fascinated by the orange and red fire eyes of his.

"I mean, when I was passed out that last time, I was surrounded by fire, and I let myself go and be consumed by that fire. Kish, word up," he said, grabbing her face, "I felt you, I heard you. It's like I could sense your whole being, Ma. I don't know what it is, but yo, after all the pain, all the fire, and even that weird-looking place, I only returned here when I thought of you. Something is telling me you're supposed to be here with me. I don't know what you have to do with this, but I know in my soul that you are meant to be here," he said, placing a light kiss on her lips, "with me." He held her hands and dropped to his knees to embrace her.

"Adam, get up! What is wrong with you? We first have to figure out why those demons are after us. At least we know what's good with you now. Most likely, they tied me with you. I mean, I know you're a god and all, but it's not like you know what to do with this power," Taki said, staring down at him as he was still on his knees. "We need to find my mentor and see what she knows and how your uncle and his friends are going to protect us. I can't stay here forever, nor do I want to be demon food," Taki said, responding to his revelation.

"Look, it would be better for you to stay with me. I don't want nothing to happen to you either. I can protect you. Don't act like I'm some bitch nig—"

"Hey, what did we tell you about that word. You're going to make me erase it from your vocabulary. A god or not. So, how do you feel, Ra?" Mikael asked in a teasing manner. "Ready to start training so you can get out into the world?" he said to Adam.

"What? Ra? Training? For what?"

"Excuse me," M interrupted, not liking the energy in the air. She walked from behind Mikael to find Kisha standing next to a tall, dark, very handsome man. Then, she recognized the energy signature. "YOU?!" she said, narrowing her eyes as she realized he was the man from the empty space. *The awakenings.* She remembered the robed man's words again as she continued to walk towards Adam.

She stepped in between Adam and Taki to get a good look at the man. "It really is you. Do you remember where you were when you awakened?" He watched him, wondering why his power was not as concentrated as before.

Adam remembered being in front of her from before. "Yes, I do. You were there. I remember you. Sorry I ran off on you like that. I was confused, and you looked real creepy back there."

"So, you can see? What do you see when you look at Mikael here?" she asked, wondering if his sight showed the true nature of a being.

"I see the pure energy he was created from," Adam answered, staring at the being in front of him. "Why are you here?"

"I was asked to be here." She turned to Taki. "Let's go. We have to talk, PRIVATELY." She pulled Taki as she spoke, with both of them walking through the double doors.

Mikael was interested in what just happened between M and Adam. "What the great heavens was that, Adam? She was there? Where? And, did you just read Melchorde?" he asked, shaking his head as he walked over to Adam. Adam stared at Mikael with fire-burning eyes as Mikael continued. "Ra, we're really going to have to teach you how to control those powers of yours. One, that was rude. Two, you're lucky we are all still breathing. She could have killed you." He patted Adam on the back as he spoke.

Guiding them both back inside, he motioned Adam to sit in the sitting area. "I can't believe it, Adam. This is incredible. We haven't seen any of your kind in eons," Mikael said as he stared at Adam with amazement as they sat in the foyer area. "Meeting your family all those years ago, I would have never realized I was raising the Sun God in the making."

Adam was slightly overwhelmed at all of the information that he was beginning to remember about his fits. "First, my name is Adam, and two, why me? I guess there's no going back to normal. So, what's next?" he asked as he looked down at himself, feeling a tingling sensation throughout his body.

"I do not know, godson. I thought all of your kind were destr— I mean, died long ago. But that story is for another time. Come on, let's go see if our friend, Xeno, has returned," Mikael answered, avoiding their current conversation and getting up to walk back to his office to search for more information.

Adam, recognizing his godfather's deterrent of the conversation, got up to follow, figuring he would get his questions answered later.

As the two walked back to the area of the castle that they were staying in, M wanted all the details of the events that happened while she was gone.

"Care to share the events of the day, Takisha?"

"Well, supposedly, my episodes are over, so we will see since it's only been a few hours. Far as how I feel, I feel fine, I guess, except I feel like I need to be around Adam right now," Taki responded as she stopped talking to stare at M. Having a residue of power leftover in her from Adam, she felt a weird but familiar energy signature coming from M.

"M, what are you?" While the rest of Adam's power faded from her, she looked at M confused, as she felt empty without the tingling sensations she felt with his power flowing through her.

M, realizing that Taki could not only dampen but siphon Adam's powers, also comprehended that Taki could be of Other. "Child, you look pale and horrid in that robe." With a smile, M stared down at the ugly monk's robe that swallowed up Taki's full-figured body.

Taki immediately looked down at her clothes. "Don't get me started, M. That sexy, white-eyed man saw me naked, since—"

"HE SAW WHAT?!"

"Hey, Hey. He was a gentleman, I think."

"What do you mean, you think?" M asked, raising her eyebrows.

"Look, let me finish! I decided to have an attack while I was bathing. I still haven't had any real sleep, and on top of that, my friend just realized he's the fucking Sun God! That's what we should be worried about instead of my wardrobe malfunction. What the fuck does that mean, by the way? Sun God?"

M lightly chuckled at the way Taki had spit all of that out. "Okay, I won't cut his eyes out," M said dismissively.

"Ohh kayyy."

"Back to your question about your friend, I told you earlier that the white-eyed creature is an angel. What makes you think gods do not exist?" M said, interested as to Taki's honest thoughts as to what was going on.

"Well, for one, I do understand what you told me earlier, but I only believe in one God. Remember, I'm Baptist, as in being a Christian," Taki said proudly.

"Humans are very annoying. First and foremost, yes, there is the Ultimate High, but before humans were created, there were other gods that walked Earth Realm. As your history books teach that they existed, they got a lot of information wrong about the different gods that came before. Enough with the history lesson. If your episodes are over, does this mean your involvement with the demons is over? You should be off their radar since you are not the one with the power they are seeking," M said, getting lost in her own thoughts.

"How long do I have to stay here? I didn't even call out of work. Hopefully, I'm not fired," Taki said as she went to grab a bottle of water off the tray the maid had brought in earlier.

"Don't worry, I sent an email to your supervisor. You had a family emergency in Japan, and you will be back next week. I even booked a flight for just in case." She was sure not to reveal her true intentions with the plane ticket she spoke of. "Are you sure you can go home after learning about all of this?"

"Thanks, M! I need a break from that place anyway. Them broads were getting on my nerves. Far as this little escapade, I mean if this means I don't wake up with sweats and feeling like my body is being cremated, I think I will be just fine!" Taki said enthusiastically.

"Well, I am very impressed with your calm demeanor about all of this. Some creatures would not be able to tolerate the mental anguish that you experienced recently," M replied. She was careful not to use the word "human." She realized that Taki may not be of the human species.

"All that meditation and training between you and Jade has me prepared for a damn alien invasion. Seeing that demons and angels exist for real does not surprise me one bit. Now when are we blowing this joint?" Taki asked as she stretched her legs on the couch. "Wait?! Where's my phone?!"

She jumped up, remembering she had it in the bathroom when she was taking a bath. Grabbing it off the old-styled sink, it was dead. "Well, that sucks!" She sat back down on the couch, upset that she wouldn't be able to call or text anyone.

"Well, as soon as I get some more information from those angels, I think we can get out of here. I want to make sure we are no longer a part of their affairs since I do not plan to get involved in this war," M said to Taki, getting up.

"Wait, don't leave me here. I want to go too," Taki said, getting up to follow.

"No, I am just going to get you some clothes. I've already figured a way around their barrier since I've been here twice, so I will be right back. Give me about ten minutes. Don't worry, I will get your version of comfortable." Then, she disappeared right in front of Taki.

"Now that, I will not get used to," Taki said out loud as she sat back down on the couch, staring off into space.

****

As X left Lucia at her place in Brooklyn, he couldn't help but feel excited as he thought about Adam's awakening. "So, the gods are back! This is going to be fun. Now we can get some real action started!" He unleashed his wings to return to the castle. Arriving at the castle heading straight to Mikael's study, he interrupted Adam and Mikael talking. "So, you ready, Baby G," X said to the sitting Adam.

"Baby G?" Mikael repeated to X.

"You know, baby god. He just awakened, so he's not all that great yet, but with some training and some weapons, we can make him into the best Sun God ever!" he said, filled with so much excitement.

"Xeno, I do believe you are moving too fast. What else did you find out from your girlfriend about our new god here?" Mikael replied, nowhere near as moved.

"Always the fun killer! All she said was be careful. He is not Ra, as in the god Ra being reborn, but this is Adam the Sun God. He is not allied with light nor dark, and his power is the most unstable and most powerful," X said with a big smile on his face.

"Why are you smiling? She said the most unstable!" Mikael responded.

"Can y'all stop talking like I'm not sitting here!" Adam said, interrupting their conversation. "What do you mean the most unstable? What happens when I get unstable?" he asked X.

"I don't know, Baby G. Maybe we can fix that by training you. We will help you, and in turn, you help us. How about it?" X asked with eagerness in his voice.

"What do you mean help you? I don't see how my newfound powers can help you," Adam said, unsure.

"Look, A, you are a fucking GOD. Eventually, you will be more powerful than Mikael and me. I don't know what they told you, but we are at war, and I rather have you as a friend than an enemy. We also need help so we can help each other. Just so happens, we are in the training warrior business so, we can help you," he said with the readiness radiating off him.

"I am sitting right here. I could have sworn I was the one in charge here," Mikael interjected, not fond of the conversation going on in front of him.

"Mikael, stop being a dick! This is the Sun God! When was the last time we had someone with this much power here to help! We are spread thin out there, and we are losing!" he said, slamming his massive hands on top of Mikael's desk. "I can't believe you and Dillon are so damn blind to your own egos to not see we are fucking losing!" X said with much frustration. "I'm outta here! A, think about my proposition." And with that, X immediately walked out of the study with weird energy radiating off him.

"In the eons that I've known him, there are only a few times I've seen him so angry," Mikael said as he sat back in his chair.

"Why is he so angry?" Adam asked.

"Just the other day, one of our bases was attacked, and a good friend of ours returned to the light. Meaning is no longer with us in spirit form," Mikael said.

"As in died? How can angels die?" Adam said, confused.

"You have a lot to learn, my boy. Don't worry, you will. Get some rest. I am exhausted after all your catastrophes over the past few days. We still have a lot of cleaning to do after that close nuclear blast you did earlier today. I won't make you pay for it," Mikael said.

"PAY? What the fuck?! How, angel credit card? Angel dollars?" he said, standing up to walk out.

"You're a jerk. Get out. I will come to get you later so we can start discussing a plan," Mikael said as he began to read a book that was left on his desk earlier.

IT'S STARTING

M popped back into the room. "Okay, here, change clothes. I do not believe we should return to your home just yet. Since you still have a few days before you return to work, you can stay with me at my apartment. It is protected from Others and humans. Come, get dressed. Let me go find one of those feathered idiots and see what else they can tell me before we go." She handed Taki a bag filled with clothes from her apartment.

Taki was still amazed at how quickly M had returned. "You really got this from my apartment?" She recognized the duffle and items inside as she began to shuffle through the bag. She settled on a black and gray designer sweatsuit and a pair of black and gray sneakers. "Thanks, M. I appreciate you grabbing my favorite pair of kicks. I feel so much better wearing a bra now," Taki added as she was tying her sneakers. "Had me swinging all of over the place in front of all these men!"

"Yes. Be lucky the white-eyed one is busy. I didn't grab anything purposely. Rushing, I picked the first thing in the closet. Now come on." Looking down at the footwear and clothes that she brought to Taki, she continued, "I still don't understand why you don't dress like a lady at all times," M scoffed, walking towards the exit to the garden area.

"I am not putting on six-inch stilettos to be chased by demons or walk around the streets of New York City. Thank you very much."

"You can dress like a lady and still handle serious business," M said as she looked down at the footwear Taki spoke of.

"M, what's going to happen now? I mean, after this, now what? Am I going to always see them?"

"They are only seen if they want people to see them. Your life has definitely changed, Takisha. After we deal with this, I will make sure you don't have to worry about seeing those vile creatures again."

Meeting X at the foyer, Taki said, "Hey there, big guy."

"Hey there, beautiful. How you doing?" he asked grimly. "What's up Mel? Not in the mood for your shit, so I'm heading off," X said as he began to walk away.

"Wait. Xeno, I must speak with all of you."

X turned around. "I'll be there in a minute, Your Highness," he said, bowing and then walking away.

"What the hell was that about?" Taki asked, staring at M.

"He will return to speak with me."

****

As he walked out of Mikael's study, Adam felt Taki as she walked towards him. Ignoring the darker swirls of colors he saw and felt, he grabbed her by the hand, staring into her as if he was diving into her soul. Interrupting their instant connection, M said, "I advise you to leave her be until you figure out how to use those so-called god powers of yours."

Gazing into Taki's eyes, his eyes turned a fiery blaze. Adam responded, "I advise you to mind your business before I send you where you came from." He turned to glare at M as his eyes of fire got more intense.

Taki immediately stepped between the two. "Hey! A! What the fuck is wrong with you?"

Mikael stepped out into the hallway to see where the sudden surge of energy was coming from. He immediately grabbed M to pull her behind him.

"Adam, what is wrong with you now?" she asked, wary as to why Adam and M were glaring at each other as if they were going to go to war right then and there. Taki held onto Adam's face. "Hey, hey, come back. It's okay. Calm down." She looked him over, remembering Mikael's assessment. "Calm down, A. It's me." She felt her body begin to tingle; she felt the warmth.

"Kish, Kish, what the hell? All I saw was fire. I saw you then fire. What the fuck was that?" Adam said through clenched teeth as he felt his mind begin to clear from the fog of anger that he experienced.

"It's okay. I'm right here. We must speak with you and your godfather. Are you okay to do that?" Taki asked him.

Adam shook his head to try to clear his mind more. "Yes. I'm fine." When he turned around, he spotted Mikael with M standing slightly behind him. "My bad, Ms. Brown. I don't know what happened." He stared at the dark energy that was almost suffocating him, making the hairs on his arms and neck stand up.

M, disliking the showdown that just happened, replied, "Mikael, let's talk."

As they all left the hall, M began. "Look, as I am aware that this situation has tied Takisha due to her ability to siphon this young man's power, I do believe she is not the reason for the demon attacks. So, I am here just for some clarification and to make sure my charge here is not associated with the current issues at hand."

Mikael replied, "What do you mean, siphon? How is that possible?" He rubbed his temple at the new information.

M said, "You said it yourself. She dampens his powers. If you pay close attention, she doesn't just dampen them. She siphons them." She looked to where Taki sat next to the standing Adam. "Takisha, what do you see?"

Taki looked up at Adam. "He looks like the sun. Oh my god, it's so beautiful." As she moved towards Mikael, she stopped in her tracks as she felt a familiar energy signature again. Taki turned to look at M as the power faded from her body. "What the fuck type shit is this?!?!" Taki said in a raised voice, scared as to what her eyes and brain could be telling her.

M wondered about the feeling she had. "Child, what did you see?"

Taki replied, "M, I don't know. It's weird. What is wrong with me now? Don't tell me I'm fucking Cleopatra reborn and shit." She sat back down, shaking her head.

Adam knelt in front of her and grabbed her hand. "We are one. I told you. You are a part of me. I feel it, Kish. I told you," he said with much excitement in his voice.

"What does that mean, A. I mean, come on. I don't want to be a god just like you don't want to," Taki immediately replied.

Mikael interjected, "I doubt you're a god as well, Ms. Mashiro. But, Mel's assessment of you siphoning Adam's powers seems to be correct after what we just witnessed. I believe you take a fraction of his power to calm him." He looked over at M, knowing she was trying to keep herself calm.

"Ms. Brown, I know you are uncomfortable with all of this, but your energy is creepy as hell, with all due respect," Adam said as he sat in the chair next to Taki.

"Stop being so disrespectful, Adam!" Taki said, speaking his full name, so he knew she was serious. "How dare you speak to her like that! You're starting to piss me off!"

Adam cocked his head to the side, sitting up to see if the glimpse of what he saw was real. "Kish? You can't feel her? She wants to kill me right now. If she could, she would. She hates it here. I feel all of that from her. How can you not? Uncle Mike?" he said, shaking off what he really wanted to say.

"Look, Adam, regardless of what you say, Mel is family. I advise you to let it go. You don't even know who you're dealing with. That's probably why you feel death pouring off her, and you're calling her Ms. Brown. Now, that she doesn't like, and you are just plain disrespectful," Mikael said, unsmiling as he walked his large frame around his desk to sit. "Mel, care to sit with us. The boy is an idiot with god powers. Give him a break. He doesn't know any better." He looked at the petite woman in the corner, remembering her last time angry in the castle.

"I am only tolerating his breathing because of Takisha here. One more insult from this so-called god, and I will cut his damn head off." She walked towards the desk and sat on the couch off to the side, crossing her legs so the blood-stained bottoms of her shoes showed.

Mikael's eyes slightly widened. M cursing meant she was past the point of pissed. "Adam, please. I have enough clean-up work to do. DO NOT SAY anything else. Understood? Unless you are asked a question. Got it?"

"Uncle Mike, come on man. I—"

"Where's the party? I just knew I was going to see somebody's head on a platter. Hey Mel, I felt you in my quarters. Boy's mouth ridiculous, isn't it?" X said as he sat down next to Mel on the couch.

"Xeno, I am not in the mood for your shenanigans. Leave me alone. We just came here to talk so we can hurry up and get out of here. Takisha, are you ready to go since you were in a rush to leave?"

"We didn't get any information. Between you and Adam here, we're almost at square one. Again, can someone give us some answers?" she asked, aggravated, looking at Adam.

X broke the awkward silence. "Um. So, we're just going to sit here. What the fuck was that about? Mel?" He stared around at everyone in the room with uncomfortable faces.

"Look, I don't like it either that some human is a sun god that has powers that could possibly start the rapture. I get it. Regardless, this is Adam. You practically raised the boy, instead of worrying about him and sexy chocolate over there," pointing towards Taki with his massive hands, "we need to be worrying about why the demons were after them in the first place. Do they know what he is? If so, what did they plan on doing with him? Didn't you say the other day he was attacked as well?" X said, finishing off his questions as if he were talking to himself.

M immediately replied, "I see you've been around Mikael all day. Excellent questions, Xeno. As I do appreciate your enthusiasm, I do not care why they are after this boy. All I want to know is if Takisha is still on their list or was she just connected to this new god here," she said in a huff, not wanting to acknowledge Adam.

Mikael, still sitting back in his chair, spoke. "Well, Mel, I cannot answer that question for you. To tell you the truth, I believe I may have to notify headquarters of this and Dillon. Adam is a sun god. All of their kind is gone. I can't keep this a secret." He put his head down, looking blankly towards the book he was reading.

M noticed the book on Mikael's desk that he was staring at, as it looked similar to the volume of books from the place where she saw Adam. "That is the part that I care not to know nor get involved in. All I care about knowing is that Takisha will be protected from his uncontrollable powers. Is there any way to know if she was being attacked because she is acquainted with him? I do not believe she is their target. She would have been on their radar if it was her they were searching for."

Adam felt overly hot and interrupted the conversation. "Can y'all stop speaking like Kisha and I are not sitting right here? First and foremost, stop talking like you're talking to the lowly humans you all believed us to be. What the hell are you talking about?" he said with much intensity and force. All three of them sat silent as if they were unable to respond. Adam interrupted the silence. "What the fuck?! I want answers!" he said, raising his voice and standing up as he spoke, body starting to glow.

X stood up. "YO!! Get the fuck out of here, Baby G! Could we really not answer because he said so?" he said with a chuckle.

M, obviously angry with her dark energy filling up the room, looked to Mikael. "I have to go. I trust you will make sure Takisha is safe. Give me a couple hours as I get our travel plans together."

"M, wait. Hold up a sec. We need to finish this conversation. And I still have questions."

"We can discuss whatever questions you have later. I am in no mood to deal with these rectrix clowns anymore."

X snorted while Mikael gave M a withering look.

"Do you even care that I wasn't surprised to know about demons and angels? It wasn't my first time seeing them, M!" Taki said as she sat back down in the chair after her revelation.

M was confused about what Taki was talking about. "Child, you never told me any such thing."

X touched M's hand. "Come on, Mel. Let's hear her out." He sat back down on the couch, gesturing for M to sit as well.

M stared at those white eyes. "Takisha, explain," she demanded, speaking through clenched teeth.

"M, what I'm about to tell you is something Adam and I don't talk about. It wasn't the fire that killed my parents, but demons that murdered them," Taki said with her head down as she stared at the floor in front of her.

Adam grabbed her hand, "Look, Kish, I told my uncle what I remember seeing. Why didn't you tell her what we saw?" he asked with sincerity.

"What could I say, A? Hey, M, by the way, my friend set the whole apartment on fire because we saw some creature-looking things eating my parents. Wait," Taki said, stopping in mid-sentence. "A, what do you remember about that night? That is the first time I was able to say that, ever," she said.

Adam confused himself as he remembered telling Mikael about some weird dogs, not demons. "Uncle Mike, I told you about the demons, right?" he asked, staring at Mikael as his memories started to form of that night.

Mikael interjected before Adam could continue. "You told me that some weird animals were in your friend's apartment and you had a fit and caused the whole apartment to set fire, and that her parents died in the fire, and that's why she moved away. You believed she hated you for killing her parents."

Adam's mind was finally clear about the memories of that night. "HIM?! What the hell did he do to me?" he said as he sat back down. "Uncle Mike, we have to find Chain Face! Pronto! He did something to me and most likely to Kish. That's why we couldn't remember," he said with excitement in his voice.

"Chain Face?" X repeated. "Who the fuck is that?" he said as he looked at Adam, puzzled.

CHAIN FACE

"Chain face? Hmmm... I don't like it," said a strange voice coming from the corner of Mikael's office. "So, you're finally awake. Yay! Now I have somebody that can play with me!" The dingy-looking man with his blanket pranced over to Adam playfully. Mikael, M, and X stood up as Mikael and X had switched to their angel army garb in a matter of seconds, with M standing with her two-arm swords unsheathed. "Hey, hey, let's play nice. I am Adam's best friend. Don't you hurt me," he said as he skipped past M and X to Adam, slightly standing behind him.

Taki, staring at the being in front of her, felt the same sensation she usually felt from A. "Who are you?" she asked, confused as to how this man is standing in front of them.

Adam turned around to speak to the man. "Hey, it's you! You came into my store the other night!"

"Hey, no yelling! DON'T TELL ME WHAT TO DO!" he responded with a lot of sass as he walked around the desk towards Mikael. "You know, he thinks because he yells, he can tell me what to do. It may work on y'all, but me and now her," looking at Taki, "that shit don't work on us—right, baby girl?" he said, sending Taki a wink.

"Who are you? How did you get past my security?" Mikael said, annoyed.

"You call this security? If I was an enemy, I could have killed you all. You haven't taught him to mask his energy yet? The whole Otherside is buzzing about a new-found power around." As X moved in to grab him, he moved swiftly next to him. "No, no, no. Don't touch. That's not nice," he said.

"Hey, you're that dude from the other day? You killed a few demons and ran away before I could get to you. Who are you?" X asked.

"Um, no. We were playing chase, and you lost and then quit. Loser," he said, sticking his tongue out.

X stepped closer towards him as Adam interjected on the weird argument. "Hey, leave him alone. Might as well get answers while he's here. So, Chain Face, what do you know? Why didn't Kisha and I remember all of that night until now?" Adam asked as he stood between X and the mysterious guy.

"You always remembered. I just replaced the demons with wild dogs. There was no need for you to awaken yet. It was too early. That's all I can tell you. Gotta go, see ya later!" Looking back at M, in a mock singing voice, he said, "Don't worry, be happy!" before disappearing from their presence.

"What the hell was that about, and who the fuck was that?" X said as he sat his large frame back down.

Adam spoke up. "He is so damn annoying. Whatever he did to me is gone. I remember everything." He stared at Taki with a solemn look.

"Well, spit it out! Don't keep us in the dark," X replied immediately.

"What do you mean whatever he did to you?" Mikael asked.

"I remember him coming to see me in the hospital before Mom and Dad got there. He told me he was my protector. He said he was doing this for my own good and left."

"You were out for a week after that. I knew there had to be more to it than that. What does he mean by the whole Otherside? Who in all heavens is putting information out there? We've been here the whole time. Are our barriers not enough?" he said questioningly.

"You know, now I really see what Dillon be meaning. What the fuck was that Mike? A bunch of fucking questions you nor I have answers to," X said, looking towards Adam as he sat back. "Now, go on with the story, Baby G."

Adam chuckled at X's insult to Mikael. "I remember dropping Kish off at her door, as usual, then I went to the stairwell to walk upstairs when I heard her scream before the door closed. I ran back towards Kish's place, and that's when I saw her screaming."

THE PAST TRUTH TOLD

"WHAT THE FUCK?!!" Adam yelled as he ran back towards Kisha's apartment door. Hearing and seeing her scream scared Adam to his soul. He ran towards Kisha to grab her from whatever she was watching. He stopped in his tracks and turned to see what Kisha was looking at directly in front of her. These creatures had scaly, burnt-red skin and gnarled wings sticking out of their backs as they attacked what looked like flesh on the ground. Blood covered their faces as they stared back at Adam with bloody red eyes.

Snarling at him when their eyes met his, Adam felt a surge of electricity going throughout his whole body. Unsure of the feeling in his body, he suddenly couldn't hear Kisha screaming anymore nor the scaly creatures. As Adam stared at the "things" in front of him, a dark mist started to surround them as he began to see the energy surrounding them. He could feel his temperature rising.

Adam spoke to himself through clenched teeth. "NO! NO! Not now. I can't have a fit right now. I have to save her!" Staring down at his hands, the fire began to rise from them. "WHAT THE HELL?!" He gazed in awe at how his hands were completely engulfed in flames. Looking up at the beings in front of him, still unable to hear them, he saw them snapping as the blood and drool mix spilled from their mouths.

Walking towards the creatures, immediately catching the first creature that dashed towards him by the throat, Adam incinerated its head as the rest of its body fell to the ground. Adam, using his left hand to grab the second one coming towards Kisha, burned its left arm off as he touched it. Seeing the creature's mouth open wide from its alleged scream, Adam placed his fire-burning right hand straight down its throat, causing its head to explode. Adam threw the headless body to the ground as he stared at the last creature in front of him.

The creature stood up and stared at Adam with intensity in its red eyes as its mouth moved as if it was speaking. Adam, unable to hear anything, gaped in disbelief at what he was seeing. Feeling the burning sensation in his body getting hotter, he felt the pain of the fire under his skin. Adam fell to his knees from the pain, closing his eyes as he yelled out.

Feeling the intensity of the fire getting hotter and hotter as he was on his knees, he looked up to see where the creature was. Adam caught fire surrounding him. Engulfed by a circle of fire, he began to hear Kisha's screams. As Adam listened to her screams, a door formed in front of him. The burning sensation intensified as his body began to feel as if it was being incinerated.

Adam began to walk towards the door, with each step causing him to fall due to the blazing fire. Noticing Kisha's voice becoming fainter as he walked towards the door, Adam stopped and turned around to return to her voice. Unable to get through the fire any longer, Adam began to feel faint from the blazing fire engulfing him. He felt like he was about to pass out and suffocate from the fire that was overwhelming him.

Taki continued to scream as she watched Adam decimate the weird-looking beings in front of her, unable to fathom the scene in front of her. Adam's hands were on fire, reminding her of something out of a comic book. He beat up the ugly, scaly things that looked like they were eating something before Adam and Taki got there, understanding that most likely the blood all over her apartment came from her parents.

Seeing the demon corpses falling not far from her, Taki screamed, "NOOOOOOO!!!" as she fell to her knees, watching as Adam fell to his knees in front of her as well. "Adam! NO! Stop it! Come on!!" Taki screamed at the kneeled back of Adam, staring as she watched a circle of fire beginning to form around him.

Taki jumped back, trying not to get burned, realizing the fire never touched her. She screamed, watching the fireball that was once her friend, and saw the last creature begin to walk towards her, snarling and baring his teeth. As the blood still dripped out the sides of its mouth, Taki yelled towards the creature and started to feel a tingling sensation as the fire began to attach itself to her hand, just like Adam. Taki was shocked that the fire was not hurting her. She screamed at the top of her lungs as the demon raced towards her. Adam's fire exploded at the same time, causing a large explosion in front of her and Adam, incinerating the rest of the apartment in front of them. Adam passed out from the blast as Taki, on her knees, barely holding herself up, watched her own hand glow while she held onto Adam's hand as everything went black.

TRUTH CAME OUT, FINALLY

"Next thing I know, I was waking up in the hospital," Taki said as she finished the story that Adam started.

"From what a neighbor told me, the girl next door and her mom pulled you and Adam out of the doorway to safety until the speed doctors came. I arrived at the building too late and went to that medical place, searching to find out you two were taken to separate places," M finished as she stared at Taki, remembering that night clearly. "I didn't feel an ounce of Other energy when I got to that building. I thought it was a legitimate fire in that hell hole of a place.

"Are you talking about the ambulance? I've never heard of a speed doctor. The power that those two exuberated singed everything. Nothing was left, not even a trace of the demons or Ms. Mashiro's parents. The whole apartment from in front of them to the windows was just complete and utter ash. Now my question to you, Mel, is why have you been in this girl's life for so long, and what is she?" Mikael asked, giving M a suspicious look.

"I don't like your tone, *Mikael.* Since she was young, I have been entrusted by her parents to watch over her, especially due to their condition. As far as I know, up until now, I believed Takisha to be a regular human. That's why I assumed the fits of pain and fire came from possession," M stated with a huff, still really angry.

"Speed Doctors? Really, Mel. And you think your cousins are trying to possess people again," X chuckled.

M, moving swiftly, unsheathed her left wrist blade towards X's neck. "Say one more word, Xeno, and you will definitely go meet your father today!" M said in a whispered tone in his left ear.

"I'm sorry, Your Highness," he said, defeated.

"Look, I am sick of the tomfoolery here. I will be back," M said as she disappeared right then and there.

"Why does everyone keep calling her Your Highness?!" Taki said, annoyed.

Mikael replied, "What do you know about Melchorde, Ms. Mashiro?"

WHO'S LADY M?

Taki stared at Mikael as she thought about his question. "She's the social worker that kept my parents from losing me to the system. She became more like a guardian when I started having the fights in middle school," she said, moving to look at Adam.

"Around the same time, my issues got worse," Adam continued.

"So, you've known Melchorde a long time?" Mikael asked.

"Yes, but you still haven't answered my question. Why the hell do you all call her Your Highness, and is she like you?"

X rolled his eyes. "That's actually two questions. And honestly, it is not for us to discuss Mel's past with you. If you know her, then you know she would not appreciate us discussing her business with you."

"In due time, Ms. Mashiro, I do believe with your involvement with all of this, Melchorde will have to explain everything to you. As far as your involvement goes, Xeno here was correct to ask if your direct attack was due to your association with Adam here," Mikael added, sitting back down in his chair as he stared at the natural beauty in front of him. "I do believe your attack was not a mere coincidence—Adam, your thoughts?"

"Huh? Me?" He looked around as everyone in the room stared at him.

"Yes, dummy. I am talking to you," Mikael replied, shaking his head at Adam's lack of seriousness.

Adam was not feeling his godfather's sarcasm. "I don't know, Uncle Mike. From what I understand, we don't know if they know what I am or if there is any connection to Kisha. So far, their attacks have been weird coincidences, including the attack on her parents. As far as we know, you guys are the only ones that know about my power, unless they know more than we do," Adam finished.

Mikael responded, "Let's assume that they know more than we do about you, Adam. Maybe they need your power for their next move and planned on using Ms. Mashiro here as bait." He raised an eyebrow.

"Honestly, nobody knows about Adam. I believe when he has his fits, somehow it leaves residual power that can attract the demons. We need to test my theory, but I don't think they know what they're dealing with. Come on, Mike. No one believes that a god is back," X said with a raised eyebrow.

"So, what do you think our next plan should be then?" Mikael said, wondering what crazy idea X was thinking of.

****

"THAT CHILD! How can he wield so much power?! WHY?! SO irresponsible! How could they have returned after all this time?" M said. "Get it together, Melchorde! What's next? I know!" She immediately thought of a place she could go to get a little bit more information on Adam.

M transferred herself a few blocks away from Lucia's shop. She began to transmit herself back to Earth Realm. Hearing slight movement behind her, M ducked as a sword swung over her head. She reached into her knee-high boot to pull out her knife as she lowered her body into a round spin kick, knocking the individual behind her to the floor as she stabbed them in the throat.

Watching the blood on her hand turn to dust as the body disintegrated, she asked, "What do you want?" speaking to someone she felt nearby. "You'll be next if you keep it up!" She smoothed out her clothes as she began to walk away. "If you value your life, Number Two," using the nickname she gave him, "you will stay out of this."

Deuce stayed silent as he watched M with an unspoken fury as his body shook in a quiet rage. In a defeated sigh, speaking out as if M was out of earshot, he said, "I will be the one to defeat you, Melchorde. Just wait and see." He then unleashed his massive wings and returned to the real task at hand.

****

Walking into Lucia's shop, M sensed the need to immediately leave but fought the urge. "Hello, is someone here?"

Lucia walked out from the back, feeling the energy. "I figured it was you. What brings you here?"

M slowly walked towards the counter Lucia was standing behind. "Look, I know you didn't tell them everything about the return of the Sun God. What else do you know about him?" M asked sharply.

Lucia responded in her heavy accent. "I told them all I know. A god has returned to our world. At least, that's what the power he wields says he is. What's your interest in him?" She tried to get a feel from the small woman in front of her.

M sensed a tingle in the air. "Impressive, young one, but you lack the power or experience to read me. You wouldn't survive if you tried. Now, do the demons know about this?"

"I doubt it. I believe they think they found something foreign and are trying to get ahold of it."

"I hope that is true, but I highly doubt it. Well, thank you for your assistance. I believe you should improve the barriers around this place because there may be trouble soon."

Lucia spoke as she watched M walk away, "I hope you got some battle shoes ready. Something's coming, and I would hate for you to dirty those beautiful boots up."

M turned to wave goodbye. "Thank you very much. I have a wardrobe ready for anything." And with that, she smiled and sent a wink as she walked out the door.

Even though it was a chilly afternoon, M felt a tingle of power coming not too far from where she was leaving Lucia's shop. "I am going to have to ask that Lucia why there is so much activity by her shop if she placed barriers and protections."

NEED PEOPLE LIKE THIS

Trystan was walking towards his victim. "Come here, human. You've been worshipping us for a long time and reaping the rewards. Time to pay up!" He revealed his fangs as he stalked the victim, crawling backward in the alley.

"She's back in Earth Realm. One more down. Not sure if you felt that or not?" Deuce said, knowing the captain couldn't care less if one of their men were killed.

Stopping in his tracks to transfer to Otherside, Trystan asked, "Why did you just interrupt me, Deuce?"

"I was reporting back on Melchorde before we returned to the boss." He made sure to bring up the fact that they were late completing their task.

"You're lucky," Trystan said, returning for the human to see. "It's your lucky day, human. I will return for my pay another time." Trystan then returned to Otherside to speak to Deuce. "Your luck is about to run out. Don't ever disrupt my fun ever again," Trystan stated chillingly.

Deuce was uncomfortable with the energy in the air. "My apologies, sir. I will not let it happen again." He bowed to show respect as he looked at the man in front of him.

"Now, let's go see this bitch and find out what she knows. The boss can wait for a second," he said confidently as they walked off to their next destination.

They stopped at a building not too far from Taki's apartment. "Is it a coincidence that she is connected to people in the incident involving you and other demons long ago?" Deuce asked, trying to decipher some information he recently heard.

"Trainee, what are you talking about? What incident?" Trystan asked suspiciously.

"Tre told me that the girl you want has to do with your friends that were destroyed a long time ago. It was her parents that you all killed or something that got you stuck training new pledges like me," he said, looking away as he told something that Tre told him to never repeat.

"I see a dead man's words still linger on your tongue. Tre always had a big mouth. Thank hell's ways that I no longer have to listen to that mouth of his," Trystan said in a chuckle. "No worries. Just some unfinished business that so happens to connect to today's business. If I'm right about what I think is going on, we may be moving up in this outfit very soon! Stick with me, kid. This shit about to get real!" he said excitedly.

Turning around to give Deuce his back, Trystan said, "Now, on to see what this dumb broad knows." He walked into the high-rise building and pushed the intercom button. "Hello, beautiful. I'm here," he said, speaking to the woman in his most charming voice. *Buzzzz.* "This will be easy. We might be able to have some fun too," the demon captain said as Deuce followed him, walking towards the elevator.

As both men walked off the elevator, massive frames lined the halls as Michelle stood at her apartment door, watching as the beautiful, chocolate-colored men walked towards her. She had a feeling of a standing orgasm as she watched the angrier looking one stare at her as if he could see her soul. Michelle started to get that hungry feeling again from wanting him. "Well, looks like I am going to have some fun today. What brings you here?" she asked, leading both men through her apartment door.

"What do you know about the woman?" Trystan asked, stopping just after the threshold to close the door behind Deuce, who entered with Michelle.

"Right to the point tonight? No spankings?" she asked as she strutted seductively down the hall to the living room that overlooked her neighborhood. Beautiful apartment, to say the least. The woman had a fetish for decorating. She sat on the chaise, positioning herself close to the large windows that engulfed the front wall. "Well, no fun for me?" she pouted as she slightly moved herself to show her bare breasts and legs from under her robe.

"Oh, don't worry, I am going to fuck the shit out of your mouth as soon as you tell me what I need to know," Trystan said as he walked towards where Michelle was laid out, stroking her face.

She moaned at the tone in his voice. "Hmmm. Well, all I know is she is some freak that the boyfriend wants to fuck but can't." Beginning to stroke his massive legs, she sat up to position herself right in front of him.

"I couldn't care less about what the fuck he wants. What does he know?" he asked, grabbing Michelle by the throat. Just then, his phone rang. He looked up at Deuce. "Here, answer this. I'm busy at the moment. Now back to you. What else does he know?" he asked again, squeezing tighter.

Answering his question with a deep desire in her voice, she said, "She exuberates massive power sometimes. He doesn't understand, as he is not aware of our world. I just know from the excess power that is lingering at her house when I can get in. Whoever is around her makes it hard for me to get in and out of her place." She began to rub her right breast and grabbed his hand to place it on her left breast.

"Good job," he said, placing his calloused index finger in her mouth as he rubbed her left nipple. "What else?" As he watched her get hotter, he was interrupted by Deuce.

"Captain, we have to go. The boss said we have to report now!" he said intensely.

"What now?" Trystan said, unbothered.

"There was a call for all of us to report in immediately," Deuce responded, adding some force at the end of his sentence.

Trystan replied, "First, watch it. Second, it must be serious for you to get disrespectful and forget your manners." He faced Michelle. "When I return, you better have some more information for me, or I promise, all the holes throughout your body will be filled with all my favorite swords." He smiled as he turned around to follow Deuce out the door.

Deuce led them out of the apartment as the captain closed the door. "The boss just received word that the commander will be holding a meeting at our base. We, as in you and me, were personally ordered to find and capture Melchorde as soon as possible," Deuce said, looking at the captain with a grim face.

Trystan was nervous and intrigued at the same time. "Well, doesn't this just get more and more interesting? Well, let's go. I've been waiting to get my hands on the bitch for a long time."

"We have to report to the boss first. Why does it seem as if you know her?"

"Oh, I just heard she was the number one traitor amongst our ranks. Her ransom is tremendous, so it will be great to collect," he lied. "Now, let's go check-in so we can get to it!" he smiled wide.

WHAT'S NEXT?

Standing in front of the brownstone on the West Side that Taki called home, X walked her towards the light wooden door. "Are you sure you will be alright? I really don't feel comfortable leaving you here alone. I mean, let us stay here with you until Mel comes back," he said, staring down at Taki.

Adam interjected. "I already told you I want you to stay with me anyway. I don't see why you have to come back here," he said, frustrated.

"Ugh. For one, M does not need to see any of you right now. I think it will be better to let her regroup and give us time to talk. I doubt very much anything is going to happen in the next few minutes. As soon as I get my phone on a charger, I'm calling her," Taki said as she looked up to the sky. "Now I see how she always gets to me so quickly. I was in the neighborhood, my ass." She turned away from the large men standing in front of her to walk to her apartment door.

Adam grabbed her hand, not wanting to her go. "Kish, come on. You're really going to make me beg you?" he asked in a low tone, not wanting X to hear.

"A, I will be fine. X here can come to my rescue if anything happens, right? I mean, we did just come back to the city on his back." She laughed at the memory of Adam's face when they were flying with X to return.

"That's not funny." Adam grabbed her face as he stood right in front of her. "I just want to make sure you're safe. All of this is new, and we don't know what them damn demons want." He planted soft kisses on her lips as he finished.

Taki felt that electrical feeling against her skin. "You know, stop that. Can't think straight." She released herself from his grasp but held on to his left hand. "A, I truly appreciate it, but I really need to talk to M. She didn't leave on a good note. I believe next time she sees you or X, she will probably make shish-kabobs out of y'all." She chuckled at the thought.

"I will do no such thing. I am a lady, and I will not allow these two imbeciles to make me come out of character again," M interrupted right behind Adam and X.

X, startled by her sudden pop-up, turned around and replied, "What the HELL, Mel? Say something when you are behind people."

Adam stood quietly due to him feeling her presence before she completed transferred to them.

M was impressed with Adam's lack of fear. "Well, you felt me coming, didn't you?" she asked, looking directly at Adam with a sense of disgust.

"Look, M, Ms. Brown, Mel, Your Highness, whatever you want to be called," Adam replied quickly in the most genuine nervous tone, "I don't mean any disrespect when speaking to you, and I don't want you mad at me or to turn me into a shish kabob like Kish said."

M stared at Adam with curiosity. "Young man, my dislike for you has nothing to do with the fact that you are the reason Takisha here is still alive and someone she holds dear. So, do not worry about being turned into a shish kabob, as Takisha said. As long as you do not harm her again." She looked towards Taki. "Again, I will ask you, did you feel my presence before I got here?" M asked, adding a creepy smile at the end.

Taki interrupted Adam before he could answer. "Just an FYI, that's her warning for you making her repeat herself. Don't do it again." Taki put her hand up and looked away from the glare that M was giving her for interfering in her conversation.

Adam looked at the petite woman in front of him, seeing the dark, swirly colors all around her. "I don't know what I felt. I did know it was you behind us." He continued to look in wonder at the being in front of him. In a childlike daze to M, he asked, "Why are you here?" as he walked towards her.

Taki, confused at his voice, grabbed Adam's arm. "Hey, what are you doing?" she asked as she pulled him closer to her, using her hand to turn his face to hers. There was that beautiful fire in his eyes again. "Adam, calm down, don't you act a fool. We in Manhattan, as in around people and buildings; we can't go boom. Okay?" She held onto his hands, feeling the tingling sensation throughout her body.

Taki quickly glanced at X. "Oh my God, you are beautiful. I forgot these damn effects A has on me." She looked towards M to see the mix of swirling colors and a very bright light in the background. Keeping the last note to herself, Taki inquired, "Yo, this is going to be creepy as hell. What am I looking at?"

"You both are seeing the auras of beings that you see. We have to teach you what the colors mean and how to decipher what creature is what. I am actually surprised you can see mine and Mel's since we are, um, high ranking in power. We can hide our true nature from novices like you two. I do believe it is time for us to get off the streets. We are getting a lot of stares," X said, without giving up his and M's exact nature.

Taki laughed at the fact that X didn't know why they were being stared at. "Well, you two do look like y'all rob a place or two," she chuckled.

X was dressed in his angel garb—black boots, black cargo pants, a black, tight-fitted t-shirt with an angel crown, and two axes facing away from each other on the front, highlighted in purple and gold. Adam still dressed like an early 2000s NYC rapper as they stood in the seventy-degree spring weather.

"So now that I know M is here, I feel a lot better," Adam said, kissing Taki's left hand. "Your Highness, please keep her safe. I know this won't be the last time we speak. I believe you were trying to teach me something just now, and I thank you. I did get lost in my power for a second, but as you know, I'm working on that," he said as he put his hand out to shake M's.

"Call me Melchorde, Adam. I highly doubt this will be my last time seeing you," she said, ignoring his handshake. "I will always protect Takisha. Xeno, let's exchange device information so I can contact you when I need to."

"You asked for my number, M? I didn't even know you knew how to shoot your shot like that. But um—" X was instantly cut short by M's kick to the knee. "Your little ass is going to stop abusing me! Now I'm not giving you shit! Let's go, Baby G!" X said, walking away from their congregation area near Taki's apartment door.

"Xeno, you will not give it to me?" M asked seriously.

X stopped in his tracks giving M his phone code. "It's 947585, Your Highness." He continued to walk away, never turning to look back.

Adam stood in shock. "Okay, well, Kish, call me later, baby girl." Adam jogged away to catch up with X.

"One day, you're going to tell me what's up with you and her," Adam said to X.

Taki opened her apartment door to let M and herself in. "So, where are we starting? You already know it's going to be a long conversation. It's been an interesting couple of days, Your Highness." They walked down the hall to her living area.

"Don't you start that!" M huffed at the use of the name she loathed as she sat on the couch.

"Are you going to tell me why they call you that?" Taki called out as she went into the kitchen area, interested in why more than one angel called her *Your Highness*.

M replied, "The same reason you call me Lady Melchorde— being funny for my lack of understanding the foolish ways that you all present to me."

Taki returned from the kitchen to the living room area with two water bottles. "Now that's the Lady M I know." She chuckled at the way she knew M was trying to hide the truth. "Maybe you should lighten up a little, and people won't call you nicknames that means being uptight," she said, still not believing M's story on the use of the title.

"It is not my fault that you guys do not know how to act," M said as she grabbed the bottle of water to open and take a sip.

Taki sat down after giving M her water. "What next?"

"First, let me apologize for my behavior at the castle. You have every right to want a full explanation about the events that have taken place. Now and again, every *creature* loses its temper. I do not want you ever to think I cannot deal with the issues that we have. Second, I appreciate your faith in me while I gathered some information and stayed with those winged degenerates. One day, when I am in a much better space, we will discuss my past. I do not care to share my history with anyone, especially about my time at that damn castle. I mean, that place. My apologies, Takisha. As you know, some old wounds still cause much pain." M stared at Taki, getting that sense of familiarity again.

"M, you know I cuss like a damn sailor. I want you to open up to me. All this time and I didn't even know any of this about you? I mean, you don't always have to carry the burden of life by yourself. I keep having to tell A that, even after all of this time," Taki said genuinely. "No need to apologize. For what it is worth, I am here for you whenever you are ready to talk about anything. This goes both ways. I truly appreciate EVERYTHING you have done for me. I don't believe anyone else would have done the same."

"I wouldn't have done it for anyone else. You are special, Takisha. I am not sure what you're going to do, but you are a special one. I knew that from the moment I met you and your mother."

M wiped the lone tear from the corner of her right eye without Taki noticing. "So, you say what's next? I say we get you out of here. My assessment of some information I received about a week ago came to fruition. You are a specific person of interest to the demons. Not on a higher-up level, but you are on a local group's radar. I haven't figured out whom yet. So, it will be in your best interest to not stay here. I believe it may be someone close to you or living in this place that knows something. Who are your neighbors?" M asked Taki as she felt for remaining energy signatures around the apartment.

"Just some old couple upstairs, and they rent two more apartments in this brownstone to two other people. I doubt they know anything. They hardly come out of their own home. I deal with the realtor to pay rent or for any maintenance issues."

"Ah, that's how. Most humans don't know that the elderly and infants are more susceptible to paranormal activities due to their state of mind. So, my assumption is correct about someone or something keeping an eye on you here." She began to walk around the living area as if she was searching for something, then stopped in her tracks. "Look, I am not sure what I feel in here, but we should go."

Suddenly, a thrown knife pierced her left shoulder, jolting her slightly back. Grabbing her left arm in pain, the culprit was still unable to be seen. "Takisha, duck! We're out of here." M took Taki's hand, immediately transferring over to Otherside to release her full powers, and transported her out of the apartment.

"What the fuck! M! What was that? Are you okay?" Taki screeched as she rushed to M's side to check on M's hurt arm as she noticed the blood dripping from it.

"Child, I am fine! I am more pissed that someone was in there and I didn't know. Being around you so-called humans is making me soft," M said in a huff as she took her jacket off. She walked into the foyer area of her apartment towards her bedroom to clean up and fix her arm.

Taki searched around. "You know, I swear I thought you lived in a cave the way you speak sometimes. This is absolutely beautiful," Taki said as she reached the living room, loving the surrounding image of the park below. "I always dreamed of living in a place like this! Breathtaking views, and the decorations are beautiful!" She walked up to the most beautiful painting of a warrior woman. Caramel color skin and hair so thick it looked like a vast, dark cloud surrounding her beautiful face. The image looked about a thousand years old. As Taki gawked, she yelled out, "M! Is this you?!"

"What are you hollering about now? I am trying to find something to wear. They messed up my jacket. Someone's parents are going to pay dearly!" Then, she realized why Taki was staring in awe. "Ah, my ancestors. I see you got intrigued, just like everyone else. It's a beautiful picture. I was told she loathed paintings and that her father made her sit there for almost a full day so the dem—artist could capture her," M said, correcting herself before Taki could catch the slip.

"She's beautiful! Oh, my god, M. You look just like her! Wow, great genes run in your family. Was she tiny like you?" Taki asked, looking at M as they both stared at the painting.

"Funny, only Amazons are your height! I am actually faster and stronger than most men three times my size."

Taki laughed since she knew it bothered M to tease her about her height. "Hey, hey, it's okay. I love you anyway." Caught in a gasp, she walked into a scene out of an old Egyptian movie: gold everywhere, purple curtains, gold busts of beautiful people, a bed made of solid gold. Taki was in awe.

"M, what in all hell? I knew you had money, but damn. Related to the Escobars much?" Taki asked, chuckling at her own joke.

"Well, can't help it. I like style. This is actually a downsize compared to my past life. Should have seen my cas—" She stopped herself from speaking, realizing it has been so long since she had a regular conversation about the past.

"Hey," Taki broke M out of her thoughts, "like I said, whenever you want to talk, I'm here," Taki said, walking towards the magnificent bed to touch it. "Do you mind?" she asked.

"Come on in. I don't mind." M knew the brief regular conversation may be one of the last ones they had if her assumptions on the involved party were correct. "Well, since you can't go home to get your things, let's go shopping. That's a regular human thing to do that always put you in a better mood," M said as she walked towards her gigantic walk-in closet off of her bedroom.

"As long as I can get some kicks I like, I don't care where we go."

M stepped out of her closet holding a dark blue, two-piece skirt suit set with a gold silk shirt. "Well, let's get cleaned up. You are putting on womanly clothes today." She turned her back to pull her undergarments out of the gold dresser drawer. "But I will allow you to at least go to that boy's store. We will need to tell Xeno what happened at your apartment," M finished.

Remembering Adam owned a store with all of the footwear and jumpsuits Taki loved, she replied in an overly exaggerated excited voice, "Yay! I get to put on pumps while I shop for sneakers." She plopped down on the oversized bed. "Damn, M, I would never get up. Whose money are we spending anyway? I never grabbed my purse."

X WORKS

"So, how far you live from here?" X asked Adam as they walked down a block not too far from Taki's apartment.

Adam looked up from texting on his phone. "Oh. I live far. I'm hitting up my driver now to see how far he is from scooping us up. Look, I already told him and Peggy you're my cousin visiting from out of the country."

"Why did you say out of the country?" X replied curiously.

"Oh, for just in case you say something weird and shit. I know you're hip, but you're still a little weird, my guy," Adam replied with a chuckle as he collected his coffee from the café they stopped at. "You sure you didn't want anything?"

"No. I'm okay. Just ready to relax, tired of your shit," he said with a laugh as they stepped back outside.

As Adam stood in front of the café, he looked to his left down the street, recognizing his vehicle. Hearing the booming system Chike (Chee-kay) had blasting coming from damn near a block away, Adam and X watched as the beautiful white car pulled over with the top down.

Chike turned the volume down. "My guy!!! Where you been?" He got out to walk over to Adam. Chike stood right six feet with a buff build and the most beautiful mocha skin. His hair locs were tied in a top. He was a little darker than X but still had a brown shade. The sun made it look like he was glistening. Not as tall as Adam or X but not a short man, he stood in front of the large men. "Well damn, A, all the men in your family big as fuck?" He reached out to hug Adam and shake X's hand.

"Haha. Funny my dude. This my cuz, X. X, this is Chike, my homeboy. We go way back to the building days. He's cool."

While reaching back to shake hands, X replied, "Hey, Chike, nice to meet you, my brother. I see you're of Other as well." He recognized Chike's energy signature immediately.

Chike nervously looked back at him. "What? I don't know what you're talking about. Ready, Adam?"

"Don't ignore me! What unit are you from?" X immediately interrupted.

Adam was not feeling X's tone nor accusation towards Chike. "Yo, my man. X? What's up? I've known Chike almost my whole life. Ain't no way he is Other. I mean, come on," he said, staring at X in disbelief.

"Care to share, Chike?" X demanded, as he knew what he felt coming from the so-called driver.

"Commander Xeno, I did not expect to see you here. I was under the impression that Adam still didn't know of our world," Chike immediately responded from the power he felt coming from X. "I was instructed to protect him and keep him out of harm's way."

Adam was standing in shock and disappointment. "WHAT THE FUCK, CHIKE?! What you mean?" He walked towards Chike, unleashing a massive left hook. When he was about to swing again, X grabbed his arm.

"Okay, okay. Let's go. Baby G, get yo ass in the car. Chike, drive. Put that damn top up, too, so we can talk!" X grabbed Adam as he opened the passenger door, acting as if a crowd was not staring at the large men and the altercation.

Chike walked over to the driver's side of the vehicle, spitting out blood from Adam's punch to the jaw. "A, I'm going to fuck you up! Fuck is wrong with you?" He pushed the button to make the car's hardtop rise.

Adam tried to get in the front seat, but X blocked him from doing so. "Nah, playboy, get in the back!" He knew it would be better for him to calm down.

"How the fuck you put me in the back of my own car? I don't even know if I can fit back here," Adam said with an attitude as he flipped the seat.

"Shut up and put your feet up. You're the one acting a damn fool! Make sure you keep that damn temper down. Taki is not here to calm your stupid ass down!" X said to Adam as he got in the back of the car. "Chike, let's go."

"Where to? I haven't received any orders in almost a week. I don't know what is going on at all. I'm in the dark here, Commander," he said, puzzled.

Adam sat in the back, staring at the men in the front seats of his vehicle. He was pissed off. He felt as if his whole life had been a lie. "Chike, you motherfucker!" He began to feel his body start to get warm.

"SHIT!" X said. "Chike, pull over. We have to get him out of here now!" he stated in a panic.

Chike immediately pulled the luxury vehicle into a side alley. X hopped out of the passenger seat, reaching for Adam. "Come on, Baby G. Let's calm down for a second." He began to feel the pure power radiate off of Adam. "Come on, Baby G. Come take a walk." X noticed Adam still hadn't gotten out of the car.

Adam was in a daze as he remembered the past couple of days. "WHAT the fuck, man? I already knew shit was crazy, but Chike? Chike? I'm going to kill that motherfucker! You lied to me all this time? You were supposed to be my man. Who the fuck are you? It's probably because of you the demons know about me." His hands were entirely on fire at this point.

X and Chike stared in awe at the massive power Adam was exuding. "You motherfucker. CHIKE, come here!" Adam angrily strode towards both men as his body was lit up like a Christmas tree. "Okay, Chike, time to tell me who the fuck you are with now! How fucking long have you been around?"

X yelled as he walked towards Adam to try to knock some sense into him. X swung his left fist to hit Adam, immediately getting burned before landing a punch. "What the fuck, Baby G? Calm down! Dammit! Why the hell didn't I get that damn woman's number?" he said, thinking of Taki and how she could have calmed down Adam's temper tantrum. Adam's energy forced X out of his way.

Chike transferred to Otherside, unleashing his full powers. "Well, what the fuck, A! I'm still your friend! You just don't know the whole truth!" He transferred back to Earth Realm in his full angel uniform—black t-shirt highlighted in purple and gold with black cargo pants and black combat boots. Chike's shirt did not have an emblem on it that matched anything that X ever remembered seeing. As Adam reached Chike to swing, Chike ducked, placing a chain around Adam's right wrist as he tried blocking the massive fire energy that Adam was projecting towards him. "Adam! Calm down! Now!" Chike screamed as he did not want to fight his friend.

X immediately grabbed Adam from behind to transfer them to Otherside to deal with his uncontrollable powers. "I knew he was a problem, but damn!" X hung onto the back of Adam, watching his arms and feathers from his wings being singed like they were engulfed in a fire pit.

Chike ducked to his left to place the other chain he had in his hand on Adam's left wrist and jumped back, yelling, "Commander, get off him now. Not sure if this will work or piss him off more."

Adam looked down at his hands to see that they were indeed chained, getting angrier as he watched the chains start to glow. In a low growl, he said, "You think this will stop me from fucking your bitch ass up!" Both warriors braced themselves to deal with the uncontrollable Adam as other players began to come to the party.

"Are you fucking kidding me?" X exclaimed as he felt what he knew they didn't have time for.

Chike felt the demonic presence approaching as well. "What the fuck type kind of day is this going to be?!" He searched for where the other energy was coming from.

The exuberating power that Adam was releasing was felt in Otherside.

"What're the chains for? Is this going to help or harm us?" X asked, unleashing his battle-ax from his back. "These ain't no lightweights coming," he said, staring at Adam directly but feeling around for the other presence.

"These are supposed to absorb his power to weaken him so we can knock him out and get him home. As I said earlier, I am not sure if it will work or piss him off more since I never had to use them before. As it looks, he's getting pissed."

Adam stood there, getting brighter and hotter as a fire-like cylinder formed around him, incinerating everything in its circle. The pure radiance of power was causing Chike and X to have trouble breathing as they watched the chains get brighter.

"I think he figured it out already. He's trying to overload the chains! Fuck this!" X jumped toward the flamed Adam with his battle-ax. He jumped back immediately as the ax became too hot to hold. He stared down, watching the ax melt. "What the fuck?" X said out loud as his hands were singed from the heat.

WHEN SIDES MEET

"What in all hellfire is that?" Trystan asked, feeling a tremendous power he never felt before exploding.

"What the fuck is that? I know you can tell. Is that her?!" Trystan asked Deuce impatiently in a hurried tone, thinking of Lady M and Taki.

Deuce immediately felt a chill travel down his spine from the power he sensed. "I've felt nothing like this before." He stood up to see if he could get a read of where the power was coming from. "Come on, I can get us near it to find out what it is," Deuce said to Trystan as he grabbed his shoulder, transferring them downtown.

Unfamiliar to the area, Trystan stared at Deuce in disgust, looking around the busy streets. "What the fuck! Why are we here?"

"Unfortunately, I'm unable to get an exact pinpoint to the power source. But I can say we are in at least a one-mile radius of whatever is going on," Deuce said. *I am only around your sorry ass to kill Melchorde. I can't wait to kill you both*, Deuce thought, continuing to play the dumb, weak role he had portrayed for the last decade.

Trystan sniffed the air as he watched all the busy humans walk past him. "Well, this seems like a nice place to be. Where are we?"

"We're actually not far from that freak bitch apartment building, but we are on the busier side of town now. Come on, we may be in luck." Feeling an unfamiliar sensation in the air that caused the hair on his skin to rise, Trystan fought the urge to want to turn away.

"What do you feel right now, Captain?" Deuce asked.

Immediately replying with a slight heavy breath, Trystan said, "I feel heavy all of a sudden, like the gravity on this piece of shit planet just changed."

"What if I told you, that's the power we are seeking, trying to keep us away." Deuce was not as tired as the captain, but his body was slightly sluggish.

"Fuck that. I want it now!" he said with excitement in his voice as he put some pep in his step, heading towards a side alleyway that felt like it was hotter than the rest of the area. "I think we may have found something," Trystan said, as he thought the wall next to him sounded like it was sizzling.

Deuce, trying to keep his real fear away, hadn't felt a power so pure since... *Grandfather?!*

They stared in awe as they walked into a scene with two angels and some burning-like being who looked like he was set on fire with gasoline. Trystan was confused about the situation.

"What do we have here? Some angels finally decided to come to the dark side?"

"Well, if it isn't Xeno, one of the commanders of those weak-ass soldiers we've been getting rid of lately." Knowing it would boost Trystan's ego as well as cloud X's judgment by using his real name, Deuce pulled his sword from his back.

"First, let's get rid of fire guy," Trystan said, jumping with his sword out to chop Adam's head off. However, he was immediately thrown back to the ground. "What the fuck?!" Trystan yelled.

X recognized one of the Royal Twins and whispered to Chike, "What the fuck? That motherfucker right there slick. Watch yourself. His twin Dante is not far behind. I'll get A and get the fuck out of here. Make it to HQ one as soon as possible! Now!"

X tried to talk Adam down one last time. "Baby G! Adam, whatever the fuck you are right now. We have to get the fuck out of here. These bastards here are no fairies to play with, and we don't have time for one of your temper tantrums!" he yelled towards the fire engulfed cylinder.

At the same time, Deuce yelled towards Adam and transferred right in front of Chike, missing Chike's neck with his sword by inches. "Fast. Not fast enough." Deuce moved towards Chike again as they began their fight.

Trystan got up from the power punch he got hit with. "Who and what the fuck is that?" He stared at the circular fire standing in front of him.

"Hey, I don't know how you know royal asshole, here but mind your business with this one! We don't want no problems right now and just want to be left alone. Our war will continue another time," X said genuinely, not sure what Adam was about to do or what in the world these high-level demons were doing in NYC at this time.

Trystan, unsure of who this X was or what he was talking about, immediately knew he was an angel that needed to die. "Another time? I believe right now is the best time!" He rushed to attack X with his sword.

X held his guard as he saw Trystan coming and sidestepped him to drop low to a spin kick. Kicking the demon to the floor, X attempted to land his kill shot with his ax as the demon rolled over. Trystan used his left leg to kick X in the chest, pushing him back.

"Ah, not so much a bitch. This one can fight! I like!" Trystan stated with excitement as the first round of their fight began.

Chike continued to swap punches, missing sword swipes from Deuce. "Look, this is getting old. Let us be on our way. I can tell by the way you're fighting me you're stalling. Why?"

"Don't get cocky, you prick! I will have your head!" He rushed in to slice Chike's head but only got the end of a lock. "Still think I'm stalling?" Deuce asked, stepping back, staring at Chike look at the loc on the ground.

"Look, demon, let us go!" Chike yelled, swinging back towards Deuce as they continued their fight. Chike sensed someone else's presence, remembering X's warning of a twin. Ducking immediately, spinning to his left, Chike barely missed the sword cutting across his shirt. He did a double-take, staring in awe at the new player on the scene.

"He is fast. That's your problem, Number Two. Talk too much." Dante, Deuce's identical twin brother, stepped in front, interrupting the fight.

"Nah, don't be rude. Let the boy talk!" Chike swung his sword towards Dante as they clashed.

"Nobody asked you to follow me, dickhead!" Deuce yelled at Dante. "He's mine!" he said, pushing Dante out of his way.

"Hey, hey, fellas, I'm only one guy—no reason to fight. Y'all are definitely not my type." Chike pulled a small metallic ball out of his pocket, throwing it towards the bickering twins. Cloaking himself from the dense smoke to catch them off guard, Chike sensed Dante too late before taking a stab to the right shoulder as the twin just missed his neck.

"You really don't know who we are. This is our element. We love the dark," Dante said in a creepy tone. As Dante finished his sentence, a burst of fire hit him, knocking him to the floor and clearing the smoke, exposing Deuce inching closer to Chike.

Chike blocked Deuce's sword with his own as another fire blast barely missed him, hitting Deuce. The blast sent Deuce farther than Dante. Chike looked to see where the fire came from, staring at an intensely bright Adam.

Adam's body was no longer on fire, just his hands, as he stood in front of Chike. "Where did X and that other one go?" Adam asked in an intense voice.

"I didn't see," Chike said, unsure of what Adam was thinking or going to do.

"Be right back. Found them." Adam disappeared right in front of Chike, leaving him there with the twins knocked out.

IT'S A DRAW

Having moved their fight to an empty garage, X threw Trystan through the wall in the alley, landing him in an office building as Trystan challenged X and pushed him through the remaining wall and placing them in the current garage. As both warriors stared at each other, adrenaline was pumping as they were a little overwhelmed from their fight.

Trystan called to X as he switched his sword from side to side, anxiously ready to strike. "Didn't expect the angels to have someone like you around. This is a good fight. Making me really use my skills. Who are you?" The demon captain leaped in front of X, barely missing his shoulder with this sword.

X guarded very well but was exhausted from all his activity over the past few days. Still sidestepping every swing Trystan gave him, he spoke, "No need to know. I promise you won't need to know once I'm done."

Adam popped up right in the middle of the large men, standing slightly taller than both. "Ain't done with this bitch ass nig—I mean, punk ass motherfucker yet," he said, remembering his godfather's dislike for the n-word.

"What the fuck, Baby G?" X replied as he stood staring in shock at the nuclear glowing-looking Adam as Adam walked towards Trystan.

"Look, he had fun playing with you and all, but we have shit to do. So, you can go. Go now!" Adam yelled towards Trystan as he threw a giant ball of fire towards the demon. The Sun God sent Trystan flying back heavily through another brick wall, destroying the area. "Damn, I didn't mean to do that. I have to get used to this shit," Adam said, staring at his hands in awe. "Yo, X, this shit feels fucking amazing. My G—Oh shit! She coming!" he exclaimed, hurrying himself up to stand slightly behind X.

"Baby G, what's up with you, man? Why the fuck is you…"

"What in all HELL DO YOU THINK YOU ARE DOING, XENO?!" M yelled from right in front of X and a glowing Adam. "And YOU!" pointing her small pinky finger towards Adam, "Every creature in this galaxy felt you. You want them to find you and Takisha? Takisha?!" She made sure Taki was right behind her.

"Don't be mad at me because you're mad at them. I'm right here, with all my bags. Not my fault you left your stuff," Taki said as she held on to the multitude of bags that she had.

Xeno ignored the angry M, waving to Taki. "Hey, sexy chocolate. Your boyfriend here was showing off. I'm innocent."

Adam stared at the petite woman in front of him. "I promise it wasn't my fault, but I did get carried away because I was angry. I was about to…" He stopped mid-sentence as he watched as M kick the man that X was fighting in the face.

"What the hell, M. I don't take you as the type." Adam couldn't believe she kicked a man while he was down. Adam started walking towards Taki, missing her touch.

"This is not someone to take lightly. Is he here alone?"

"Them punk-ass twins that are always stirring up trouble. I know their parents hate them. Oh shit, we left Chike fighting them freaks!" X said, running away from the garage area back towards the alley.

"I knocked them bitches out before I came to rescue you," Adam yelled towards the running X, holding on to Taki's bags that she instantly gave to him when he reached her.

"Twins? Let's go! Now! What is this chickie X is going to get?" M said.

Taki laughed. "No, M. Not chickie, Chike. That's his name. Wait a minute. Why is Chike here?" she asked Adam.

"Yo, Kish, don't get me started. I am bout sick of all this bullshit. Somehow, Chike works with the angels or is one himself. I was too busy trying to take his head off, but when his bitch ass gets over here with X, we can get back to me whooping his ass."

I'M CHIKE, SO?

Chike watched as he walked and talked with X towards a beautiful, petite woman the size of a child and brickhouse female standing next to A. As soon as M saw the insignia on his shirt, she instantly grabbed Chike and X and yelled towards Adam and Taki, "LET'S GO NOW!" M felt the presence of the twins approaching and was able to transfer all of them to her apartment.

"I'm so never going to get used to that," Taki said as she immediately sat down in the nearest chair, this time not losing her stomach.

M looked around. "Don't get comfortable. I will be right back." Then, she disappeared.

"Okay. At least we can breathe for a second. A, you good? I know you got baby girl right there, so you not going to kill us all, right?" X asked, remembering trying to fight Adam in the alley.

Adam replied, "Nah. My bad. I lost it." Then, he looked towards Chike. "Yo, back to you. How you in this shit? I promise I won't fry you like an egg. Just tell me what's up."

"Nah, A, we good. Y'all can talk later. Y'all are not including me in fighting in M's house. Get your necks broke on your own time. Let's go, A. Calm down. No light shows in here today," Taki said, grabbing his hand. She began to lead him towards the room that M told her she could have while staying there.

Chike, happy at the save, finally recognized Taki from the old neighborhood. "Oh, shit. Kisha? Wow, should have known how that motherfucker was all over you. Nice to see you."

Taki yelled from the hallway, "You already know!"

"Wow. I can't believe them two are involved in all of this. I knew A was something special, but Kish too? This just keeps getting better and better," Chike said excitedly.

"So, I see you have a history with Baby G and sexy chocolate over there. In that case, how is it? You have angel garments? I've never seen you before, rookie!" A little bit of force was in his last sentence.

Chike immediately answered, keeping calm, "Commander X, I'm here because I was asked to keep an eye out on Adam here. I can't tell you much more."

"Your cover is blown. You might as well give it up. Who sent you? I am not going to ask again." X stood up glaring at Chike, tapping into the powers he rarely used.

"Look, Commander, I just—"

"Call me X. Don't give me that commander bullshit. I want the truth before I send you to the light." Unsheathing his battle-ax on hand, he said, "Keep fucking with me," as he continued to use his other powers to get a quick read on Chike.

M popped back in with numerous bags in hand. "Xeno? What are you doing? Why are you doing that!?" M took the bags and walked towards her bedroom. "If you ever do that in my presence again, I will explicitly become YOUR walking nightmare. I'm going to get dressed. Be ready to go when I'm done," M said before closing the door, leaving X and Chike to finish their conversation.

X spoke so low so that only Chike could hear. "She's already my fucking nightmare! You know what, my bad. But what I will say is this. I am giving you a chance to tell me the truth. If I think for one second that you are not honest with me, I will show you how I can force it out of you," X said to the warrior in front of him. "So, let's sit." He gestured Chike to the sitting area not too far from where they were standing in the living room.

"Where you want me to begin?" Chike asked.

"Depends on how long the story is going to be, because I am not in the mood for a long, drawn-out one," X said with a slight attitude, still reeling himself in from using those other powers.

Chike felt a hint of power that was unfamiliar of an angel. "Look, what I can tell you is this. I've been in A's life for a long time. I grew up with ol' boy. But something happened to me a while ago, and then I was told to still be around him while I check in from time to time." He looked directly at X to show his sincerity. Chike was unsure what his body was telling him, but he knew he had to be honest with the angel sitting across from him. "Commander X, I can tell you, I'm here to help in any way I can. As you have seen, I'm well trained, and I want nothing but to make sure my boy is good. I never wanted to tell him what happened to me. That shit was wild."

"I can imagine. You had to die to become one of us. How did A not know you died, man. Damn," X said as he continued to contemplate Chike's story.

"He was there when I died, X. He didn't even know I didn't make it. Somehow, I woke up in this strange place, and the rest is history. Shit, man, that was almost fifteen years ago. This was when he was just a weirdo doing crazy shit with the fire," Chike said, reminiscing about the early days with Adam.

"That insignia on your shirt looks weird, but I know you are at least part of our army. Whomever you work for told you about me, so with that being said, as long as you show that you are on our side, I will leave you alone for now. Quick question, who made those chains for you?"

"Actually, the chains are something that I am working on. I believe we can use them for higher-level demons and start to rid them of their leaders."

"You said you've been dead for about fifteen years, right?" X said.

Chike nodded his head to confirm.

"What made you develop something like this?" X was really curious about the rookie angel in front of him. He knew that there were times when commanders would find dying humans and leave them in the human world to handle their business. What X was confused about was how this rookie had a part in the army he's never seen and who trained him to fight.

"Well, Chike, you handle yourself very well. I would definitely fight with you any day. Who trained you?" X asked, just to see what the rookie would say.

"Sorry, Commander. I can't tell you that. What I can say is—"

"Look, as soon as I get in touch with Mike, you are going to tell me everything I want to know." Of course, he was assuming that Mikael was his boss.

"I hate to put you in the middle, but how can I talk to A without totally blowing my cover? I mean, I have to tell him something," Chike said with a defeated look. "That's my friend, man. Even while I was so-called getting better when I died, he always checked on my moms, sister, and little brother. Like, the bro really looked out. I always have to make sure he straight. I feel bad for not telling him, but he would just blame himself."

"Look, tell him the truth. He knows our world is full of mystery. Tell him you can't tell him everything. He will have to understand for the time being. Fuck it, he acts up, we'll jump him and put those chains on him again," X said with a laugh.

"We didn't have much luck last time, but thanks, I appreciate the courage," Chike said with a chuckle.

OH SHIT, WE DID IT?

Taki closed the door behind her after letting Adam walk in with her shopping bags into the room, she temporarily called home. Adam placed all the bags in the enormous walk-in closet.

"Yo, Kish, this shit fire! This just the guest room? M got style. She got the hookup on some real estate over here?" Adam looked out the large window, admiring the view of Central Park.

Taki walked to stand next to him. "Can you believe we are standing here?"

"You mean as in standing here overlooking the park, or in the house with angels, me a sun god and demons chasing us? I don't know what's real about life right now," Adam answered, turning to Taki, grabbing her hands. "Kish, all I know is I want us. I'm not letting you get away from me this time. I let the streets, my powers, and other bullshit determine that I wasn't going to tell you how I feel. Then you left. I was sick. Now I got a chance to say something. I'm not letting it go by. I want and need you in my world. Especially with all this new bullshit, I don't want to go through this alone," he said passionately. His eyes started to turn that fire red she loved. "I'm telling you, Kish, I can protect you, I can provide for you, I can love you and be there for you like no one else. Whatever you want in this universe, I can give you," Adam said confidently.

Taki stared into those fiery eyes. "Adam, we've known each other almost all of our lives, man. We've never crossed the line that you want to right now. You're my best friend. I don't want to lose what we already have due to some petty bullshit. Also, how can you be trying to kick it to me right now, and we don't know if we're going to make it into tomorrow," she said as she started to get lost in those lovely eyes.

"Did I just say love?" Taki said out loud, not realizing she wasn't keeping her thoughts to herself.

"Love? I love you too, baby girl. Always have," Adam said as he grabbed her face and began to plant light, soft kisses on her luscious lips.

Taki got lost in the tingling electrical feeling his kisses gave her. "Hey, what I tell you about that!" She pulled away from Adam to think clearer.

Adam grabbed her hand. "I'm sorry. I can't help it." He rubbed her hand as he still stared at her with those eyes.

"Look, A, I told you, I have a man. I can't just go messing around with you. Bad enough, your flirting has been on a thousand. You know I don't even get down like that," Taki said as she went to walk to the closet.

"He ain't hitting that, and you know it," Adam said, smacking Taki on her ass as she walked in front of him.

"Shut up! It's none of your business who I'm fucking!" Taki said with an attitude as she smacked his hand away. He was irritating her now, so she started angrily putting away the clothes she purchased.

"Uhh, uhh." He shook his head, coming up behind Taki to grab her waist from behind and whispering in her ear. "No. Be honest. What have you felt since you saw me the other day? Isn't it more intense than when we were younger? We always wanted to be around each other. Since I've been reborn in this universe, I know you're my twin flame. The soul that rests with mine." He planted soft kisses on Taki's neck with each word he spoke.

"Reborn?" She was starting to feel the tingling sensation he gave her when his powers were active.

"Yea, reborn. I mean, what else would you call it? I know for a fact I am not the Adam I woke up as the day before yesterday. Kish, you don't understand. My mind is racing with information that would not have made sense yesterday. I remember everything we ever did and all the time we spent together. You were always going to be mine. I can't wait to get a better handle on all this shit so I can show you," Adam said as he continued to plant soft, kisses on Taki's left ear and neck.

"A, what are we going to do now?" She felt the surge of power flowing through her and was getting lost in the sensation; she felt as if her soul was becoming one with Adam's. Taki felt like she was going to explode with an orgasm. Taki looked at the most beautiful being she had ever seen. "A, is this really you?" Taki asked, speaking to the being standing directly in front of her.

Adam stood as the Sun God in full glory. The air rippled around him, showing his heat. "I guess so. I am telling you now, there's no stopping this. You better walk away from me right now. I am trying my hardest not to touch you right now," he said through clenched teeth.

"Come here," she said, pulling him closer as she placed her lips on his. Adam kissed Taki with a fiery touch, causing her to moan against his lips. She fell deeper into his kiss, with a feeling of an electrical sensation that flowed throughout her body as if his powers were touching every part of her. Adam moved his lips down her neck to the top of her breasts, using his right hand to hold Taki's left breast in his right hand that began to glow.

"Am I hurting you?" Adam whispered against her skin as he planted kisses on her bare chest.

Taki, unable to completely answer, shook her head no. Getting lost in the fantastic feelings, she moaned back, "What in the world are you doing?"

"I am about to change your world," Adam instantly replied as he had already unbuttoned her blouse and began kissing down her stomach. Using his massive size and strength, Adam placed Taki's left leg over his shoulder, slightly raising her up to give him access to her womanly sweetness. Using his hand to raise her skirt and move the underwear blocking his target, Adam began to devour Taki as if she would be his last meal.

Taki instantly moaned aloud as Adam used his other hand to cover her mouth so they wouldn't reveal what they were doing to the rest of the penthouse. As Adam continued to get lost in Taki's taste, Taki became lost in the blissful connection. The two started to glow like fireflies in southern nights. Adam, feeling as if his mind and spirit were becoming one with Taki, stood up as he licked and swallowed the sweet juices running down his face.

"I told you. You are mine." He reached down to kiss Taki passionately, pressing himself against her, pinning her against the wall.

Taki responded to Adam's kisses, panting as the fiery tingling from the first orgasm he gave her made her legs weak and shaky. Resting herself against the wall as Adam continued to kiss her, "Oh my God," was all she could muster as he continued to kiss her all over. Using her free hands to unbutton his pants, Adam froze.

"I want you too," Taki said, reassuring him as the last thing separating them fell to the floor.

"Baby, I hope you ready for me. I've been waiting on this for a long time," he moaned as he entered her.

Taki gasped loudly as she felt hot and cold at the same time. Adam kissed her to soften the loud moaning as they immediately started a rhythm, getting lost in the power of lovemaking.

"So, she assisted them in escaping?" Dante asked, already knowing the answer.

"Yea, I feel it too," Deuce replied as both twins walked to find the passed-out captain.

"I truly think your little pet project should be over with. You've been playing this charade long enough. It's starting to get boring," Dante said in an exasperated tone as they stared at the down captain.

Sensing him about to awaken, Deuce reached down. "I'm still having fun. You're just impatient since Grandfather is around." He sent an electrical shock into Trystan to awaken him.

Immediately reacting to the twin's shock, Trystan stood straight up. "What the fuck? Kid, what the fuck did you do to me? I feel like I drank like a thousand of the hot drinks the humans be drinking to wake up."

"He gave you the energy to wake up. For a low level, it gives you an extra boost of power for a short while," Dante replied snidely.

"Who the fuck is this?" Trystan replied angrily.

Deuce stepped from behind Dante so the captain could see that there were two of them. "This is my twin brother, Dante. He's visiting from his platoon and sensed me fighting and came to assist."

"Well, it's two of you annoying little fucks," Trystan said, insulting the twins.

"My twin is not as meek as me. I would advise you to not insult him again," Deuce replied, smiling.

Dante interjected, "Keeping playing," before immediately disappearing.

"Well, I guess he didn't like my jokes. Now, I feel her excess energy. She helped them, didn't she?" Trystan said, irritated.

Deuce relied on that anger for his next move. "Yes, my twin woke me up, and I felt her presence as well. She is still working with those imbeciles."

"Who were they? It seems they were acquainted with you." He was starting to remember bits and pieces of the fight that he noticed between the twin and the white-haired angel.

Deuce covered his tracks. "They are some high-ranking angels that keep track of all recruits. I recently came across both at the last raid." He lied since he knew Trystan had nothing to do with war affairs.

Trystan made a mental note as he felt Deuce's underlying power slightly emerge when his twin was around. "Well, whatever. Next time I see him, his head is mine. What do you think that man on fire was?" Trystan wanted to know the recruit's opinion.

Deuce did not want to share his actual assessment. "I don't know, never seen or felt anything like it. Is that the power source you're looking for? It felt similar to that girl we're watching," he said, diverting the conversation back to the captain.

Trystan immediately replied, "You know what, you're a smart kid. It did feel like that bitch. I wonder what's going on with these humans. And why all of a sudden are those feathered bitches around them. Better not mess my plans up. I only have one more thing to do. Come on. Let's see what the boss wants."

****

Mikael paced back and forth in his study. "You have to be kidding me?! Sun GOD! The damn SUN GOD! He was such an arrogant prick. I hope Adam doesn't become like him." He slammed his massive fist on his desk. "Now, my following questions are why and how?" He remembered the book and snatched it up off his desk to read a few pages. He stood in shock as he read something that he thought could never happen. "You have to be kidding me! Reborn? Where did this book come from? I have to tell Dillon." He reached for his cell phone to make the call he dreaded. Unfortunately, going straight to voicemail, Mikael knew he had to go figure out where to get some more information from. *Chain Face. I wonder, can I find him?* Mikael then got up and left the castle to return to Earth Realm to find the mysterious man.

****

Back at M's penthouse, Chike and X continued their casual conversation. "Imma have to teach Baby G in there to control those powers of his. They better be lucky Mel's not here." He burst out laughing as he finished his sentence.

Chike remained calm-like. "Man, don't mention it to either party. Fuck around and blow the whole damn building up," he said with a smile as M popped back in on them.

"Where's the other two? We have to talk. NOW!" she said in a hurry as Adam and Taki entered the living room. Adam was still slightly glowing, and Taki was just as bright, sitting on the couch next to each other with sheepish looks.

M looked at both of them. "Why are you both glowing?" *Silence.* "Anyway, I have some information that may help us. Supposedly, something is going on in the ranks of the demons. From what I gather, the situation with Takisha and him are on a local level. They have their own internal power struggles going on. There's no talk of power searching or anything that could tie the upper ranks with this."

X immediately replied, "So, Mel, you sure your—"

"I am not in the mood for your stupidity today, Xeno. What you don't understand is this. There is a rogue faction out there doing this, meaning it could be any one of them."

"You just told me not to use those powers, and you have the fucking nerve!"

"Do not test me, Xeno."

"Okay, um. What can we do with this new information, Ms? I don't believe we have been properly introduced. I'm Chike." He reached his hand out to M.

"Who are you, Chickie?" she asked, mispronouncing his name. "Never mind, I don't care to know. That man that Xeno was fighting is trouble. Those other two are unequivocally a menace. We need to regroup with Mikael and find out who can be behind all of this," M stated.

"Who is he? What do you think he has to do with this?" X asked, cocking his head to the side.

"From what I know, he's a walking menace for the demon army. But he's not part of the upper ranks from the information I gathered."

"Well, look, you have the right idea about us regrouping with Mikael. I've been trying to get a hold of him since we got here, but he hasn't responded yet. We do have to remember, there's still a war going on. This is not our only set of problems," X said, finishing his rant slightly angry.

"Xeno, is that anger I feel coming from you?" M said, concerned.

"No, Your Highness. I am just presenting facts. I don't want the other demon factions to think this is a time to attack due to our low numbers in the field and in Otherside. We've been spread thinly out here, but that doesn't matter to you as this is not your war," X said, shooting M a not-so-nice look.

"You're right, Xeno. I don't give a damn about YOUR WAR!" M said, slightly raising her voice at the end.

Taki interjected, "You know what. It has been a long day for all of us. How about we call a timeout and relax for the rest of the night? I mean, come on. None of us has had time to chill since all of this happened today."

"Some people have been doing more chilling than others around here," X said, looking back and forth at Taki and Adam sitting on the couch.

"Mind your business, X. I'm just saying we all need to rest, that's all. All of you are acting cranky as hell, and it's pissing me off."

"Takisha, have you been siphoning his power?" M asked.

"By accident, I believe. I'm okay," Taki replied.

"You are right. Adam, Xeno, and Chickie, get out. We will see you another time." M said, immediately kicking the Sun God and angels out of her home.

"Hey, wait, that's not what I meant, M. Come on." Taki rushed to M.

"I wasn't leaving anyway, sexy chocolate. I know for a fact meathead here isn't leaving, so it doesn't make sense for me to leave, and Chickie over here ain't going nowhere until I get with Mikael. Looks like we are one big happy family here, Mel," he said, adding a laugh at the end.

"There is no reason for you to be here. Taki is safe with me. We don't need you here."

"Look, I want A to stay with me, and far as X and Chike," he emphasized the correct pronunciation of his name, "it'll be better to stay here just in case anything happens. I mean, you did say even you don't have a clue on who or why they could be after A and myself."

"No. Get out," she stated matter-of-factly as she walked towards her kitchen area.

"I don't care what she says. I'm not leaving," X said, pointing towards Chike. "You are not leaving either. So, get comfy." He plopped himself on the couch.

"Look, that's her 'I said, get out, but I won't kick you out' tone. So, come on. There's another room here. This place has three bedrooms plus the master. Chike and X, you both have rooms to crash in. Come on," Taki said, leading the two warriors to their respective rooms, leaving A sitting alone in the sitting area.

As Adam was about to get up and return to Taki's room, M returned to the living area. "Where are the feathered imbeciles?" M said in a huff.

A, snapping out of his own thoughts, said, "Why is this happening to me? Do you think we can go back to that place to get answers?"

"I have not tried to return there. Have you?" M said, looking up at the tall man standing in front of her.

"No, I've only been there that one time. Can you help me try to get there? I don't know how to use that power," Adam said, glancing down at his hands.

"I noticed you have a similar transfer power that I do. You will have to learn how to master that before you can learn how to travel to that place, as it is neither Earth Realm nor Otherside. I have never fully been inside that place until I saw you there. So, I will teach you to master that power. It might just give us the information we need to learn about your awakening," M said curiously.

Adam responded excitedly, "Thank you! I really appreciate it. You know, regardless of that hard exterior, I know you're a softy inside." He laughed.

Left in the hallway, M thought of the brief conversation with Adam. *I wonder where Mikael is, and why hasn't he popped up?* She began to feel for his essence to see if she could pinpoint him.

"One day, Mel, you'll have to deal with all of this. I'm getting really pissed that you're taking all your hostility out on me. Look, we love you, always will. We can't change what happened back then. Times were different. Anyway, when we speak with Mikael, we will figure out our next plan and be out of your hair," X said.

"Unfortunately, as long as Takisha cares for that boy, you will never be out my hair," M said, turning to walk away. "Good night, Xeno."

With that, she turned and walked to her bedroom, leaving the tall, dark angel standing in the hallway in her foyer area.

TRYSTAN'S PLAN

"It's two of them. Ugh. I just know I'm going to have to get rid of that Deuce. Especially now that it's two of them. Once they're gone, I can go on to the other part of my plan. He thinks I don't know his plan to use me for whatever it is that motherfucker and his twin are up to. He should have known not to cross me. I knew he was a problem." Trystan felt a cold chill come over him as he ended his rant.

Sensing someone coming for him at his door, Trystan pulled out a cell phone to send a text as Deuce approached his door and knocked. The captain opened the door before Deuce could knock. "I knew your dumb ass was at the door. Can't even mask your presence. How do you expect me to train you, and you can't even get the fucking basics right?" Trystan said, speaking irately as he walked past Deuce, ignoring him as he brushed past.

Deuce was not in the mood to play his charade. "I am in a foul mood today, Captain. I'm not in a training mood," he said, speaking with extreme sarcasm. Remembering the evening before and the information he collected while assisting his father, Deuce said, "What do you know about gods?"

"They were pains in the asses. Some ended up on our side, but eventually, all of them were destroyed by their own kind. We didn't have anything to do with that. Don't let nobody tell you any different," Trystan added to his statement.

Deuce was curious as to how the captain had so much information. "Well, isn't that interesting. I heard some demons are god killers. Not the other way around," he said, playing the dumb role again to get the captain talking.

Dante immediately popped in. "Two, let's go. We have to go now!" he rushed.

"How the fuck did you get in here? My barriers are the strongest in the area. Answer me, soldier!" Trystan asked, raising his voice.

Deuce immediately cut his charade act. "I advise you to lower your tone, captain," he said, putting a large amount of force in his last statement to make sure the captain felt the power in it.

Trystan was frozen by the power he felt coming from the recruit he remembered as an incompetent idiot. *Who the hell are these kids, and why do I sense I'm in deeper shit than I know?* The twins had disappeared in front of him.

****

Mikael paced back and forth in front of Lucia's shop, hoping to run into the strange creature they called "Chain Face." After a while, Mikael stopped as he opened the door, feeling the mysterious presence behind him.

Chain Face. "Looking for me, feathers?" He laughed at the end, adding, "I sounded like a villain!"

Mikael studied the man, feeling the sensational power swirling around him, finding himself reading the creature out of curiosity.

"NO! Ah-Ah! Don't do that. I don't like when people do that. Just ask me what you want to know. You make my body tingle," Chain Face said, laughing and waving his hands over his body as if he was being tickled.

Mikael was surprised that this chain-faced man could feel what he was doing, as he did not forcefully read him. "So, you're more powerful than you look. I can see how you did that to a young Adam. He is such a novice," Mikael said, bringing up Adam's memory problem while easing into a casual conversation.

"I was only able to do that because he is a novice. Once he accepts what he is fully and what he was born for, he will be the most powerful of them all. He will lead them all to defend us for the end," he said casually as he stood in front of Mikael, rocking back and forth wrapped in a dirty blanket.

Mikael rolled his eyes. "Defend us? What end? What are you talking about?" he scoffed at the being in front of him.

Chain Face was lost in a daze. "As they all begin to be reborn. The beginning of the end is to begin. They all will lead to defend all that is to end. Whoo. Damn," Chain Face said, swaying side to side, "too much that time. Sorry, gotta go." He instantly disappeared.

"What the heavens?! Come back here! What does that mean?" Mikael yelled at the spot where Chain Face was standing.

Lucia stepped out of her shop. "He always does that when he reveals too much." She motioned for Mikael to come in. "Come, let's chat." Lucia led Mikael into her shop, locking the door as she closed it.

"And, why the paranoia? You know that won't stop them," he said, staring at her.

"My locks work for humans and the supernatural. I protect this place at all times. That is not why I want to speak with you," Lucia said, nibbling her lips in a worried tone.

Mikael looked at her seriously. "You know Chain Face?" he asked, wondering what Lucia's connection to the mysterious man was.

"Chain Face?"

"The man that was just talking to me in front of your shop! My apologies, Lucia. That's the name my godson gave him, and it stuck," he said, chuckling as he rubbed his hand on his head to calm himself.

Lucia chuckled, understanding Adam's humor. "He does have interesting sets of jewelry," she said. Referring to the earrings and chains across his face and wrapped around his wrists that the eye can see poking from under the blanket when he was moving around.

"Yes, he does," Mikael immediately replied. "How do you know him?"

"No, I don't know him. He comes by here and gives me work advice and leaves. He is the one that told me I would meet God's children, and I would have to help them. I believe he was talking about you all. He described my X down to the scar."

"What do you mean? When did he tell you this?" he asked, wondering if they were too connected to Adam and Taki.

"Ahh, give or take twenty years ago, handsome. Why?" Lucia asked, shrugging her shoulders as she walked towards her counter area to have a seat. "Come, sit. We can chat for a bit." She offered Mikael one of the customer stools that was sitting in front of her counter.

"Lucia, who and what are you?" Mikael asked, putting enough force in his statement to make sure she was telling the truth.

"No need for that. I'm willing to tell you what you want to know. You guys never asked me. I never kept a secret about what I am. I must do so at times to make sure I am not targeted by ones such as yourself, but I believe I earned a few favors with the angel army to live," Lucia said, staring at Mikael from across the counter.

"What do you mean, target?" Mikael said curiously, answering his own questions in his head as he immediately recognized her energy signature.

"Mikael," she raised her arms, "we will not go into a history lesson, but I am what you think I am. I feel you reading me," Lucia said with a smile.

"I want you to tell me what you are, Lucia," Mikael replied seriously.

"Too bad I am telling you before I tell my handsome X. But I am half-god, half-human, Mikael. Just as you thought. The question is, can you tell me what god, and which was each parent?" she asked excitedly.

"Please, do tell." Mikael wondered.

"Shit, I was hoping you could tell me," she said, clapping with laughter. "I was hoping you could tell me since you can do readings too. I can do readings, but I read by the feel of the power and tell what power source it comes from for humans; it's different. Let's just say they can't hide anything from me."

Mikael was shocked at Lucia's revelation of her true nature. "How can this be? How do you know you're a demigod?"

"Look, Mikael, I'm over a thousand years old. I've been around long enough to know what I am. For your information, I was raised by a true psychic. He taught me the ways of the mind and how to dig deep and find out what the power that you hold is true. I can feel the purity radiating off you, angel. It feels amazing!" She stared into Mikael as if she was diving into his very being.

"Hey, don't get lost; most people don't come back," he said, speaking of his light.

"Whoops, my apologies. I am old, but it is hard to resist the light of an angel."

Mikael returned to the subject at hand. "Again, how do you know the man with the chains on his face, and what exactly did he tell you twenty years ago?"

BREAKFAST

Walking towards the kitchen, Chike grabbed the refrigerator door to search for breakfast, only to grab a bottle of water. Strolling towards the pantry to search for a snack, he opened the door. "Oh, SHIT!" he yelled, immediately closing the door in an attempt to erase an image out of his mind he would never forget.

Taki and Adam emerged from the pantry area, both of them glowing like skyscrapers at night. Taki immediately rushed out of the kitchen as Adam walked towards Chike. "My bad, son. Can't help it when her fine ass around." He began to wash his hands.

Chike responded, unable to look Adam directly in the eye. "It's all good, my g, but dog, what the fuck is up with your eyes? You not about to blow us up, right?" he asked as he remembered Adam's look from the alleyway.

"Oh, hah. We good. It just gets like that when I'm excited and shit too. Don't worry. I'm not fucking you up today. Remember, we still need to talk," Adam said seriously.

"Look, A, I don't want no beef with you. Just know I didn't lie to you," Chike responded, now facing Adam directly.

"Look, we got other shit to worry about. We'll talk. I'm about to go back to the room with my shorty," Adam said and began to walk away as Xeno and M entered the kitchen area.

"So, what party did I miss? I feel some weird shit going on here," X said, looking back and forth at Adam and Chike. "What kind of bromance did I just walk into?" X added on.

"Where is Takisha?" M said.

"In her room, ma'am. I will go get her."

"That's fine. I'll go get her. Stay here with your feathered friends," M said as she left the kitchen area to head towards the bedrooms.

"Baby G, the first lesson we will teach you is honing your powers. You wouldn't be able to go anywhere in Otherside like that. Too potent there. Fuck around and be a walking nuclear bomb, going off everywhere. Also, remember, demons are looking for you. I know we're in Mel's house, but you gotta be careful. You're getting stronger fast," X said as he felt the potency of Adam's powers grow since they had left the castle early yesterday.

"Look, I didn't mean for Kish and me to get out of hand. It's just I feel magnetic to her. Like I need her around me to control this shit," he said as he felt the need to be near her intensify. "I'll be back," he said as he began to walk out of the kitchen.

"Nah, Baby G, stay right here. Mel got her. She good," X said as he yelped from being singed by Adam's arm.

"Don't ever stop me from seeing Kisha. Got that?" He stared at X with fire-blazing eyes.

X was getting annoyed with Adam singeing his hand. "Who the fuck you think you are? Don't make me hurt you, rookie. All that power and don't know what to do with it." X stood up, unleashing his own other power, causing Chike to stare nervously as the two beings were standing directly in front of each other.

"Yo! Stop before Lady Melchorde comes in here and makes us leave or worse," Chike said.

"Tell Lite-Brite here to calm the fuck down before I make him," Xeno said, responding to Chike.

"Yo, A, chill. We ain't got time for this, my guy. Like you said earlier, we got other shit to worry about," Chike said as he stood between the two large men.

"I am fine. I just need a second," Adam spoke through clenched teeth as he began to try to calm himself down.

As the women began to walk into the kitchen, M grabbed a bottle of water. "So, what did you lose your temper for this time?" she said, speaking to Adam without looking at him.

"Mel, the baby god here was mad you went to get sexy chocolate over there, and when he went to go get her after you left, I stopped him."

"Snitch!" Adam sneered at X.

"So, why didn't you get past Xeno to get to Takisha?" M said, curious as to how he controlled himself.

"I just thought of my new happy place," Adam said.

"And where is that?" Taki asked.

"Besides *your* happy place," Adam said with a smile, "the sun vision I told you about. That's how I ended up in that place. Remember, M?"

M stared with intensity. "I don't know what you're talking about."

"Okayyy," Adam said, unsure of M's response.

"Forget happy places and testosterone contests. What's our next move?" Chike asked, speaking to everyone in the kitchen.

Adam, no longer standing in front of X, moved next to Taki on a stool. "Well, I don't know. Apparently, I'm ready to go nuclear at any given moment."

"I don't believe they were talking to you, handsome," Taki said as she grabbed two bottles of water out of the fridge for her and Adam.

"YO! Where in the entire fuck is Mikael? I've been trying to reach him all night and all morning since I couldn't sleep due to some people being a little noisy," X said, looking towards Taki and Adam.

"I was out trying to get some information. I didn't hear any noise when I came in here." M disappeared when she finished her statement.

"Do all of y'all do that? Why did we have to fly with you, X?" Taki asked, curious as to how M can do the disappearing act.

Adam changed the topic, realizing Taki still didn't know about M. "Who knows with these weirdos. But I'm hungry. Where can we get some food around here?"

Taki noticed what he was doing. "Don't do that. I was asking X a question." She looked towards X sternly.

"Look, baby glowworm, don't put me in y'all little lovers' quarrel. I don't know shit except that I'm hungry too. I want some human food," X said, not wanting to answer Taki's question either.

"Fuck it. What are we eating before I curse both of you out this morning?" Taki said, slightly angry that X ignored her question as she sat on the stool next to Adam.

"Son, the food in the pantry is contaminated. So, we either gotta go out or order something," Chike said.

"Contaminated? You act like it's full of lice or something," X said with a chuckle.

"My nig—I mean, my gee, chill. Don't make it seem as if it was that crazy. Relax," Adam said.

"You and Kish were the ones—"

"Takisha, come, get some nutrients. We will use this downtime to get some training in today. I believe it will be beneficial to you if you trained more often," M said, startling everyone but Adam and Taki.

Taki had siphoned enough of Adam's powers to have been able to sense M coming close. "You know, this time I felt you coming too. Probably has something to do with me getting used to being around A. Anyway, we can do that. After I go see Mark, though," Taki said sheepishly.

Adam whipped his head towards Taki with literal fire in his eyes. "What the fuck? You going to see that bitch ass?"

"Adam, I advise you to watch your mouth and tone. Takisha, why is it you need to go and see this Mark?" M asked as she stood in front of the couple sitting at the kitchen island counter.

Taki looked at both of them with a weird look. "Um, for one, I'm grown. Two, I really don't appreciate feeling like I'm being questioned here. And last," looking directly at Adam, "I told you I didn't want to cross that line with you until I ended things with him. Of course, you didn't listen, and well, now I am going to officially end it." She turned back to M. "Also, we need to make sure regular humans are not involved with what we got going on. Never know, they probably used him to get to me," Taki said, finishing her explanation and thinking about her last statement.

"You may be correct in your assessment, Takisha. I will accompany you while you go and speak with this Mark."

Taki laughed at M's response. "You always sound like he's a disease. This Mark," she mocked, chuckling as she laid her head on Adam's shoulder.

M noticed how close they had gotten since they'd returned to Earth. "So, this doesn't mean you two should immediately start something either," M said grimly as she stared at the two and the energy that started to form around them.

"Too late! Sexy chocolate over there and Baby G already did the damn thing! Surprised the building still standing." X laughed at Chike as he spoke.

"Chill, X. Come on, we got enough problems. I don't know about y'all, but I'm about to get into this grub Ms. M brought back." As he walked with the bags of breakfast that M dropped on the counter to the smaller table area in the kitchen.

"Chickie is right. Let's eat," she said tightly. "Xeno can explain what he just said when we sit down. Come, we will eat in the dining hall." She walked out of the kitchen area, leading Chike and the others to the large dining room area on the opposite side of the kitchen and the sitting area they were accustomed to.

Taki loved the luxury that the dining room showed. "M, this is absolutely beautiful," she said, staring at the gold plates and beautiful pictures on the wall of the most beautiful family and places she has ever seen. "Wow, M, these are gorgeous. They all look like ancient treasures," Taki said as she sat down next to Adam.

X, recognizing some of the paintings, said, "Wow, Mel, didn't realize you still had some of these." He began to walk around and look at the artwork on the walls but stopped short of discussing them.

"Are these real paintings of people you know?" Taki asked M as the group began to dismantle the packaged food and make their plates.

Not wanting to discuss her decorations, M said, "This place was like this when I moved here. Some pieces are from my past life that I do not care to discuss."

Taki stopped eating and spoke to M. "These taste like the breakfast we used to get from the restaurant in Japan. Omg. M! I missed these! Where in NYC did you find these?" She was excited about the Tamago Kake Gohan breakfast platter in front of them.

M smirked. "The breakfast here is from the same exact place we used to eat breakfast when I came to visit you. I thought you needed something familiar this morning." She continued to eat.

"Thanks, Mel. I appreciate the breakfast. I believe it would be a good idea for us to try to find Mikael. I still haven't heard from him," X said, putting his chopsticks down and pulling his phone out.

"I think that is a good idea. The only information I came across last night is that ranks in this area are in disarray. Whoever is supposed to be in control is losing it. The twins in the alleyway were just around searching for something. I believe that something may be Takisha, and they don't know she's not what they're looking for," M said as she thought about the little information she could find.

Taki said curiously, "What do you mean searching for me?" then placed her chopsticks down.

"Meaning they are looking for a way to get this area under their control and want power. That's all. They don't know what they're dealing with, to my understanding. I say we get this talk done and over with that human boyfriend of yours and get to training. I know you're rusty," M said, standing up. "I will be ready to go within the hour."

"Wait, I'm going with Kisha to see this dude," Adam said.

"No. You are not. You will go with your feathered friends here to find Mikael so we can come up with the next steps of action to keep Takisha safe and find out why you are the Sun God," M said, putting some force behind her words.

Adam stood up from the table, revealing his massive frame. "Look, you know your powers don't work on me, so don't do that. Kisha is not going to that dude's crib without me, and that's that," he said, grabbing Taki's hand.

Taki, aggravated at Adam, felt his power leach onto her. She began to feed more of his power into herself. She felt the sun and somehow began to feel hot herself, falling into a daze and seeing a fire turn a cool blue flame around her.

"Oh, shit! Do you guys see this? This is beautiful," Taki said, forgetting she was angry. Instantly snapping out of her blue fire vision, she looked around and saw Adam holding her. "What are you doing?" she asked in a whisper.

"Kish, what the hell? You just scared the shit out of me and M here. What the hell is wrong with you? I know I was being a dick, but damn. No more taking my powers," Adam said to her.

Taki looked around, realizing she was wrapped in the tablecloth and that Adam was only touching the parts of her covered with the cloth. "What happened? I remember the red fire, and then this pretty blue fire started to come around me, and then I saw you holding me," she said as she looked around the fire-scorched room. She jumped out of Adam's arms. "What the fuck?! Did I do that?" Taki asked as she looked around the destroyed dining room.

M came around Adam so Taki could see her. "Not just you. Adam here as well."

"Taki! You the shit, Blue Flames. When this motherfucker gets out of line, I am so calling you. I need your number. I want what you got. I guess you and him getting it on got you in tune with his powers, so you can take his ass out!" X said with a grin as he shook his head.

"What did you say, Xeno? Getting what on?" M asked curiously.

"Xeno! Shut up! You talk too much!" Taki said as she looked at M with a sly look. "Don't mind his stupid talk. Like you said, these angels are dumb."

"I'm hurt, sexy chocolate. Ain't my fault she gonna be pissed at you."

Feeling the shake of the building, Chike looked over at M. "I told y'all to shut the hell up about it. We all about to die."

"What the hell is that? An earthquake in New York?" Taki asked.

"Nah. I think that's Mel trying not to kill y'all," X said, laughing at the blank look on M's face.

"I will be dressed in one hour. All of you better be ready to get the hell out of my house!" M said forcefully. The power behind it even sent chills down Adam's spine.

"Um, I am so staying away from her for the rest of the day. Kish, you can go to that dude's crib with her. Meet us back at my place. You have your phone, right?" Adam said.

"I do. Don't worry. I'll be fine. M's not that mad," Taki said. *She's been madder...* Taki couldn't help but remember the weird things that used to happen when Taki used to get in trouble and do stupid things.

"Look, she'll probably turn me into a shish kabob later. I'm just going to stay out her way. You be safe. I'm going to help X find Uncle Mike," Adam said as he grabbed her hand with the cloth between them.

"Get off me!" Taki said, snatching her hand away. "Later, A. Get dressed when I leave," Taki said, letting him know she didn't want him in the room while she was getting ready.

"Damn, son. She said, 'Don't come in here'." Chike chuckled as X added to the laughter.

"Shut up!" Adam said vehemently, lashing out at the angels. Instantly stopping laughing and being quiet, Chike and X stared at Adam with angry faces. "Oh shit! My bad. My bad. Y'all can talk again! Ya'll can talk!"

X grabbed Adam's shirt and yoked him up. "Look, Baby G! I know you're learning how to use them powers you got, but those words better not ever come out your mouth again until you learn to control them. Got it?" X said harshly.

"My bad. I won't. You got my word."

"Okay, now. After the ladies leave, we can go," X said to the other two.

"Where are we going, and where are we going to start to look for this Mikael?" Chike curiously asked, not knowing whom they were talking about.

"Cut the charades. You know who he is. I can't wait until we find him so I can know your story, rookie," X said, staring at the slightly shorter man.

"Yea, son. This isn't the time, but we definitely having a conversation when Uncle Mike back around." Looking towards X, Adam continued, "Where's that Dillon motherfucker? I haven't seen him around."

"That's a good question. I haven't seen him since right before I saw ya girl and Mel. As a matter of fact, it was when he made you pass out in the garden the last time you almost went nuclear on us. That was officially the last time I saw him. You know what? He disappears from time to time, searching for shit. So maybe it's one of his moments," X said.

"Well, I need Mike and Dillon to get their asses back around so we can figure out what our next move is going to be. I'm ready to see what's up with these demons that are getting out of control," he said as X's phone began to ring.

X, seeing the caller, instantly answered. "Where you been? It's been a little wild on this side, Mikael! Mel and Taki were attacked, and we had a run-in with the twins and some old demon. WHAT?! Where do you want to meet?" X yelled into the phone. "Okay, okay. Funny, Baby G just said his house would be a good idea. Alright. We'll meet you there." X finished the call.

Adam, curious about X's outburst, asked, "What's wrong? What was that about?"

"To be honest, we might as well get the whole story from Mikael when we see him. Let's just say his day has been just as interesting as ours. Just not as exciting," X said as he turned to go find M.

TIME TO END THINGS

Taki was still reeling from being pissed at A but also intrigued about what happened to her. Speaking to her reflection in the mirror, she said, "What is happening to you?" She felt the remnants of Adam's power.

"Takisha, are you ready? I am dressed and ready to get this over with. I have training equipment and clothes at the dojo. We can change there." Turning to walk away, she yelled back, "You look lovely," as she continued walking down the hall.

Taki stared at herself. She had on an all-white, body-fitting, mid-length dress, pieced with a lavender-colored, to-the-floor duster with matching colored stiletto sandals. The diamond hoop earrings, bracelet, and necklace set she paired it with sparkled in the light as she moved around the room, checking herself out. Taki, readying to leave, pulled her phone out to text Mark. She wanted to let him know she was stopping by. Taki left her temporary bedroom and joined the others gathered in the living room area.

"Hey, M. I'm ready," she said, looking at the three men staring at her.

Adam walked over to her. "Girl, this how you dress when you go break up with someone? Shit, how they let you talk them out of that?" He grabbed her hand and planted soft kisses on it.

Taki was feeling a bit petty. "Oh, so you're touching me now?" She snatched her hand away and walked towards the area Chike and X were sitting in. Chike and X looked away as if they didn't hear her diss Adam. "I'm ready when you are," Taki said to M as she sat next to Chike on the edge of the couch so Adam couldn't sit next to her.

M stood up to leave. "Look, you all can leave now. We will reconvene after this meeting to see what's next. Here is the address to my dojo, and you can meet us after you find Mikael."

"Oh, Mikael's found. We are meeting him at A's house to get some information. Worth checking out immediately. So, most likely, we will meet up with you two right after," X said.

"Kish, look my bad. We just don't know what else my powers could do to you. I don't want to accidentally hurt you again." Adam grabbed her hand again to kiss it.

"Look, A, it's fine. We'll talk later. "She allowed Adam to kiss her hand and gave him a hug.

M grabbed Taki's hand. "Leave my house," M said, speaking towards the angels and Adam. "Come, Takisha. We are leaving." And in the blink of an eye, she and Taki disappeared.

"OH SHIT!" Adam yelled.

"What? What happened?" X asked.

Adam threw his hands in the air. "I should have asked her to take us to my car first!"

"Let's go. I don't think Ms. M wants us here when she returns," Chike said to the large men, ignoring A's statement.

X looked at Adam. "You're a dumbass. And Chike? You're the one that probably encourages his dumbassness. Come on. Let's get Baby G's car and then meet Mikael."

****

Taki and M arrived at Mark's apartment building. Not too far from her brownstone, Taki had a key to the building door because she would sometimes wait for him after work for their dates if he worked later than she did. "I'm so never going to get used to that," Taki commented on their way of travel. As both ladies waited for the elevator, Taki paced back and forth nervously.

"Why are you so nervous if you don't care for him in that manner?" M asked.

"Honestly, I don't know. I have a sick feeling in my stomach right now. I know I've needed to do this," Taki said as they arrived at the floor that Mark lived on. As both arrived at Mark's apartment door to knock, Taki checked her phone to see if he read her message. *Read.* Putting a little more force in her knock, she tried again. "I know he's here. He's always home on the weekend."

M replied, "Maybe he finally made plans." She started getting an ill feeling herself about their surroundings. "I feel another creature of Other around here. It's coming from inside Mark's apartment," M said to Taki.

"That's what I feel?" Taki asked, feeling an eerie chill in the air. Preparing to knock again, Taki was stopped by the door swinging open, Mark standing there with just a pair of sweatpants on. Muscled, chocolate chest bare, slightly glistening with sweat.

"What?! Oh shit? Taki, what are you doing here?" he asked, panting as if he was doing some exercising.

Taki was shocked at him answering the door with such aggression and noticed he was not his regular well-put-together self. "I texted you a while ago. I really need to talk to you. It says you read it."

"Oh, Ms. Brown. I'm sorry for letting you see me this way," Mark replied, looking down at the short woman. "Taki, I am a little busy right now. I wish you would have called and not just texted me. I didn't see your message, and I'm—" He was suddenly interrupted by a woman's voice calling for him from behind.

Michelle walked from behind Mark, grabbing his chest. "Honey, who's at the door. The food's here already?"

M recognized her energy signature. "Why are you here?" M asked Michelle.

"Your Highness, I do need sustenance," she said, taking a couple steps back.

Mark stood there confused. "Taki, I am sorry, I am so sorry. I didn't mean for this to happen like this." His speech was more than jumbled.

Taki stood there, shocked but not angry at what she was seeing. "I knew something was up. I couldn't put my finger on it. I knew I couldn't trust you. Probably why I wouldn't give you no pussy!" Taki said, raising her voice at Mark. "Let's go, M. I don't need to talk to this piece of shit anymore, especially with the dingy bitch. Always a little too friendly for my taste anyway."

M gave Taki her full attention. "Takisha, wait. What do you mean? You know this creature?"

Taki turned around. "YES! This is the woman who is at work fucking with me all the time. Always in my face and shit. Come to find out this is who he was sleeping with."

M looked directly at Michelle, who hadn't moved from her spot. "I will ask you one more time, why are you here?" she asked, putting force behind her sentence.

"The captain had me use this human here to get close to the power we seek." She covered her mouth as soon as she finished speaking.

Mark, disoriented, listened to what the women were speaking about. "Captain? Who's that, Michelle? What power?"

M was interested as to what other information Michelle could give them. "Mark, do you mind if I come in and have a conversation with Michelle? I believe she knows some people that may want to hurt Takisha here." M decided to use his obsession with Taki to get them behind closed doors.

Mark was curious about what Michelle had to do with Takisha. "Sure. Come in. We can all talk." He moved from the front of the door to let Taki and M into his apartment.

Michelle had already walked down the hallway to the large opening of a living room. M used her powers to speak with Michelle. "Have a seat. Why are you here in Earth Realm?"

"I am here to help the captain get power and revenge on the ones that killed his comrades and the ones that stripped him of rank and power. You making me tell you this information will get me killed," Michelle said as she put her head down.

"You weren't worried about that when you were getting these two in Otherworld activities. You know that is forbidden for low-levels such as yourself. What are you supposed to do with them?"

"I am supposed to get close enough to Mark here to get him close to Taki. I don't know the plans of what he was going to use for her," Michelle said to M.

"What's going on here? Who is this man? Why is he setting me up?" Mark asked in a freaked-out tone.

Taki, trying to keep herself calm, understood why he was freaking out. "Look, Mark, there are things in this world we don't understand, and this is one of them. If you weren't so worried about getting your dick wet, you probably wouldn't be in this situation.

"What we can do now is figure out how to get him out of this. He has nothing to do with all of this," Taki said to M.

"That he does. He's the reason I was able to come to this realm. I do not know how. But he has a connection to Otherside. And I was able to come through to him." She turned to Taki with attitude. "For your information, if you were fucking him, I wouldn't have to."

Mark looked confused. "Michelle, what are you talking about? Can someone tell me what is going on here and what the hell is Otherside?"

M was getting annoyed at the lack of truth Michelle was telling at the moment. "Michelle, right? Since you seem to recognize me, that means you are an older one. So, you know what it means to make me upset," M stated, standing up from her seat, unsheathing both arm swords as she walked closer to Michelle.

Michelle quaked with fear. "I don't get what you're so upset for? This is just a lovers' quarrel. No need for knives. But I actually like getting cut," she said, putting on her seductive voice.

M looked at Michelle with disgust. "Look, no one in here but him wants anything to do with you. Just finish answering my questions. What did you tell him about Takisha, and where can I find him?"

Michelle was very angry that M was so much stronger than her, even after all this time. "Look, I already told you what I know. Let me continue to have fun. Mark here will be fine," she said, rubbing the back of Mark's neck as he sat in a chair, slightly dazed.

"What the fuck did you do to him? You dumb bitch!" Taki said to Michelle.

Michelle chuckled at Taki's anger. "He's fine. He doesn't need to know all of this. Why you mad anyway? I smell another man all over you anyhow. Oh my. He smells good. What's his name?"

"You are really starting to make me dislike you. You have no claim on this human."

Michelle burst out into a laugh. "You think I didn't make a deal with him as soon as I got here? I am not that dumb. Even if the captain wanted to take me from here, he can't until my deal is fulfilled. So, I am completely his," she said, returning to Mark's side.

Taki, angry at what Michelle said, walked towards her and used her left hand to swing, landing a loud, sharp smack across Michelle's face. Taki yelled, "How dare you?! Why would you involve him in something he doesn't understand?" Taki began to feel the fire from her siphoning Adam start to fester.

Mark snapped out of his daze. "Taki? Taki? What's going on? My mind, it's so foggy."

M used her powers to search for anyone else in case Michelle was lying about who else was involved.

"Michelle, I advise you to leave this man alone. Let the deal be done, and let's go. You are going back to Otherside. I know you don't have permission to be here."

"Look, you're not as scary as you used to be. I can take care of myself now. I think I will stick around for a bit." She placed her arms around Mark and glared at him, returning him to a dazed look.

Taki was past the point of angry now as she watched Michelle do something to Mark, unsure of what she was looking at. "Bitch!" Taki walked towards Michelle and grabbed her by the long, black, curly hair covering Michelle's back. Michelle was not a small woman, as she and Taki both were around the same height with Michelle barefoot.

Michelle began to scream. "Get off me! I should kill you, human!"

Taki began to throw punches as Michelle began to use her own powers to stop the attack.

Mark suddenly got up. "Taki! What are you doing? Get off of her? You're hurting her!" He grabbed Taki's wrist as she was still trying to attack Michelle. M intervened by pushing Mark out of the way, sending him flying to the other side of the living room and smashing into the wall.

Michelle snatched herself away from Taki. "Mark, come on! You're supposed to protect me!" she said, looking at Mark to get up.

Mark got up. "Taki! Stop! Don't make me hurt you. I will." Then he ran towards Taki, grabbing her by her throat. Taki's defense training kicked in. She used her arms to break his grip on her throat. She jumped up, wrapped her legs around his arm, and wrestled him to the floor, kicking him in the face as Taki rolled over to miss Michelle from kicking her in the face,

"Oh, so you a sneaky bitch!" Taki yelled as she swung at Michelle.

Ducking from Taki's punch, Michelle said, "I am too old to get my ass kicked by a human," as she landed a punch to Taki's left rib. Taki took the force to the ribs, grabbing Michelle's head, planting it on her right knee, and finished with a right hook, causing Michelle to start spitting blood.

Michelle laughed. "Bitch, you could never defeat me. Don't be mad at me that Mark takes good care of me and loves me now. You're old news!" she hissed at Taki.

"The fucking bitch!" Taki jumped towards Michelle to hit her again, missing her punch, with Michelle landing a left hook to Taki's face.

M watched the two women fight and saw how Taki could improve and noticed the kind of training Michelle had. Not seeing anything out of the ordinary, M yelled to Taki, "You are getting soft, Takisha. If this was the dojo, I would have deducted points for the lack of skill."

After getting up from Taki's kick, Mark said, "Michelle, my love, I am going to kill her for you!" He ran to Taki, grabbing her throat with both his hands.

M rushed to Taki's aide but was interrupted by Michelle. "I think I am going to allow him to do something he will ultimately regret when he wakes from my control." M realized Michelle was playing with Taki the whole time, beginning their fight.

Taki was choking from Mark's large hands around her neck; she felt him squeezing as tight as he could. She struggled against his hands and continued to try to stop him. "Mark, Mark, wake up! What are you doing?" Taki tried to yell in his face as she fought for breath.

"I am protecting my love, Michelle. My love, Michelle. My love, Michelle," Mark said, sounding like a dazed broken record.

Taki began to feel lightheaded as she felt that tingling sensation return. Her whole body began to feel hot but cool as she continued to think of A, believing that would assist her in getting Mark off of her. As she continued to struggle, Taki began to see the blue fire again. As Mark's face disappeared and the blue fire got brighter, she began to feel like she was free and could breathe again.

The cool breeze of the blue flame that made her feel light as a feather was abruptly interrupted by M's voice directly in front of her. "Takisha! Takisha! Are you okay?"

AND SO, THE END BEGINS

Adam, Chike, and X arrived at Adam's penthouse shortly after leaving M's place. Adam asked for assistance from Peggy to get someone to retrieve his car. That helped them from having to go all over town before meeting Mikael.

"Damn, Baby G live nice I see. Mikael said he'll be here shortly," X said as he looked around the fancy penthouse, returning to looking around.

Chike was sitting in his usual spot in the kitchen, resting on the stool at the island in front of the fridge. "So, what's next?"

"We wait for Mikael. Once he gets here, we exchange notes and see who the fuck those twins were with and what they are up to," X said, thinking about the twins at the battle.

"Do you know them?" Adam asked.

"I know if those two are involved, it's bad news. Anytime one of them is around, it's always some bullshit, and the other is not too far. The times I've run across them, let's just say they are a major pain in the ass," X said, shaking his head as he got up to go to the fridge. "So, Baby G, what you got in here?" he asked, rummaging through the refrigerator for a snack. *Knock, knock.*

"That must be Uncle Mike," Adam said, walking towards the front door.

"Creepy. He got upstairs without the doorman calling," Chike said as Adam walked away.

X chewed on an apple. "Once we get the real problems out the way, we are definitely going to get to your ass."

"Xeno, I would like to know what you are doing?" Mikael asked sternly.

"I am trying to get some information out of this rookie that you sent to spy on A," X said, stumbling over his response.

"What are you talking about?" Mikael looked at X and Adam stare at each other.

"Who the fuck is this, Mikael?" X pointed to Chike as he yelled at Mikael.

"You tell me, Xeno! I do not know this soldier. From his attire, he's from a special unit. What's your name? Who's your commander?" Mikael asked, putting power behind his questions.

Chike was nervous as the two famous angels he always heard about were questioning who he was. "As you know, Commander Mikael, I'm not able to tell you that information," he said, putting his head down.

"As I thought. My power won't work on him. We will never know unless his commander permits him to reveal his identity. Well, heavens." Mikael shrugged his shoulders as he looked at X.

"How do we know we can trust him? He lied to A all this time," X stated.

"Adam, what do you think, almighty Sun God?" Mikael asked, curious about Adam's thoughts on Chike.

Adam stuck up his middle finger at Chike. "I don't know, Unc. Chike has been around a long time. Wait a minute. How do you become part of y'all little gang anyway?" Adam asked curiously.

X responded before Mikael could. "Look, kid, just tell him what happened, and you good."

Chike gave X the death look. "This is not the time for this conversation." He looked at Adam with a long sigh as he put his head down.

Adam was curious about why Chike was hiding how he became an angel as he was interrupted by a tremendous feeling of power. "Um, guys. I know I am not the only one feeling that?"

Mikael was searching for what it could be. "I feel it too, godson. It feels familiar but different. Before we get distracted, I saw this Chain Face. He gave me some rather interesting information. Something about this one being the most powerful of them all," he said, pointing towards Adam. "And as they are reborn, this is the beginning of the end." He looked around at the other men.

X was confused by what he had just heard. "What? Reborn? That means there's more of these motherfuckers coming back?"

"Reborn? Who will be reborn?" Chike asked, interested in what he was hearing.

"Meaning the gods are returning. Supposedly, this will start the end of all, what you humans know as The Rapture. Whoever is in charge at the end will have all four levels of existence's fate in their hand."

"Four levels of existence? What does that mean?" Chike asked, questioning what Mikael was trying to explain.

"He really is a rookie. That's proof that he is not my protégé, as this information is taught in your early lessons. Right, Xeno?" Mikael said with a smile at the end.

"Unfortunately, yes. Mikael makes you into a bookworm before he trains you to fight. But yes. There are four levels of existence now due to the wars that have been raging on for eons. You have Heaven, Otherside, Earth, and the other place, Hell," he said, ending in a creepy voice.

"Little back story. At the beginning of time, there were only two, Heaven and Earth. Then Otherside came along to protect *other beings* and then hell as the fallen ones were kicked out," X said to Adam and Chike.

"Wait a minute. You're telling me that other worlds were created because of the wars? That's not what they taught us," Chike said, remembering what he learned while he was in his training.

Adam was confused at everything, but his mind understood as his power gave him small visions of what X spoke of. "X, is it safe to say that demons know this?"

Mikael interjected. "I doubt it."

Mikael was interrupted by X. "Nah, they don't. Mel already confirmed that the higher-ups don't know anything about this. Somehow, those twins are using that other dude to do their dirty work," X said, telling Mikael parts of their day. "Also, there was an attack on Mel at Taki's house. So, it's been an exciting time since we got back," he said with enthusiasm.

"That's interesting. With all that power, you would think I would have felt it. I was in Lucia's shop having a fascinating conversation with her." Mikael turned to X. "I believe you and her need to have a talk. This is serious, so there is no way we can keep this secret. Today, I found out that Lucia somewhat knows Chain Face and that she is a demigod. She doesn't know her real parents, and she knew we would one day come for her help," he said, looking at X with sympathy.

"I know. I mean, my readings aren't that great, but I can feel what she was when I met her. Just thought I didn't need to say anything since you didn't," X said, looking at Mikael with a smile.

"Honestly, I never paid her any mind to read her," Mikael said, admitting his arrogance around humans.

X was curious. "What else did you find out from Lucia?"

Mikael was stopped by the massive power he felt coming from a distance. "Again? What in the heavens is that?" he asked, turning to search for the source.

Adam immediately went into panic mode. "That's Kish! I gotta go! How that stupid shit work?!" He concentrated on what he felt as his body began to tingle. X instantly grabbed Adam's wrist as both men disappeared from the penthouse's kitchen, leaving Mikael and Chike.

"So, now we have to find where they are," Chike said, confused.

Honestly, we will feel them soon enough. This will be interesting. Let's go, rookie! I hope you can fight," Mikael said, unleashing his massive wings as both angels prepared themselves to travel to the source of the power surge.

Taki heard M's voice. "I hear you, I'm here. What? What? Is Mark alright?" she asked, remembering he was choking her from being under Michelle's control.

M held Taki's wrist as if she was stopping her from something. "Child! You are worse than the boy! You lost complete control, and the power you unleashed damn near killed both of them!"

Taki looked around, noticing they were no longer in Mark's apartment and were instead standing on the side of the building on a dead-end street. She looked down at herself. Her white dress was a little wrinkled from the tussle with Mark, and the lavender duster was slightly dirty from fighting with Michelle. That's when Taki noticed the sleeves of her duster were singed.

Taki remembered the blue fire that she felt had helped her free herself from Mark's grasp. But then she saw a hazed memory of her singeing Mark's hands as they were on her throat and using her left hand to set Michelle on fire. "M, how did we get out of there?" Taki asked, realizing she lost herself for a moment to the power.

"I know you're confused and scared, but right now, take your shoes off and that sweater," M said as she prepped to fight. "The ones coming are not to trifle with," she stated as she began to remove her shoes and wrap her long, sleek ponytail into a bun.

Taki nervously prepared herself as she began to feel a butterfly effect feeling at the pit of her stomach as if her body was waiting for something.

M yelled, "NOW!" as the three popped up directly in front of Taki. Deuce swung his sword towards Taki. Trystan immediately rushed M, and Dante attacked M as the captain missed his first two swings, starting the fight between M and Taki versus the three demons.

"Oh shit. Who the fuck are you?" Taki asked the handsome warrior she was fighting as they went back and forth with blocked and missed swings. Noticing he was a twin, he looked like one of the demons fighting M. "Why are you attacking me?" She used her strength as an advantage since she noticed he was faster but weaker than her.

"I see you are of Other to Ms. Mashiro. Too bad we are meeting like this," Deuce stated as he used his sword to swing towards Taki's head.

Leaning back, using her long legs to kick forward as she fell to the ground, Taki used Deuce's disorientation to knock his sword out of his hand with her left foot and got back up to land a right hook.

Impressed with her skills, Deuce taunted Taki. "I see the bitch taught you some shit. I like!" he said in an excited tone as he could no longer contain his disguise as a weak recruit. "You are going to make me pull out all of the stops." Deuce noticed he was getting some competition out of the woman he was fighting. He glanced over to see how the captain and Dante were faring with M. "Make sure you get her real good, twin!" Deuce yelled towards the two-versus-one fight.

Taki felt a bit insulted, swinging and landing a two-piece to the gut and jaw. "I believe you should pay attention to your own fight right now," she said, showing off a bit.

"So, since I know you are not fully human, I guess I can go all out," Deuce said to Taki as he rushed her, causing the two to get entangled with their arms.

Taki used her legs to jump up and wrapped her legs around his waist, immediately using her hands to slide around as if she was riding his back, placing her arms around his neck in a chokehold. She rode Deuce's back and whispered in his ear. "I don't care if you think I'm human or not. You are not whooping my ass." She jumped down to continue choking the twin to the ground. Taki's senses immediately reacted, letting go of the twin to duck the sword from her right. "Oh, so we switching?" Taki said, seeing Dante coming to Deuce's rescue.

Deuce yelled at Dante, "I got this! Go back to the bitch!" as he stared at Taki with hate and admiration. "I should have met you earlier!" he said as he grabbed his sword and began attacking with double the intensity, causing Taki to back up.

M took on both ferocious demons. She understood Dante's anger but was unsure of the other demon swinging with such ferocity. M observed Trystan's aggressive fighting style and immediately remembered her days of training, then questioned, "Trystan?" M stopped, taking a swing to the right side of her face and a cut from his knife on her stomach.

Trystan stopped in his tracks. "Didn't think you would remember me. What's up, Melchorde?" he spoke, swinging towards her again.

M saw the twins stalking Taki as they argued amongst each other. M did not want to be bothered with Trystan. "Why are you here?" she asked, distracting him with her question as she rushed him, sliding between his massive legs, using her left arm sword to cut his right upper thigh, and unlinking the blade to stab him in the left foot. M got up to rush Dante, yelling, "Not today!" and swinging her right hand at the twin, landing a right hook to restart their fight.

Taki saw M's assist and said, "Let's go, pretty boy!" as she swung on Deuce.

Deuce kept up with Taki with no problem. "You know, twin, we may have to turn it up a notch," he said, yelling towards Dante.

"These bitches don't deserve to see our greatness. I can kill this broad now!" Dante said arrogantly.

"Why are you two here? You're not supposed to be here!" M said, raising her voice at Dante.

Dante swung his sword towards M's neck. "Doesn't matter. As long as we kill you, they will forget that small indiscretion." Missing her neck, he switched the way he was holding the sword to swipe back immediately, landing a cut across M's chest.

M saw the cut across her chest and clothes from Deuce and Trystan. "Now, I must hurt you." She took a look at her disheveled clothes again, striking towards the bigger man immediately. M landed herself under Dante, swiping her sword across his neck and chest, causing blood to leak from his neck and a gash diagonally across his chest to match hers.

Dante was surprised at how fast she was able to penetrate his defensive stance. "Bitch!"

M chuckled at his temper. "I always told you, calm down. That temper will be your end," she said as she felt the swing from behind her, ducking and rolling to the other side to face her new opponent.

Trystan, standing in front of M, was back on his feet. "Won't get rid of me that easy, Melly!" he screamed, using his hate for M to attack her continually and aggressively. "I've been waiting a long time for this, Mel! You think you can really defeat me?!" he asked, using his size and strength to try to overpower her.

M, using her speed and strength as well, replied, "I see you haven't changed! What do you want from me?!"

BACK AT IT AGAIN

Trading blows, slight cuts, and misses, M and the captain continued their fight as Adam and X were launched violently to the ground. They landed about one hundred feet from the battle with the women and the demons. Adam sensed Taki's fight with the twins and rushed towards her to assist. At the same time, X watched as he noticed the crazed man attack M with aggressive swings and punches.

X used his massive wings to arrive at the fight, interrupting the demon's attacks on M. "Hold on a second! Let's deal with someone your own size!" Unleashing his battle-ax as he reached the demon, he missed his first swing but landed a cut on the captain's arm. "Aww, nice. You haven't lost a step since I kicked your ass the other day!" X said to the panting captain.

"I believe it was me that was doing the ass-kicking," Trystan said, swinging his sword towards X as he began to back the angel up with his ferocious blows.

Using X's interference to check her injuries, M looked over at Taki and noticed Adam and her charge were in battle with the twins. Adam gave Dante a run of stiff competition as Deuce continued to go toe to toe with Taki. With her source of power, M stopped her wounds from bleeding and used her incredible speed to reach Dante as he fought with Adam.

"Help, Takisha!" M yelled, swiping her blade across the demon's hand, stopping Dante from landing a punch to Adam's rib. "You will deal with me, Number One!" M spoke directly to Dante.

Angry at what she called him, Dante immediately attacked M with a swing of his sword. He missed as M knocked the sword out of his hand and used her speed to instantly grab the blade before it landed on the ground to press against his neck while perched on his shoulders. "If you move, I will send you back to where you came from. Don't disappoint your parents, One!" M whispered in his ear.

"MELCHORDE! It will be me that will defeat you. Leave them out of this!" Dante said through clenched teeth as he was about to turn around to attack.

M, showing her seriousness, immediately pressed the sword's blade to his neck. "Do not think the past will stop me," she said, causing blood to spill from a wound.

Dante paused, unsure of what to do, stood there nervously waiting for an opening. Just as Deuce rushed to his twin's side and aligned their backs together to unleash a power circle directly in front of them that revealed Otherside.

M, amazed at the feel of power the twins created, jumped off Dante's shoulders as Deuce began his circle and Dante completed the power circle on his side.

As the twins disappeared from Earth Realm, M immediately sensed their power coming from Otherside. She yelled towards the angels and Adam. "Do not let your guard down!" While they watched the whole area begin to crackle with power and reveal a large area of Otherside, demons and other creatures of myth were released to the New York City streets.

Taki was shocked at the view in front of her. "M, what the hell is going on?" X immediately stopped his fight with the captain to eliminate a few lingering demon creatures coming through the portal.

Trystan was confused about how Otherside was being revealed. "Get back here, you feathered bitch. We're not done," he said, chasing X to continue their fight. Adam, Taki, and M searched around for the twins as they continued to feel the power of the merge of Otherside and Earth. Just as M was about to walk towards Taki, she immediately ducked low, detecting an evil presence directly in front of her.

At full strength of the Royal Fallen Ones, Dante was a member of one of the elite families of the original fallen angels. M recognized the release of power as she released her own since she knew she would have to fight at one hundred percent as well. The sense of energy coming from the fight with M and Dante made Adam's own power tingle as he sensed the fallen angels' power in the air.

Taki was confused at what she was looking at. Still, the power flowing through her told her precisely what she was seeing. Suddenly, she gasped for air as she was pierced through her stomach from behind by Deuce.

"I wish I could have met you differently," Deuce whispered in Taki's ear, shoving her off his sword as he stared at Adam with a grin, licking Taki's blood from his sword. Deuce was immediately consumed by a memory of Melchorde screaming at his mother, she was interrupted by a massive hit to the face and ribs, feeling an immense heat coming from in front of him.

Adam watched in slow motion as Taki fell. The demon licking his sword turned Adam's vision to red immediately, setting free the massive sun powers that he tried to hold in check. With his maximum power from merging their current area with Otherside, Deuce began to get hit with what felt like the sun itself. Adam was unable to see anything but red as his whole body burned internally. The demon in front of him was beginning to look bloody and bruised in front of him. Adam ignored the heat his whole body felt, as he wanted to kill the thing in front of him that hurt Taki. Swinging his massive arms, he began to feel hotter, melting everything in his vicinity and causing the rift to merge Otherside and Earth to get larger.

M immediately felt Adam's massive god powers from afar and used her powers to throw Dante off of her. She swung her sword towards his chest. As he moved, she quickly sidestepped him to make sure she was next to where he would dodge to. M landed a kick to Dante's gut and a slash to his face, just missing her goal of chopping his head off.

"I see you've gotten better, nephew," M said to Dante, as she could tell he was frustrated. Not allowing herself to let up on him, she continued, "Come on. You said you would kill me, Dante!" M unleashed more of her own power, causing a vigorous shake in the area around them as she continued to stare at the demon.

"You really think I won't kill you because of who you are. You have another thing coming!" Using her massive power to make her stronger and faster, she attacked Dante with electrifying hits and cuts.

"No, not today, Mel!" Trystan said, unleashing his true power as he went up against Mel and Dante fell to his knees. "So, I see these little brats are related to you! I couldn't put my finger on it, but I knew something was up. And this power! Hell is my savior. I want it!" he said as he added more power to his attacks, pushing M back.

Using her quickness, she landed multiple blows to the demon as the demon captain continued to release brutal attacks on M. Just as Trystan was about to land a crushing blow to M's chest, Chike came swooping in from the sky, landing a massive blow to the captain's face and shattering the left side facial structure of the captain.

Mikael landed a few seconds after Chike searched for Adam as he fought off creatures from Otherside. Mikael yelled towards M, "What is this?"

"The demon twins' power," M responded, panting between breaths as she watched the loc-haired male give Trystan a solid fight. "We have to close it now. For some reason, it is getting bigger," M explained to Mikael as she felt the power of Otherside become more potent.

Mikael sliced the head off of a scaly demon. "Where are Adam and Takisha?" He felt Adam's massive power but could not pinpoint exactly where he was with all the commotion.

"They were fighting the other one last time I saw them. Adam has gotten a tremendous power boost. Maybe that is causing the rift to get larger," M said, thinking the combination of all the power was causing the instability.

"We need to find them now. We can't continue to hide all this commotion and power from humans any longer. I placed a barrier as soon as I got here, but I doubt it's working since the realms are merging," Mikael said, feeling Adam's rage and pain. "Mel! Come on, Chike got that one!"

He ran towards the power surge he felt coming from Adam, stopping in his tracks as he watched Adam hold a limp and bloody Taki, screaming at the top of his lungs. Mikael, unnerved, tried to stop M before she ran on the scene.

The picture became more apparent as M saw the bleeding and unconscious body of Taki. Feeling herself let go of all the pain she buried long before she had returned, M yelled, "TAKISHA!" unleashing her true powers that could be recognized in all realms. Eyes bloody red, gigantic, black, leather, bladed tipped wings with shining lights of regal blue pulsing with energy came out of her back. Then, the area began to shake around them.

Deuce passed out from being battered by Adam, and Dante could barely stand up as he felt his aunt's power unleashed. "Grandfather," he whispered to himself as he tried to stand to reach Deuce.

"Don't you move! I promise I will make my sister have to live without her children! Make it stop now!" M said as she pressed her sword to the already bleeding wound on Dante.

"I can't. It's never been this big before. I don't know how." Defeated, Dante put his head down as he felt the power and rage roll off of M. "You can have anything in this universe but choose to be a coward." He stared at her with intensity and hatred in his eyes.

"Goodbye, One," M replied as she used the hilt of her sword to knock the remaining twin out. "Now to kill Trystan. Most likely, he is the reason why all of this is happening," M said to Mikael. "Go help her!" She looked back towards the angel as she started to walk towards the fight with Chike and the captain.

Mikael yelled towards M as she walked away, "These are your sister's kids? How can this be?"

"Obviously, the time has gone by, Mikael. I can't tell you why they are here. I know my sister better pray to our father that Takisha survives this, or she will be childless," M said before flying off to the fight with Trystan and Chike.

Mikael spoke to Adam, "Come on, godson. Let's help her. Let me make sure she is okay." Mikael slowly approached Adam holding the limp Taki. "How is she?"

"Help her. I saved her," Adam said through clenched teeth as he gave the limp Taki to Mikael and walked away.

"Where are you going?" Mikael asked, speaking to the burning god.

Adam turned around, trying not to lash out. "To destroy." Then, he disappeared.

Mikael looked down at Taki, supernaturally feeling around for life in her body. Noticing that Adam had stopped the bleeding in her stomach and had partially healed parts of her other injuries, he heard a slight heartbeat. Mikael placed the unconscious Taki on the ground to see if there were any other life-threatening wounds. Feeling a massive power surge, Mikael looked up to see parts of the building they were near were crumbling due to the merge with Otherside, revealing a rocky mountain area that exposed scaly demons that started to cross through the large circle. He was stunned at what he saw, so he picked up the unconscious Taki to leave the area merging with Otherside.

Chike was trying to hold his own against the captain, but he was no match for Trystan "You must be a rookie. The warrior I was just fighting wasn't this soft," the demon captain said as he rushed the rookie angel with a cut across the chest and a kick to the face. Trystan watched the angel writhe on the ground. "I am really thankful for them twins. I see they added some spice to my plan. I just wanted to kill Melly here. But look," he said as he walked towards Chike to grab his locs.

"Son of a bitch!" M used one of the twins' swords interrupting Trystan's fight with Chike. She used her swift speed and full strength to land a few blows and cuts, as it looked like she was beginning to overpower the demon.

Just as it seemed as if M would defeat the captain, Trystan blocked her last punch, grabbing her hand. "You know, I waited for this," he panted between breaths. "There is no way I am letting you win!" he said as he began to unleash dark energy throughout his body, getting bigger.

M, shocked at what she was looking at, jumped back towards Chike to check on the angel as she watched the demon in front of her. "What the hell?"

Chike sat up, looking around at the battlefield. "I'm good, Ms. Melchorde. I will help X with the demons coming over. Take care of this asshole," he said as he got up and towered over the small woman.

M was surprised the young man was okay to still fight. "Tell Xeno to figure out how to close that circle. Wake one of those twins up if need be!" she said as she returned to look at the massive-looking Trystan.

Trystan fully unleashed his maximum power that showed him slightly larger in size and added horns and claws to his look. Trystan stood proudly, about to attack M. She was amazed by the massive energy coming from the demon. She began to feel the area get scorching hot and added power that caused the ground to sizzle. Trystan, unable to move due to the massive power that Adam exuberated as he walked towards the battle, glared at the demon as he stood a few feet from M.

"Is he our enemy?" Adam said, speaking through clenched teeth in a strange, trance-like voice.

M, overwhelmed at the power she felt coming from Adam, slowly swallowed and fought off the power. "He is..."

Adam instantly disappeared and reappeared directly in front of the demon, landing a cosmic punch to the face, causing a spark and blood to fly as Adam continued to pound on the captain. The captain brushed off the critical hits that Adam was throwing and hit Adam with a few punches of his own.

Chike and X fought side by side as the numbers of scaly demons coming through the large portal were not easing up. "Melchorde said we have to find a way to close this circle. She said we may need to wake one of the twins up!" Chike yelled towards X, slashing the head off three scaly demons that were trying to run past him.

"I know. I haven't figured out how to do that yet. Fuck no! We are not waking them up! They're the reason we are in this mess," X replied as he continued to hack at the creatures coming through. "What the fuck? What area of Otherside did they merge with?" he asked, wondering why there were so many creatures trying to get through.

Chike, continuing to fight, said, "I have an idea. It's similar to what we did with the chains. We need a conduit or something that would cause the opposite to attract the excess power. Tricking the circle to close." He landed a final blow to a scaly creature and searched the battlefield for something to use.

X fought while replying, "I like how you think, rookie. I was thinking the same thing. I believe they created a portal and figured out a way to merge the area for a short amount of time." He stopped to take a breath but was cut short by a creature swinging his claws and landing them on X's shoulder. "Alright now! I know y'all have better shit to do!" He said as he continued to fight the creatures.

Mikael tended to the rest of Taki's wounds as he watched the fight between Adam and the demon, surprised at how a demon captain could hold so much power. M walked towards Mikael. "Is she okay?"

"Thanks to Adam, she will live. She lost a lot of blood, so she will need to rest. We need to get her to the castle as soon as possible," Mikael said as he looked up at the petite woman.

"I will take her now." M swayed as she tried to pick up Taki.

"Melchorde, do you have enough strength to move her and yourself?" Mikael saw the battle had worn her out.

"I still have some reserve left." She looked down at herself. "I know someone is going to pay for messing up my shoes and clothes today. All this blood I have to wash out of my hair is really pissing me off, too."

"Melchorde, who is this demon that Adam is fighting?" Mikael asked, reminding her of their predicament.

"I know him from my way distant past. He's looking for power." M looked away at the fight between the new Sun God and the demon captain, confused at why he was involved.

Adam used his powers to strengthen his punches at the captain, landing heavy blows that drew blood. He was learning how to use his powers with his fighting skills, "You fucked with the wrong ones," he said, speaking to the demon as they continued to trade blows.

Spitting out blood, landing a couple of his own hits, the demon replied, "Looks like I found the right one!" He started unleashing more energy, making himself stronger.

Uncaring of the massive energy boost he felt, Adam said, "Nah, son. I'm telling you. You definitely got it wrong." He then started unleashing more of his own power, feeling as if he had a bottomless pit of energy in his body. Adam felt himself getting hotter and loved the feel of his cosmic transformation as he continued to pound on the captain. Getting lost in his power, Adam released all of his anger on the captain.

THIS IS IT

As the power continued to grow, the circle began to get larger, causing part of the buildings to disappear and continued to reveal more of the Otherside. As the horde of scaly demons endlessly came through the merged area, Mikael's barrier no longer protected the area, causing damage and possible witnesses.

M, feeling Adam's power, told Mikael, "Adam is getting out of control. I don't think Trystan can hold him anymore."

Mikael looked around for Chike or X as the two angels quickly ran to him and M.

"The rookie's a genius. We got this. Hopefully, you can get Baby G over there to calm down," X yelled, pointing up towards Adam's fight. "His power is making it more unstable, causing the rift to get larger," he said to Mikael as he ran off to continue to fight the demons coming through.

Chike continued with the idea. "I believe if we can get A away from here, we can use this here," he said, holding a set of chains. "I am not sure if these can contain all the power, but we can try."

Mikael contemplated what Chike was saying. "You may be right, rookie. Causing the power to flow to a specific target may cause the merger to go back to its original power source. Since they're both knocked out, it should actually close. Great idea! Unfortunately, since it is Adam's power causing it, we're going to have to cipher his energy into the chains," Mikael said to M and Chike.

"I have an idea. Give me the chains," M said, reaching for the heavy chains.

"Melchorde, what are you thinking?" Mikael questioned.

"THEY ARE COMING! WE HAVE TO END THIS NOW!" She snatched the chains, rushing towards Adam and the demon captain just as a wave of demon soldiers arrived, attacking Mikael and Chike.

"Got dammit! We don't have time for this!" Mikael said as he began his battle with two of the demon soldiers.

M used her wings to get to Adam. "We have to end this now! Let's go, boy!" she spoke to the Sun God. Adam, lost in the sun's powers, constantly hit the demon captain as Trystan laughed.

"I would have never thought one of you returned. I need this power. I WANT THIS POWER!" Trystan yelled as he unleashed more of his power, causing the area to shake.

Using her swift speed, M wrapped the captain's arms around his back with the chains as she began speaking in an ancient tongue to get the chains to absorb some of the power Adam was releasing. M yelled towards the god, "You must end this now, Adam! Takisha is alive! We have to go now!" She slammed the chains to the ground to hold the demon captain.

Still unable to understand M, Adam yelled, "DESTROY, I must destroy.", in the trance-like voice as he began to glow brighter.

M released the chains as they began to burn bright with Adam's power. "Adam, let's go. We have to get Takisha out of here, NOW!" she said, speaking directly to the god, attempting to use her powers to get through to him. The demon captain rolled and screamed on the ground as the chains burned him so he couldn't get them off. "LET'S GO, NOW!" M spoke in a more menacing, dazed voice towards Adam.

"YOU!" Adam said, grabbing M by the throat as he began to get more enraged.

X saw the captain on the ground as he finished off a few demon guards and scaly demons. Watching the scene from afar, he immediately reacted to seeing Adam choking M. Arriving at the battle area, he attempted to grab the Sun God's arm. "Baby G, what the fuck are you doing?! This is Mel!" X screamed, speaking through the pain as he continued the hold on Adam.

"I must destroy them all!" Adam spoke towards M. "WHY are you here?"

M gripped Adam's hand as she spoke to X. "Help Chike stop the merge. I got this. We have to go before they get here."

"No. I am not leaving you here. Come on."

"You know. I always lied to you about your eyes. Now get the fuck out of here so we can get this back under control," M said, speaking as she fought from getting her head popped like a cherry.

Hesitant in letting her deal with A on her own, X said, "Hurry up and deal with this baby god here like we used to do their bitch asses. You got this, Your Highness."

"Now to you," M said as she released her wings, causing the area around them to sizzle, wrapping her wings around her and Adam. As his power and her power began to merge, the area around them sparked with light, and the ground shook.

"We have so much more to do. Let go now! Do not get lost! Return now!" M said, speaking directly to Adam as his eyes were lit with fire. Unleashing a massive light from inside her wings, she caused a white circle around Adam, as he had let go of her.

Adam, unable to speak, raised his thumb up as he disappeared into the light. M, exhausted from the power she exerted, looked around to search for X and the captain, then passed out.

Chike ran towards X with the burning demon captain. "Hey, is it working?"

X dropped the yelling captain. "I don't know. I just know his voice is fucking annoying at this point. Mel is dealing with Baby G and his temper tantrum again. You know, I'm definitely going to kick his ass when he is himself."

"You and me both. Where's Mikael?" Chike asked.

"I told him to get Taki out of here. We can't fight with her here. Mel kept talking about somebody coming and started spazzing. Yo, what's up with that hole? It feels like everything just stopped," X said, looking around the battlefield. He watched the merge of Otherside and Earth begin to close as a bright light shined towards where he left Adam and M.

"What in all names?" Chike asked as he stared at the light, noticing M passed out. "Oh shit."

He ran towards her to pick her up. Walking with the passed-out M, Chike spoke to X. "Now what do to with that piece of shit," he said, talking about the demon captain passed out from the burning chains.

Just then, the area began to sizzle with unexplained power. The already burnt-out streetlights began to sizzle, and the air commenced to thicken and become crisp, making the hairs on all bodies stand.

M popped up. "Grab my hand now!" she said as she held on to X and Chike, disappearing from the battlefield in the blink of an eye.

AND SO, IT BEGINS

More than three days had passed since the battle in Manhattan. As the news stated, humans were unsure of what caused the buildings to rust and disintegrate. All the demon bodies were burned, and all that was said was there were minor injuries to the workers assisting in cleaning the area.

M sat listening to the moving picture box, as she called it, in the background. "We have to start now. It's coming. I can feel it," she said as she got up from her spot and walked out to her dining area. Looking around at all the people in her home, she was happy but sad at the same time. "Where's Takisha?" she asked Chike as he was cooking them some food his mother taught him how to make from their country.

"Hey! What's up, Auntie! She's in the living room with everyone else."

"What did you call me?" M asked in a whisper.

"Oh, Auntie? I don't think Mel or Your Highness would be fitting. You a G for real! I wish I had an aunt like you. So why not?" He turned back around to continue cooking and turned his music back up. M shrugged her shoulders as she walked to the living area, walking in on Mikael and X arguing as always.

"Mikael, stop being a pussy and let it happen! We got this, my guy," X yelled at the angel, picking up slang from Chike.

"You don't have anything. We have been sitting here losing the whole time," Mikael responded as he placed the card on the table.

"Takisha, should you really be up?" M asked, sitting down next to Taki on the couch as she placed a card on the table.

"I'm tired of laying down. I want to hang out with everyone else too," she said, making a pouty face and smiling at the end. "Anyway, I feel fine. My boo here made sure I was good," Taki said, placing her hand on Adam's large hand.

"Oh, don't get lovey-dovey with me now after that cuss out I got this morning. You're lucky we beating these two birds in spades. That's the only reason I'm being nice to you right now," Adam replied to Taki. "Good morning, Your Highness. Can I talk to you for a sec?" Adam asked, placing his cards down. "I will be right back, y'all. Don't be cheating. Especially you, X!"

"Sure, are you okay?" M said to the tall Sun God.

"I'm good. Just need to holla at you," Adam said.

"There will be no hollering in my house. I have had enough ruckus for a while. You can be quiet," M said to Adam, not following him when he walked away.

Adam turned around laughing. "I mean, I want to talk to you in private. Believe me. I will never holler at you," he said, speaking to M in the sincerest tone. "Now, can you please come? Promise it won't be long." He reached out his hand to her.

She placed her hand in his large one. "I see you and your feathered friends made yourselves comfortable here. I don't like that," M said with a smirk Adam was unable to see since he was leading her.

"I know you don't mean that. It's okay. We all needed to rest. To be honest, it's hot out there. Mikael said the demons are looking for you and me right now. You have the best barriers from what Chike and X said," Adam said to her as they sat at her dining table.

"What do you want?" M asked, staring at Adam, sensing his power was more stable. "I see you feel a lot better."

"I do. I have you to thank for that. Whatever you did to get me out of there... Let's just say I have a new perspective on things." He looked back at M, cutting to the chase. "I know who and what you are."

"I know you do. Do you know why I am here?" M asked, smiling.

Adam smirked. "Yes. To guide and protect," he said as his eyes lit with fire.

"Calm down, sunshine," M said as she grabbed his hand from across the table.

"Don't worry. I got this. I am just excited to finally know what's going on. I know the others can't know now, so that's why I wanted to speak with you alone," Adam said excitedly. "I returned to that place and learned so much. I got back here yesterday. Kisha and Uncle Mike were worried about me, but Kish said she knew I was good for some reason."

M realized they may be anchored to each other already. "How is she?" M asked, looking at Adam with her fierce eyes.

"She's good. I promise you. I can control my powers more, so she doesn't absorb as much as before. Little demon figured out how to siphon without me being all wild and shit," Adam said, laughing at the end.

M smiled. "Well, good. We will have plenty of time to discuss things. I have more to share with all of you. We might as well get everyone else in here, so I don't have to repeat myself." M went to go get the others.

Adam stood up. "Queen of the Golden River Realm, I truly appreciate your help in all of this. I promise we will accomplish our mission."

****

Chike and X placed the food on the dining table as everyone else took their seats. M sat at the head of the table as always, with Taki to her right and Adam next to Taki. Mikael sat to the left of M, with X and Chike following.

As the group made their plates and began to eat, M started her story. "Look, I want to thank all of you for participating in that unforeseen battle. I know there are more to come. I believe there are more questions than answers at this point. To give you some insight into all the information I have, first, I would like to introduce myself. I am Melchorde, daughter of Belial, Queen of the Golden River Realm. Well, former queen. For you so-called humans that don't know what all of that means, I am the oldest child of a Royal Fallen Family. My father is the original Fallen Angel Belial," M said, staring directly at Taki.

"I relinquished my title and assisted the angels in the last Angel-Demon War and the Days of Hunts," she said, pausing to look at Mikael. Mikael nodded his head, giving her permission to continue.

"I have been enemy number one on the elite guard list for over two thousand years. Those two that opened the rift to Otherside are my nephews. They are one of my younger sisters' kids. I am telling you all of this to let you know what we are dealing with. When I had to unleash my powers during the fight, that alerted my father to my presence. They will be searching for me. This brings me to Adam here," she said, looking directly at Adam.

"Are you telling me you are a demon, M?" Taki asked, putting her chop chicks down.

"Actually, Ms. Mashiro," Mikael answered, "Mel here is a fallen angel. She is what we considered fallen since her parents are of the original fallen. The generations I believe after her are what we all consider the demons, as they do not have a connection to the light."

"I do not need you to answer for me, Mikael. Thank you very much." She paused to calm herself. "Do not ever attach me to those vile creatures, as I do not agree with the ways of Hell anymore. I will not be compared or put in the same category as those beings. As Mikael stated, my father is one of the high-ranking original fallen angels. As my power is drawn from the dark, its original source still comes from above. No, Takisha, I am not a demon, nor am I an angel as you asked me before.

"Back to Adam, they know he is a god. I believe Trystan survived the chains. He has his own problems, as he was responsible for the twins."

"Responsible for the twins? You sound like he was their babysitter," Chike said to M.

"This is my last time telling you. Never interrupt me." She paused to glare at Chike. "In our world, the training is equal, meaning the army trains together regardless of rank or status. Each demonling is assigned to a trainer. Most trainers are retired generals or commanders. They train for a time and then start their ranks in the army," M said.

"Oh damn," Chike said, sitting back quietly.

"Yea, their training sucks ass, and that's why they always in some shit here in Earth Realm," X said.

"Correct, Xeno. Some of the recruits are wealthy and can get in and out when they want. It's supposed to be off-limits, but this area is not organized at all," M said.

Mikael scoffed. "Not organized. This area has the highest human raids in the country. For some reason, New York State has been the demon hub for the past fifty-plus years."

"I am telling you this place is in disarray. All those from Hell who are looking for more power are trying to take this place over from what I've heard over the years. I—"

Knock! Knock!! Knock!!!

All three angels immediately switched to battle gear. M herself unleashed her wrist swords. Adam's hand began to glow as the loud noise startled everyone.

M walked towards her door. "Who is it?" she yelled.

ANOTHER ONE?

"Hiraku, Hiraku (Open Up, Open Up)!" *Bang! Bang!! Bang!!!* "Tasukete, Tasukete (Help me, Help)!" she screamed as she kicked the door while the man that helped her escape laid passed out next to her. She was nervous, as she thought the woman, she needed would not be home. "Nande Watashi (Why me)?" she said, as the door snatched open, causing her to jump.

M was surprised as she opened the door. "Michiko Tanaka? Naze anata wa koko ni iru nodesu ka (Why are you here)?" The young girl fell into Mel's arms.

Taki, recognizing her friend's voice at the door, ran towards Michi and M, listening to them go back and forth in Japanese as the angels stood in surprise as well. Having a strange feeling of another presence, Taki walked towards the door and saw someone lying near the doorway. Taki yelled towards Michi, "Kono Otoko wa Michi (Who is this man)? So that we are all on the same page, I am speaking to you in English, Michi; my friends don't understand Japanese."

"It's okay. He's a friend. He got me here. I was so scared, Taki. They are coming for me. Cho, Ma, Pa, they're all gone," she said, crying in Taki's arms.

"Oh, my God. Baby girl. I am so sorry. Why would anyone want to hurt you and your family?" Taki said as she consoled Michi.

Dillon stumbled through the door. "Because her powers have awakened, and she knows who she is." He passed out again as he crossed the threshold.

Mikael instantly grabbed Dillon. "How in the heavens is he involved?"

Michi rushed over to Dillon. "Oh no. He is exhausted. It took us forever to get here, and they won't stop coming out the wood words. Did I say it right, Taki?" she asked, chuckling.

Taki laughed with her, knowing the pain her friend was in. "No, dummy. It's woodworks," she said as she hugged Michi again. Mikael and X picked Dillon off the floor and laid him on the couch.

M stared at the cinnamon-colored man passed out on her couch and started speaking to Michi in Japanese. "Naze kare to issho ni iru no? Kare wa Anata o kizutsukemashita ka?"

Taki interrupted her. "That is rude. You can ask her that in English. Michi, how do you know him, and did he hurt you?" She was wondering why M's demeanor had changed.

Michi was confused. "No. No. Why do you think that? He's the one that taught me how to use my power to get us here. They were going to kill me. He stopped them."

"Why is he here?" Mel asked through clenched teeth.

"I know, Mel. We will get him out of here as soon as possible. You have my word," Mikael said, shaking his head apologetically, wondering as to why Dillon was in Japan.

"Last time we saw this mofo, he was here in NYC. Why the fuck would he go to Japan?"

"I went to Japan to get answers on our Sun God here," Dillon said, opening his eyes to stare at Mikael. "You thought you would keep that information from me?" he asked, closing his eyes again.

"I didn't even know! You wouldn't listen to anything I would say anyway," Mikael yelled at the resting angel.

Dillon swiftly sat up, cringing in pain. "That's because you would want to coddle the boy. We don't have time to coddle. The murder of this one's parents is proof those vile creatures have more power than before. For some reason, they are seeking her power," he said before laying back down.

Michi stood up. "Lady M, they are coming, do you feel them? I feel them. They are close. They are coming to get me, and they're angry," Michi said as her eyes turned to a solid gold color.

"I am Luck! I am the reason you all will survive today," Michi said, laughing as she danced around and touched everyone. "Nothing shall harm you. Be wary. One of my six wants my power, a power she can't have as she is only one of my many." Then she giggled one last time before passing out.

THE END

Made in the USA
Middletown, DE
30 October 2022

13779384R00156